Thug H[oliday]
Valentine's Day
Edition

Written by:
Twyla T.
Patrice Balark
Dani Littlepage
J. Dominique

Copyright:

© Copyright 2018

Text <u>ColeHart</u> to <u>42828</u> to be notified of all New Releases!

To stay up to date on new releases, plus get information on contests, sneak peeks, and more, *Click The Link Below…*

http://bit.ly/2BtGCXH

Text TwylaT to 21000 to stay up to date on new releases, plus get information on contests, sneak peeks, and more!!!!

Last Time in Thug Holiday 2…

Christmas Eve

Alyssa woke up early Christmas Eve morning filled with the Christmas spirit. She jumped out of bed and headed to the bathroom to handle her hygiene before getting dressed for the day. Yoga pants, a tank top, and a pair of slippers was her outfit of choice. She grabbed the wrapping paper and began wrapping the presents she purchased for her family. Alyssa couldn't wait to see the looks on her family faces when they opened their gifts.

When she was finished with the gifts, she carried them downstairs and placed them under the tree. After the last gift was tucked away, Alyssa began to cook brunch for the family. She wanted to get her family into the Christmas spirit as well, but she wanted to see if her family would notice what she was up to. She was in the middle of mixing the batter for the waffles when Kyler entered the kitchen with a pouty face. She watched him as he flopped down in a nearby chair and folded his arms across his chest. She chuckled at the sight of him and couldn't help but wonder what was wrong.

"Are you okay, nephew?"

"No. Mommy won't let me see my gifts until tomorrow."

"Aww. Well, maybe I can convince your mom to let you open a gift tonight, okay?" she smiled.

"Okay!" he cheered up instantly.

"In the meantime, would you like to help me cook?"

"Yeah!"

Alyssa and Kyler's conversation, laughter, and aroma of the food drew everyone from their rooms and into the kitchen. The holiday sisters, Victoria and J.R., eyed Alyssa suspiciously as they watched them cook.

"Alyssa, what is going on in here?" Victoria quizzed.

"I'm just preparing brunch for everyone. Nothing special. Is something wrong with that, mom?" she smirked.

"You ain't fooling nobody, Lyssa. The Holiday tradition is in full effect." Andrea smiled.

"The holiday tradition? Anastasia asked with a raised eyebrow.

"Damn. It's been years since we did that. What made you think of that?" Lexi took a seat at the table.

"Well, I figured since we're all home, we could celebrate Christmas like we used to. I know dad isn't here to be a part of the festivities, but I think it would make him happy that his family is celebrating the holiday the right way and not fighting." She eyed everyone in the kitchen.

"I hate to admit it, but she's right," Andrea nodded.

Everyone nodded their heads in agreement, which put a smile on Alyssa's face.

"Aight. Let's get started, but nobody better not touch ANY of my gifts." Lexi pointed at her sisters.

They shared a laugh before they began to set the table. Alexis filled J.R. in on the Holiday Tradition and what it was as well as its meaning. After giving him the run down, he nodded his head in understanding. The house was full of the Christmas spirit and there was nothing but good vibes floating around and it reminded Alyssa of when they were younger.

Every Christmas Eve, they would wake up and eat brunch before their mother prepared dinner. They would also bake Christmas cookies, watch movies, and open one of their gifts before they went to sleep and Alyssa wanted to relive all of those memories. When the food was finished, Alyssa placed everything on the table and before they all sat down, Aunt Shirley walked in.

"Well, check y'all out. I was prepared to whoop some ass so I could get y'all into the Christmas spirit, but I see someone done got the ball rollin'." She took a seat at the table.

"I brought some eggnog to livin' things up around here." Aunt Shirley placed two containers on the table.

"Aunt Shirley, this one is almost empty." Anastasia shook one of the containers.

"I got started early." She lifted her flask and winked at her.

Alyssa chuckled at her Aunt.

"Ummm, before we eat, I just want to apologize for the way I've been behavin'," Victoria spoke up.

"I'm not goin' to lie and say that I'm happy with the decisions you girls made, but y'all are still my daughters and I love y'all dearly. I'm very worried about your father, but I know that his surgery is goin' to be just fine. I'm glad that y'all are here with me durin' this tryin' time. I know I can be stubborn, but I need y'all right now." Victoria began to sob.

Alexis jumped up to console her mother, while the others told her that it wasn't a problem. After a brief prayer, they didn't hesitate to dig into their food. Alyssa's phone chimed letting her know she had a text and she checked it immediately. She was a bit disappointed when she saw it was Tara texting her instead of Corey, but she didn't let that put a damper on her mood.

They sat around the table telling embarrassing stories about the girls' childhood. Like when Alyssa had to be rushed to the hospital for sticking beads up her nose and how Anastasia got her ass whooped because Lexi lied and said Stasia broke her favorite toy. Aunt Shirley told a story of how Andrea pissed on herself when she took her to a haunted house for Halloween, that made everyone laugh until their stomachs hurt. The women shared stories and laughs as they ate for about an hour and none of them were too concerned that a man was at the table or that they sat there longer than intended, until Alyssa announced it was time to move on to the next tradition.

Andrea and Alyssa cleared the table before washing the dishes. Alyssa expressed to her older sister how excited she was about the twins and how much she was going to spoil them. Andrea inquired about Corey and she informed him that he would be making an appearance some time that day. The holiday sisters had been getting along quite well since they all arrived and it felt like they were starting to form a bond they never had.

They all stayed in the kitchen sipping eggnog as they prepared to cook dinner and bake Christmas cookies. Anastasia pulled the Christmas shaped cookie cutters from the drawer while Aunt Shirley, Victoria, and Lexi cooked the food. Kyler seemed to be enjoying himself as he helped his mom with the cookies. Andrea pulled out her phone and provided the house with some Christmas jams and when *I*

Saw Mommy Kissing Santa Claus by the Jackson 5 came through the speaker, they all sang along to the music while they danced. J.R. watched the women carry on for a few minutes before he excused himself to the living room. Everyone had smiles on their faces and that holiday feeling that Alyssa was trying to recreate had finally made it presence in the house. Alyssa didn't want to tell her family about her suspension, but she was tired of being secretive and she wanted her family to know the truth about her job. So, she told them what happened to her and how she was under investigation. They all stared at her with wide eyes as she confirmed what everyone was thinking, which was that their father was right about law enforcement, but instead of harsh remarks, they consoled her.

As the day went on, Alyssa stepped away from the family to call Corey a few times, but his phone went straight to voicemail. Each failed attempt made her anger grow a little more, but she managed to hide it. They communicated throughout the week and he reminded her that he would be there. So, she didn't understand why he hadn't arrived yet. After she made the last failed call to Corey, Kyler found her on the porch and informed her that dinner was ready. His excitement made her cheer up a little as he dragged her to the kitchen table to eat.

After filling their bellies with cornbread, collard greens, fried chicken, honey ham, string beans, and Mac and cheese later that evening, Aunt Shirley and Victoria put the food up while the girls gathered around the Christmas tree to open their gifts. As *Santa Claus Goes Straight To the Ghetto* by James Brown played in the background, Alyssa handed each of her sisters their gifts as she let Kyler chose from one of the three she purchased for him. She watched as they all opened their gifts from her and the looks on their faces were priceless.

"Damn Alyssa, these bracelets are the shit." Andrea admired her Pandora charm bracelet with the "HS" charms on it.

"Yeah, Lyssa. I think this is one of the nicest gifts you ever got me." Lexi placed the bracelet on her wrist.

"Let's be real. That's the ONLY gift she ever brought your ass," Anastasia stated.

They all laughed.

"Wow! Auntie Lyssa brought me a PS4 and the latest games!! Thank you!!" He squeezed her tightly.

"You're welcome, baby." She kissed his cheek.

"How you get these raggedy heffas gifts and didn't get me anythin'?" Aunt Shirley entered the living room.

Alyssa reached under the tree and grabbed her aunts gift and handed it to her. As she waited for Aunt Shirley to open her gift, the doorbell rang. No one seemed to be worried about the doorbell so, she answered the door. Alyssa opened the door without looking through the peephole and when she saw it was Corey, she jumped on him causing him to stumble back on the porch.

"Oh, my goodness. You don't know how much I missed you." She closed her eyes and squeezed him tighter as his hand cuffed her ass.

"I missed you, too, bae."

They shared a passionate kiss that lasted for a few minutes. Corey placed Alyssa on her feet, but she kept her arms wrapped around his neck.

"What took you so long?"

"It took me awhile to pick up ya Christmas gift," he smirked at her.

"What gift?"

Corey stepped to the side and a black 2018 Cadillac Escalade was parked in front of the house with a red bow on it. Her mouth flew open as she rushed down the porch steps to examine the car. Alyssa shrieked when she opened the door and saw all the features that the car came with. She knew Corey was going to get her something for Christmas, but a new car wasn't what she had in mind.

"I love you so much, baby! Thank you!" She kissed him again.

"It took you all day to get this?"

"Yeah. I bought it at one of the dealerships down here. I was gonna get you the car when we got back to the NY, but you need a gift a now and don't worry, I'll have your truck shipped home," he chuckled.

"Good because I'll be damned if I'm leaving my truck down here," she stated seriously.

"Oh, and about that baby thing, it was scam," he stated with confidence.

"What you mean a scam?"

"Shawty sent me a text talkin' about the baby ain't mine and the only reason she accused me of bein' the father is because her nigga got booked and she didn't want to raise the baby alone." He pulled out his phone and showed Alyssa the text.

She took her time reading the message his fling sent him and he was indeed telling the truth. The chick said that she felt bad setting him up like that and apologized for her actions. Alyssa handed him back his phone with a smile on her face. She threw her arms around him again hugging him tighter than before.

"So, when is that date for the weddin' again?"

"I wanted to get married in the spring, but I want to get married sooner than that. We can go to the justice of the peace to get married and the ceremony later."

"That works for me because I can't wait another day to have you as my wife."

"But, let this be known, if you cheat on me again, you're going to either end up in a hospital or in a grave. Do you hear me?"

Corey bit his lip before he peaked hers, letting her know that he understood her.

"Get a damn room you two," Anastasia yelled from the screen door.

"Stasia, call the family out here so they can see my new truck." Alyssa pointed

Anastasia shouted to the family to come outside and they all came out the door one by one. Corey greeted Victoria with a hug and a kiss on the cheek and he greeted her sisters the same way. Alyssa introduced Corey to J.R. and they shook hands before Corey wrapped his arms around her waist. Alexis didn't hesitate to hop her ass behind the wheel of her truck, leaving the door open. After she got finished checking out her truck, she told Alyssa that she looked good behind the wheel and that Alyssa should let her borrow the truck. She dismissed Lexi with a hand wave and she motioned for everyone to come back inside.

Aunt Shirley thanked Alyssa for her rose gold customized flask and the bottle of whiskey as they made their way into the living room to watch movies. *Home Alone*, a classic holiday movie, was just coming on as they all got comfortable in their seats.

As Corey and Alyssa snuggled on the couch, she couldn't help but to recap her day. The day she planned was a success and it made her feel like it was a step in the right direction for their future as a family. The love and good vibes that flowed throughout the house was different for her and her sisters, as well as their mother. Reliving the Holiday Tradition was to get them to forget their differences towards each other and to remember what it was like to be a family. She wanted to build the foundation for an unbreakable bond for the four of them and felt that she accomplished that. Alyssa secretly wanted a relationship with Andrea and Alexis, but was too stubborn to take that step until that day. They say that miracles happened on Christmas and Alyssa was in agreement because the day she just endured with her family and the news about Corey's fling was proof of that. The last miracle that she needed to happen was for their father to return home in a healthy and happy state.

Christmas Day

Just when Lexi began to get into the holiday spirit, Ebenezer Scrooge came along and fucked things up. The time she spent with her family yesterday was amazing, but she couldn't get her mind off the fact that her boyfriend had plans on killing her sister's baby daddy. The saying "small world" never hit home until right then. Lexi laid in the bed fidgeting with the neckless that Alyssa had given to her as a gift the night before. Her and her sisters never exchanged gifts as adults and she didn't expect them to this year either, which made Lexi relieved that she went ahead and got them something too.

"Wake y'all asses up and MERRY CHRISTMAS!" Drea yelled, followed by three hard knocks on the bedroom door.

J.R. stirred in his sleep while Lexi attempted to get out the bed.

"Why the fuck y'all wake up so early around here?" he asked in a groggy voice.

Lexi grabbed her phone off the nightstand to look at the time, "It's 8:00 a.m., it's not that early; besides, it Christmas morning. Get up!"

Lexi went inside the connecting bathroom and hopped in the shower. After she was done, she rambled through a Target bag and pulled out the Christmas sweater that she recently purchased. She laid it across the bed along with some black leggings. She then grabbed the black Christian Louboutin peep toe boots she brought with her and placed them on the floor next to the bed. By the time she was done lotioning up and applying her make-up, J.R. walked out of the shower with the towel wrapped around his waist. Lexi admired his fit frame, which caused her pussy to get wet instantly. She watched him grab his MCM duffle bag and pull out a pair of ripped up Balmain jeans with a Gucci collar shirt to match.

"Wait. Wait. Wait. I forgot to show you what I brought for you," Lexi said, getting up from where she was sitting and going back over to the closet, pulling out a Christmas sweater for him.

"What's that?" J.R. asked, eyeing her.

"When we were younger, we all got dressed up in Christmas sweaters on Christmas day," she explained, handing him the sweater.

"Well, good thing I ain't a part of this family," he replied, tossing the shirt back to her.

"Jerrreeeemmmmyyyy   pleeeaassseeee!" she whined, poking out her bottom lip.

"Allleexxiiissss noooooooooo!" he mocked her while he pulled the Gucci shirt over his head.

"You dead ass ain't gon wear it?" she asked, getting upset.

"I'm dead ass not wearing that ugly ass sweater," he informed her.

"Whatever, FUCK IT!" she snapped, tossing the sweater back in the bag.

"Bruh, don't nobody give no fuck cuz you mad over some stupid shit."

"We know, you don't give a fuck about nothing."

"And what that supposed to me Lexi?" he asked.

"Nothing man, let's just get dressed."

The couple got dressed in silence. That was not how Lexi planned on starting her Christmas day. She figured maybe she was overreacting about the sweater incident, but truth be told, she'd been annoyed since J.R. dropped the bomb about killing D. After they got dressed, they met up with Drea in the living room before the three of them headed next door.

"What's wrong with you?" Drea asked her baby sister, noticing the grimaced look on her face.

"Shit, I'm cool…. Just hungry," Lexi informed her.

"Hungry? All yo ass do is eat. You sure you ain't the one pregnant?" she asked, rubbing Lexi's flat stomach

"Hell yeah, I'm sure," Lexi replied, smacking her hand away.

"Yeah, I heard y'all the other night, fucking in my house," Drea said looking at J.R. that time.

"Nah, she bet not be pregnant. I'll have to kill Lexi, she'll be on that crazy baby momma shit," he joked.

"Kill me, huh? That's what you do, huh?" Lexi smirked, hoping that J.R. caught all the shade she was throwing at him.

When they entered their parents' house, the sight of breakfast being prepared made her feel better. Mrs. Holiday along with Anastasia and Aunt Shirley moved about the newly remodeled kitchen while Kyler mixed fresh blueberries inside the pancake batter.

"Merry Christmas y'all!" Alyssa yelled as her and Corey walked into the house.

"Merry Christmas!" Everyone turned towards the front door and said in unison.

"Come on, lil man," Lexi heard J.R. say to Kyler, grabbing him by the back of the head, ushering him out of the kitchen.

J.R., Corey, and Kyler went inside the living room while the Holiday ladies prepared breakfast. Once everything was done, everybody sat down and ate. It seemed as if every single person at the table stuffed their faces fast as fuck, attempting to get to the gifts that was under the tree. Lexi was no different, she couldn't wait to see the looks on everyone faces when they opened their gifts from her.

"DONE!" Kyler yelled, jumping out of his seat first and running over towards the tree.

Everyone laughed and followed his lead. Tradition in the Holiday house meant, everyone opened their gifts, from oldest to youngest and that year was no different. Drea grabbed four boxes from under the tree and passed them out to each sister.

"1…2…3," Alyssa sounded off like she did when they were kids before each sister ripped through the gold wrapping paper.

"Biiiittttccchhhhhhhh, how you know my MacBook Pro was on its last life!" Lexi screamed.

"ALEXIS…. WATCH YO MOUTH!" Mrs. Holiday warned.

"I'm sorry, ma." Lexi said followed by a light chuckle.

"Drea, these are so dope. I been wanting one for the longest," Alyssa stated.

Drea spent good money on the latest Apple MacBook Pro's that she got for her sisters.

"I love it. Thanks, sister!" Anastasia said as she walked over to the tree to grab her gifts.

"Look, y'all know I'm going through a divorce soooooo…."

"A mug, Stasia? You got us a fuckin coffee mug," Lexi blurted out before peaking around the corner to make sure her mother didn't hear.

"It's the thought that counts," Stasia laughed.

"Bitch, I don't even drink coffee," Alexis replied, causing everyone to laugh.

"I love my mug, thanks sister!" Lyssa said, buttering her up.

"Thank you. At least someone appreciates it," Anastasia replied, cutting her eyes at Lexi.

"Y'all crazy! Ok, since we opened Lyssa gift's last night, it's your turn Baby Holiday," Drea stated.

Lexi stood to her feet and went in front of the tree and cleared her throat, getting everyone's attention.

"As you can see, there is no gift from me under the tree…."

"That's not shocking," Stasia said, cutting her off.

Lexi stuck up her middle finger before continuing.

"Ever since Thanksgiving, shit... I mean, things ain't been right amongst us…"

"Shit ain't been right with y'all since birth," Aunt Shirley shouted out.

"DAMN! Can I finish, PLEASE? Ok…. Y'all made me forget where I was going with this," she said pulling out her phone.

"Aw ok, I remember now, check y'all emails," Lexi said, smiling.

"Check our emails?" Stasia repeated.

"Just do it," she replied, placing her hands on her hips.

Lexi did a silent countdown in her head and just like clockwork, all three-sister jumped up yelling. They all rushed Lexi, forming a group hug.

"What? What? What?" Aunt Shirley looked on and asked.

"Lexi paid for all of us an all-exclusive trip to Jamaica!" Drea screamed.

"Wait… Waiiittttt. I don't even have an email. How am I supposed to get my shit?" Shirley questioned.

"You ain't no Holiday sister, baby. You ain't invited," Stasia replied, dancing around in Shirley's face.

"Mommy, I have a special trip planned for you and daddy once he gets well," Alexis informed her mom who looked on smiling.

"Seeing my girls loving on each other like this is all the gift I need," Victoria said as she wiped tears away.

All four girls went and gave their mother a hug. Their embrace was interrupted by the ringing of the house phone.

"I got it," Lexi broke away and went inside the kitchen to retrieve the cordless phone.

"Merry Christmas, Daddy!" Lexi bubbled as she joined the rest of the family back in the living room.

"Let me talk to daddy." The other three pushed their way past each other to speak with him.

"Wait, I answered, so I talk first.... Go ahead, Daddy, what was you saying?"

"I just wanted to call and speak with y'all while y'all all opening gifts and everything. I know y'all will be here before they take me back for surgery, but I wanna hear all my girls' voices now," Abraham informed his youngest child.

"It's sooo good to hear your voice, daddy, and we will be there very soon. I love you." Lexi grinned, sticking out her tongue at her siblings.

"Be nice, Lexi. I love you, too. Let me speak to everybody else."

Lexi laughed because her father wasn't there, yet he knew she was doing something spiteful to her sisters. She passed Drea the phone first and from there, it went around in a circle. Lexi went over to the couch and set next to J.R., who grabbed her by the neck, pulled her close, and gave her a kiss on the cheek.

"I'm proud of you," he whispered.

"I hope so, because I'm going to need my ten stacks back since that trip was your idea."

"I got you, shorty, and I got yo gift, too. But I don't think it's appropriate to give it to you at yo people's house." J.R. told her.

Lexi wondered what it was and she felt kind of bad because with all the shit she had going on, she forgot to get him something

"Ok baby, and I'm going to give you your gift when we get back home," she replied.

"I want a baby," J.R. said, shocking the shit out of Lexi.

"You want a baby and I want a ring. I guess we both just gon be wanting shit," she responded back, causing him to laugh.

"Ok, I will see y'all at the hospital in about an hour. Kyler, Granny will be back to play with you and all your new toys," Mrs. Holiday informed her grandson before walking out the door.

Their mom left early so she could be there with their dad a little while before he went under the knife. The surgery could take anywhere between one to three hours. Once Kyler opened his gifts, they were going to head that way, too. For the next thirty minutes, the girls sat around and talked while J.R. and Corey helped Kyler put his train set together. Lexi excused herself from her sisters and went onto the front porch to smoke a blunt. Not long after being out there, J.R., Corey, and Shirley joined in on the smoke session. For it to be December, the weather was beautiful, it had to at least be almost sixty degrees. Alexis closed her eyes and allowed the smoke to fill her lungs while the cool breeze crept under her sweater.

"Who that pulling up in that Beamer," Lexi heard J.R. ask.

She popped open her eyes just in time to see Richard getting out the car and storming towards them.

"That's Stasia's bitch ass husband," Aunt Shirley replied, taking a hard pull from the blunt.

"Anastasia, yo bitch ass husband out here," Lexi cracked opened the front door and yelled.

Richard came onto the porch looking like he was out for blood. He wore a pair of gray jogging pants and a Champion hoodie that was two sizes too small. Lexi moved in front of the door, guarding it because she knew that's where he was headed.

"MOVE!" he yelled into her face.

"It's excuse me," Lexi snapped, rolling her neck.

"It's get the fuck out my way," Richard snapped back.

"Hold on, buddy. You got me fucked up," J.R. said, grabbing Richard by the back of his neck, damn near tossing him out of Alexis's face.

Richard stumbled, falling onto Corey, who pushed his ass onto the ground.

"What the fuck is going on out here?" Stasia asked, finally coming out the house.

"Aye yo, sis, I'm about to pop yo husband if he don't chill out," J.R. informed Stasia.

"Do yo thang bro," Stasia smirked, folding her arms across her chest.

"I'm going to ignore your hoodlum ass cousin because I came here for a more important reason. Where the fuck is my son?" Richard fumed.

"Richard, get the fuck on somewhere. My son is fine and now that I think about it, he ain't ask about yo tired ass not once," she said matter-of-factly.

"You taking him away from me is kidnapping and -."

"SHUT UP, BITCH! SHE CAN'T KIDNAPP HER OWN SON DUMMY!" Aunt Shirley stated, causing everyone, but Richard to laugh.

Richard looked at Shirley and rolled his eyes like a little girl.

"As I was saying…." He tried to continue, but was silenced by Drea and Lyssa running out the house screaming.

"I just got a call from mom, dad went into cardiac arrest, they don't think he gon' make it."

Everyone one on the porch ran to their respective cars and headed to the hospital with hopes on what they just heard not being true.

***

Anastasia and her sisters rushed out of the house and straight to Alyssa's truck with tears streaming down all of their faces. The last thing they had expected to hear was that something was wrong with their father. As she hopped into the front seat with Alyssa behind the wheel, Anastasia wiped the tears from her eyes, but they kept coming, and she could hear both Alexis and Drea in the backseat breaking down. The only one who seemed to be keeping their cool was Alyssa, because although she was crying, she was still able to maneuver them to the hospital. Anastasia figured it came with the territory of being a Fed, but at that moment, she was glad that somebody was level headed. All that ran through Stasia's mind was how her and her sister's petty beef had been the reason for him even going through all of the illnesses. It seemed like just when things were starting to look good for the sisters, something else came and threatened their newfound bonds. She could hear Alexis in the backseat trying to calm Andrea down, so that she didn't stress out the twins, and more tears slipped from her eyes. Sure, Anastasia and her father had their moments, but she loved him and knew that she wanted him to be okay.

Alyssa pulled up to the hospital damn near on two wheels and Stasia held on for dear life as she watched her sister park her big ass truck. Once they parked, everyone stepped out and Anastasia reached for her sister's hands. She stood in between Alexis and Andrea while Alyssa stood on the other side of Drea. They walked inside holding hands and climbed into the first elevator that was available.

"Y'all I swear I don't know what I'm gonna do if something happens to daddy," Drea wailed, pacing the small space.

The look of worry and dread on her face made Anastasia even more worried about their father's condition. That time Alyssa went and attempted to console her.

"Please, I know you're worried Drea, but I don't want you stressing the babies out. Daddy will be just fine. What did he tell us to do in times of fear?" she asked, her voice getting stronger as she spoke.

"To pray," They all mumbled in unison, bringing a small smile to Drea's worried face.

"That's right, and that's exactly what we're gonna do," Alyssa told them with a nod as the doors dinged open.

Be strong y'all."

They all walked off of the elevator together still crying silently, but saying their own personal prayers. They were damn near running to see what was going on with their father as fear gripped them all. As they got closer to his room they could hear yelling and it sounded like their Aunt Shirley.

"I don't give a damn, Victoria! You should have been told that girl!" she screamed at her sister while Stasia heard her mother crying.

"Don't you stand there and tell me what I should have done, Shirley! There was never a reason for her to know any of this shit!" her mother yelled back and Anastasia's eyes bucked in surprise. Their mother never cursed unless she was extremely upset.

"She has lived her entire life trying to please y'all and doing everything she can to make y'all proud! The very least you could have done was tell her the truth! Andrea deserves to know!"

"Do you think that somebody can just come right out and tell their child that the only father they've ever known isn't really hers? How could I tell her that the man she's called Daddy all these years isn't? Huh?"

The sister's stopped just behind Andrea as she opened the door on that last bit of information, and immediately her back stiffened. Their mother and Aunt Shirley stopped their heated argument and their eyes landed on her, but she still didn't move or say anything.

"Andrea," Their mother tried to talk, but she clearly seemed at a loss for words.

"He's not my daddy?" she asked in a meek voice, still not walking into the room any further.

"Listen to me honey..."

"No! Are you saying that... that my daddy isn't MY DADDY?!" she demanded as tears rushed down her face.

Alexis stood back with her hand over her mouth shaking at the revelation while Alyssa held her and whispered comforting words into her ear. Stasia too wrapped her arms around her big sister trying to console her and ease her back out of the room.

"Is daddy dead?" Alexis wanted to know, drawing all eyes to the bed. Their father lay under a white sheet with his face covered.

"And you didn't even call to say that he had died, Ma! Was y'all that busy in here arguing that y'all failed to call and tell us that our father was dead!" Drea shrieked wildly.

"Andrea please... just calm down," their mother said, hoping that her daughter would give her a chance to explain.

"Is… the daddy I've known all my life… not my daddy?" Andrea asked again and that time instead of saying anything, her mother merely shook her head no.

Anastasia and her sisters stood quietly still crying until she confirmed their fears and they all shrieked in shock.

"What?"

"Oh, my God, Ma!"

"Are you serious?"

They all shouted at the same time looking at their mother in confusion. The very last thing they expected to hear was that their oldest sister didn't share a father with them. Their mother stood off to the side silently crying while Andrea ran out of the room. Anastasia and Alyssa were too shocked to move, but Lexi ran after her.

***

Drea took off running with no particular destination in mind. Her eyes were blurry and burning as tears continued to stream down her face. She just couldn't believe the news that she heard. It felt like her whole life turned upside down in the blink of an eye. Her whole life had been a lie. How could her parents keep such a deep, dark secret like that? Drea heard her mom saying something, but she couldn't stop. She needed to get away. As soon as she got to the elevator, she fumbled with buttons until it finally opened. When she stepped on, someone grabbed her.

"We gonna get through this sister," Lexi comforted her.

No words came out of Drea's mouth, only uncontrollable sobs. Lexi pulled her closer and squeezed her tight. They stood there for what seemed like an eternity with Drea's cries being the only noise that was heard. A few minutes later, her phone started ringing. She wasn't in the mood to talk to anyone, but Lexi grabbed her phone and answered after the first call ended and it rang again.

"Hey brother-in-law... my sister needs you... we lost our dad... and some other stuff... yeah... University of Mississippi Medical Center... straight down Lakeland to State Street... okay, bye."

She halfway listened as Lexi talked to who had to be D, since she called him her brother-in-law at the beginning of the call. Lexi reached over and hit the button to go to the first floor. Right before the doors closed, J.R. appeared and got on the elevator. Drea tried her best to get herself together. She knew that she had to be strong no matter what, and that was exactly what she was going to do. Everyone always depended on her and she couldn't let them down despite the circumstances. Even with the news that they had just heard, Abraham was still her daddy, no matter what. He was all that she knew. Abraham Holiday had his ways, as all parents do, but they loved him in spite of. It was crazy how they all had just talked to him and then, boom. Life sure was funny. The lawyer side of her wanted answers, while the soft side of her just wanted the entire day to be a dream that she could wake up from instantly.

"I don't even know what to say to y'all... but, I do know that the love that y'all have been showing this past week has been real. Y'all gotta keep that goin and move forward," J.R. advised.

"He's right, Drea… on the way over last week he was telling me that we gotta stick together no matter what. All families go through bullshit, but we fuckin Holidays and we gon get through this… TOGETHER!!"

"Thanks y'all! Both of y'all are absolutely right!" Drea finally found her voice.

"I just need some air… let's go outside for a while please."

When the elevator chimed, Drea stepped off first. She saw a sign for a bathroom and told Lexi and J.R. that she was going to get herself together for a minute.

"You need me to go wit you sister?"

"Nah, I'm good Baby Holiday. I'll be right back. I just need to get myself together right quick."

Drea made her way to the restroom. Thankfully, no one was inside, so she really had a moment to herself. She stared into the mirror and wondered what God's reasoning for the chain of events that had just transpired could have been. Things had been going to great, only to take such a drastic turn for the worse. On Christmas Day at that. Drea loved her family dearly, but she was actually happy that Lexi had told D to come to the hospital. There was something about a male companion that made things a little better during hard times. Drea hadn't had that in almost never, so she appreciated D. She had no idea what it was they were doing, but everything about him and the situation felt so right. She wanted to feel his strong arms wrapped around her.

After she cleaned her face, she noticed that her eyes were still red and puffy, but there wasn't anything that she could do about it. They would probably be that way for days to come. Drea made her way back out and she saw Lexi and J.R. standing near the door. When she walked up, Lexi gave her another hug, and then they walked outside. It was December, and the Christmas season had officially started three days ago, but the sun was shining and it was fifty-five degrees. The light coats they had on was all that they needed.

"There go ya maannn!" Lexi sang.

As soon as she said it, Drea looked to her left and saw D headed her way. The swag that he had was out of the world. No one could even blame Drea for sleeping with him and getting pregnant on the first night. He came up to her and grabbed her and pulled her into his arms. Just like before, his cologne hit her nostrils and drew her in further. Even though she had told herself that she was going to be strong, as soon as she was deep in his arms, Drea's tears started back.

"I got you, ma… I promise I got you!" He squeezed her tight.

He comforted her and everything was alright, if only for the moment. Out of nowhere, Drea heard her sister's voice and it wasn't pleasant.

"What the fuck is going on?" Anastasia yelled.

"Stasia, what the fuck wrong wit you?" Lexi stepped to her as soon as Drea turned around.

"Move Lexi! Get outta my way!"

"First, you wit a random ass bitch and now you hugged up wit my sister!!" Stasia fumed.

"What the fuck you talking bout?" D queried.

"I'm sick of you playing me to the left like I'm some random ass bitch. Just because I couldn't leave when you asked, you play me to the left while I'm going through a divorce!"

Drea couldn't believe what she was hearing. Was D her sister's lover? As if everything that had happened wasn't already enough, it appeared that more had just been added.

"So, you really thought that this thug could replace me? Look at you standing there looking just like the stupid bitch that you are!" Richard walked up and said.

Before anyone could say another word, J.R. made his way to Richard and punched him in the face. Richard fell straight to the ground as blood splattered from his nose and he screamed like a bitch. D removed himself away from Drea and went and gave Richard another blow that caused him to lay all the way out on the concrete.

"Don't disrespect women you punk ass nigga!" D spat.

"What the fuck you think you doin, nigga?" Anastasia stepped to him and pushed him upside the head.

"Look, lil mama… I don't even…"

"D'Mani, Ima fuck you up if you keep acting like you don't know me," Stasia yelled and pushed him.

"Stasia!! Keep ya damn hands to ya self!" a voice rang out from behind.

Drea turned around and couldn't believe her eyes. D had told her that he had a brother, but he failed to mention that he had a twin brother.

"Oh my God… what the hell?" Stasia said and covered her mouth with both hands.

"I don't know what my brother did to you, but I ain't him… I'm D'Mari, but everybody calls me D."

To Be Continued…

Chapter 1

Andrea stood there shocked as hell as she heard the revelation that D had just made. He had told her that he had a brother, but he never said "twin brother". To see how Anastasia was acting and then to grasp the fact that her secret lover was actually the twin to who she was pregnant by was crazy as hell. The meaning of "it's a small world" instantly came full circle. Andrea looked between the two of them and she couldn't tell the difference in them at all. Identical twins were supposed to look the same, but damn. No wonder her sister was acting a damn fool.

"Yooo what the fuck?!?! My sisters fucking twin brothers!" Lexi exclaimed.

The twin who Anastasia referred to as D'Mani made his way towards her while Andrea's mind and thoughts were all over the place. She had no idea what was being said, but she saw her sister jerk away from dude and start yelling. Andrea went into lawyer mode and assessed the situation. Her dad who she had just found out wasn't her dad was now dead, Richard was laying on the ground knocked the fuck out, Lexi was screaming, J.R. had a mean mug on his face, Alyssa looked perplexed, D was saying something to her, and people had begun to watch her family and take in all of the drama.

"We gotta get outta here. This isn't the time or the place to handle this business. Let's go to the house," Andrea pointed out.

"That's the best news I heard all day. Let's get outta here. All these nosey mfer's in our business!" Lexi agreed.

"We all rode together, so let's go," Alyssa finally found her voice.

Andrea started walking, but D grabbed her by the arm. Normally, Drea would have cussed him the fuck out, but his touch actually felt comforting. He seemed to be just the peace she needed in such a chaotic time.

"I'll take you home," he verbalized.

"I'd like that," Drea replied and began following his lead.

"My sister ain't riding alone wit you. We don't know you like that!" Lexi vacillated.

"I understand that… you can ride with us if you'd like. I see my brother is following your sister anyway," D pointed out.

"Yo Lexi… yo sister a grown ass woman and can take care of herself," J.R. chimed in.

Drea didn't have an issue with J.R. at all, but the way he said that made her feel some type of way. She knew that she was grown and all, but who was he to stop her sister from looking out for her?

"Drea, just come ride with us and ol' buddy can follow us to the house," Lexi told her sister.

"Or you can just ride with us and J.R. can follow. He knows his way around anyway, he's been here a week," Drea challenged.

"Lexi come on!"

"We'll just meet y'all there Drea, okay?" Lexi said and walked off.

"So, it's like that?"

"Like what? You riding wit yo man and I'm riding wit mine," she shrugged and made her way towards J.R.

Andrea didn't know if it was the hormones from being pregnant or what, but she was really in her feelings after Lexi walked away. How was it that she went from being her sister's keeper to dick riding in a matter of seconds? Drea saw Anastasia, Alyssa, Corey, and D'Mani get into Alyssa's truck, while Lexi and J.R. were together and Richard's ass had finally gotten up and was staggering in no particular direction.

"Don't be mad at your sister… it just seems like she was in a tough situation," D said once they were seated in the car.

"It's not just that. It's everything. I never admit this kinda shit, but I just feel overwhelmed and now all of a sudden, I feel like an outsider in my own family," Drea sobbed as tears began to roll down her cheeks.

"All families go through shit. I haven't known you long at all, but I can tell you the rock to this family and they gonna need you to get through whatever it is y'all goin through ma."

D'Mari pulled away from the hospital and made his way towards her parents' house. He already knew the address because he had visited her the other day. Andrea openly expressed her feelings about the entire situation to D and he never interrupted her. The chemistry between them had been great from the start, but Drea had no idea that she would need him emotionally, and so soon at that. She expressed her love for her dad and how she didn't even want to know any details of who her real father might be or where he was if he was still alive. Abraham Holiday had been all she knew, and that was all that she wanted to know.

They pulled into her driveway and Drea pulled her key out of her purse before getting out of the car. Thankfully Hannah had pulled up right when they heard the news about their dad and agreed to keep Kyler. Andrea figured that she was going to take him to her house, but seeing her car still there confirmed otherwise. She got out of the car and D walked around to her. He pulled her in for a hug and she melted in his arms. Once again, she cried. She not only cried for her, but she cried for her whole family. She knew that she needed to get it out so that she could once again be the strong person that they needed her to be.

"Try not to stress, remember you got more than just you to think about," D said as he rubbed her stomach.

"You're right… you've helped me to feel better already. Thank you!"

After a soft kiss, Drea led the way inside. She knew that the rest of the family would be arriving next door soon, but she wanted to fill Hannah in on everything ahead of time.

Chapter 2

The entire way home, Anastasia tried to ignore D'Mani's lying ass. He kept making excuses, but the truth was that he should have told her from the beginning that he had a fucking twin. She had managed to embarrass herself on more than one occasion because he had failed to inform her of something. Finding out about his twin, Richard popping up, and most importantly, her father having passed away was a lot to deal with for Anastasia and she really didn't know which problem should have been tackled first.

"So, you just gone keep fuckin' ignoring me?" D'Mani asked, grabbing her face so that she could look at him with his face balled up in irritation at her lack of interest in what he was saying.

Anastasia met her sister's eyes in the mirror and silently let her know that she was alright. Sure, D'Mani probably looked extremely scary when he was upset, but he had never put his hands on her and she was positive that he never would. She could tell that Alyssa wanted to say something, but was happy that she remained quiet and only sucked her teeth before returning her attention back to the road. Once she wasn't worried about her sister prying, she snatched her face out of his grip and frowned deeply.

"Yeah, actually I was, just like yo ass been doin!" she growled angrily.

The nerve of him to pop up out of nowhere after he'd been giving her the silent treatment and not mention his fucking twin, that just so happened to be her sister's baby daddy.

"Stasia." He closed his eyes and ran a hand down his face.

"I apologize about not telling you about D'Mari, but it ain't like we was doin much talkin' when you came around."

She sneered at him joking about the situation, and then attempted to turn her back, but he turned her small frame right back to facing him.

"I wasn't finished yet! You so fuckin' selfish, Anastasia. Off top, you assuming that the whole reason I stayed away from you is because I'm in my chest bout yo pussy ass husband when in all honesty, I don't give a fuck about that nigga! I'm tryna keep you safe! Niggas is at my head right now and they'll use you to get to me.... all I been tryna do is protect you ma... that's it," he finished dramatically.

Anastasia didn't know what to say to that. On one hand she felt flattered, but on the other, she was beginning to wonder if being with D'Mani might not have been in her and her son's best interest; especially while she was going through this divorce with Richard.

"What do you mean niggas is at you, D'Mani?" she questioned, and he looked at her like it was obvious.

"Don't try and pretend that you ain't know the type of lifestyle I lived when we started this shit, Stasia." He kept his voice low, but Anastasia still saw her sister watching them from the rearview mirror and instantly shook her head at him. True, she knew what he did, but that didn't mean that she wanted her FBI agent sister to know.

"We'll talk about this later. Right now, I need to go check on my son and my sister," she told him sternly and again let him know that they shouldn't talk so much in front of her sister. Even though she had an attitude with him over not talking about his brother, she knew damn well that her not informing him about Alyssa working for the FEDS was going to be a major problem.

Catching her hint, he sent an uneasy glance her sister's way, but nodded and remained quiet, as they pulled up to her mama's house. Without waiting for her sister or D'Mani to step foot out of the car, she made her way up the sidewalk and into the house where Andrea and D'Mani's twin sat in the living room while he tried to console her.

Upon seeing Anastasia come in, D immediately stood to his feet so that he could be ready in case she tried to get physical again.

"I just wanted to apologize for earlier. Your brother never mentioned that he had an identical twin soooo… it kinda took me by surprise," she tried to explain as soon as she entered the room. He gave her a stiff nod and then looked behind her at D'Mani and Alyssa walking in.

"Yeah, this nigga is known to keep a secret or two." He gave her a half smile and then dapped his brother up as he approached them.

"My bad y'all. Stasia, this is my brother, D'Mari, D'Mari, this is my girl, Stasia."

D'Mani introduced them quickly. D'Mari gave her a light handshake before turning his attention back to Drea, who was still crying uncontrollably on the couch.

"Awwww boo it'll be okay," Anastasia cooed, taking a seat on the opposite side of her sister and wrapping her arms around her tightly.

"Has mommy at least tried to call Drea?" Alyssa asked with a voice full of concern, to which Drea's head snapped up angrily.

"Hell no! Of course, Mrs. Prim and Proper hasn't called to check on us when a thirty-year old secret comes out after the way she blamed me when Daddy first had that heart attack!" Drea spat, shocking everyone in the room.

Anastasia couldn't lie and say that her reaction wasn't warranted because she knew that their mother blamed Drea for their father having to go to the hospital in the first place. Still, it was strange to hear Drea talk that way about their mother when she was the main one campaigning for their parents to begin with. Andrea had always been a daddy's girl, so for her to find out that our father wasn't hers, on the same day that he died was probably too much for her to take, and she was obviously lashing out. Anastasia didn't say anything, but Lyssa decided to speak up.

"Drea, I know that this was a lot to take in today, but mama needs us right now just like we need her. I don't believe that they kept this a secret to harm you…"

"But, that's exactly what it did, Alyssa! The most important man in the world to me is dead and on top of that everything he's been to me is a lie!" she shouted, jumping to her feet and pacing the floor in frustration.

"Andrea, calm yo ass down before you stress out my shorties, man!" D's voice vibrated through the room. Stopping her movement, she turned and face him with her brows knitted together.

"Don't tell me to fuckin' calm down! How am I supposed to act with all this shit goin on? Huh?" He crossed the small space that separated them and both Alyssa and Anastasia stood to their feet also ready to jump his ass if he started acting up.

"Drea, I'ma let that slick shit slide cause I know you under stress, but you need to sit down and calm yo damn nerves before you hurt my kids like I said." The look he gave her must have let her know not to test him because she placed her hand in his outstretched one, and let him lead her back to the couch. Alyssa and Stasia shared a look at how easy it was for him to get through to their stubborn sister.

"I know this ain't how your day was sposed to go, but just calm down and breathe for a minute and when yo OG come up in here, I'm sure she gone tell you everything you need to know."

He wrapped an arm around her shoulders and she nodded as she buried her head into his shoulder silently crying. D'Mani, who sat on the couch across from them still hadn't said a word as he observed the scene. Anastasia would have preferred for him to remain silent since the drama alone was embarrassing enough. They all sat quietly with only the sounds of Andrea's heavy breathing and occasional whimpers filling the room before the sound of the door opening drew all of their attention.

Alexis and J.R. stepped inside, and looked around at everyone sitting there in silence. "What the fuck else done happened?" She immediately wanted to know, going straight to Andrea's side and almost knocking Stasia out of the way.

"Damn bitch, ain't nothing happened; he had just got her to calm the fuck down," Anastasia said, sucking her teeth at her baby sister who didn't seem to care either way.

"And she's still calm, so shut up, Stasia." Lexi stuck out her tongue and turned her back to her so that she could put an arm around her sister.

"Daddy ain't even been dead a whole day and y'all bitches already arguing like we got something to argue about, shit!" Alyssa fussed, shaking her head at them.

Both Anastasia and Lexi felt bad for fighting over stupid shit while they should have been dealing with their sister and their own grief.

"You're right; I'm sorry, Lexi," Stasia replied sullenly, letting out a heavy sigh.

"I won't argue with you about that bitch," Lexi quipped, being childish to which J.R. cleared his throat and she let out a groan.

"Ughhh, I'm sorry, too." She placed a kiss on Drea's head and then moved over to where J.R. was sitting and plopped down on the armrest next to him.

"Well, I guess now we just need to wait for mama." Alyssa grumbled quietly, but loud enough for everyone to hear before taking a seat in the armchair closest to Anastasia.

The sister's looked at each other not sure of how things were going to turn out once their mother got there, but Anastasia knew that regardless, she was going to have her sister's backs against their mother. She just hoped that Andrea was prepared for whatever revelation that she was going to drop once she arrived.

Chapter 3

Lexi sat on the arm of her parent's cream leather couch, rocking back and forth. J.R. placed his hand on her knee, soothing her for the time being, causing her to stop moving. She had a headache out of the world and with all the shit going on, she could tell it was only going to get worse. Within a matter of minutes, she found out that her father passed away, her favorite sister was now only her half-sister, and that Drea and Stasia were getting dicked down by twin brothers. There was no way possible the day could get any worse. Lexi listened to her sisters argue and for the first time, she wished she could go back to the time when they were kids. She would make shit different between them; she would ensure that all four of them would be closer.

Just as Lexi was about to get up and head over to Drea's house to lay down, her mother and Aunt Shirley came walking through the door, causing the entire room to freeze. Mrs. Holiday looked around the room briefly at everybody before dismissing herself.

"Imma go get some rest," she said, turning to leave.

"No, you not; you about to talk to your children," Aunt Shirley replied, grabbing her by both shoulders.

Victoria stood still before releasing a deep breath. Lexi hopped up from where she was sitting and ran to her mother's side.

"Yeah mommy, Auntie is right. You can get all the rest you need after we have a civilized conversation like adults."

Lexi led her mother over to her father's favorite loveseat, forcing her to sit down. Everyone cut their eyes at the person next to them, with hopes of someone breaking the ice and addressing the elephant in the room first.

"Ok, since the rabbit got everyone's tongue, I'll speak up," Lexi said, using the rubber band around her wrist to pull her hair into a pony tail.

"You about to fight or talk?" Aunt Shirley asked, while taking off her earrings.

Lexi along with everyone else in the room, chuckled for the first time that day and it actually felt good.

"I'm about to talk, Auntie, chill," Lexi replied, holding up her right hand, stopping Shirley from going any further.

"Excuse me y'all, but I think this is an intimate ordeal in which y'all should handle amongst family. Lexi baby, I'll be in the truck if you need me. I'm sorry for y'all loss," J.R. stated before standing up to walk out.

"I'm with lil homie on this one. Anastasia, hit me up if you need me," D'Mani informed her.

D'Mari, stood up, following his brother's lead, but instead of saying anything, he kissed Drea on the forehead and walked out quietly.

"Wait a minute, it's two of them fine mother---"

"AUNTIE!" All four sisters yelled out at the same time.

"Well shit, I'm just saying…. My bad, carry on Baby Holiday."

Lexi shook her head and picked up where she left off, "Not only am I about to bury the only man to ever love me unconditionally, it's confirmed that daddy is not......"

Lexi paused and looked over at Drea who looked as if she was going to breakdown just at the sound of those words. Alexis hated to see her sister hurt, she hated to see any of her sisters hurting for that matter and it killed her most that Drea was dealing with more than one type of pain. Sure, they were all mourning their father's death, but Drea was dealing with that and plus some.

"Mama, I just want answers." Drea began to sob uncontrollably.

Anastasia and Alyssa both ran over to Drea's aid, consoling her as if they weren't just arguing minutes ago. Lexi rubbed her mother's back hopefully giving her the courage to be honest; not only to Drea, but honest to herself.

"Baby there was never an easy way to tell you such a thing. You were Abraham's world, Drea. That man couldn't have possibly loved you more," Victoria finally explained.

"But- but-but... who is my.... why .... How could y'all keep such a secret?" Drea asked, stumbling over her words.

"Andrea, your mother and father are human chile, and just like the rest of us in this room, they make mistakes. Both my sister and Abraham did some things before you girls were born that led them down this path. Their consequences are leading us to have this conversation right now. Everyone knows that I'm not the President of Abraham's fan club, but I give respect where respect is due. He was an awesome father to all you girls and even more of an awesome man for taking on a responsibility that wasn't his. Now Drea, you can cry all day and night, but that's not going to change shit and to be perfectly honest, y'all worried about the wrong shit right now. Y'all mother just lost her husband of thirty-three years and y'all lost y'all daddy. The skeletons are out the closet, but it's up to y'all to allow those skeletons to hunt y'all for the rest of y'all life."

No one in the room moved, let alone blinked after Aunt Shirley read them that scripture. It was like everyone was in their very own sunken place and slowly trying to gather themselves after the day's events.

"Drea and Victoria, y'all need to go upstairs and talk," Shirley said, breaking the silence.

Lexi watched her mom rise before walking over to where Drea was sitting. Victoria helped her stand to her feet before the both of them disappeared up the stairs.

"I'll be back, too," Lexi announced before grabbing her leather jacket off the couch and heading towards the door.

"LEXI WAIT!" Aunt Shirley yelled out.

"What up?" she asked, turning back around facing her.

"You got some weed?"

"Byyeeeee Felicia," Lexi laughed as she took off down the block to J.R.'s truck.

Doing a light jog a few houses down, Lexi hopped into the passenger's seat of her man's ride and snuggled up in the warm leather seats. J.R. seemed to be engaged in a heated conversation, but that still didn't stop him from glancing over at her smiling. Lexi waited patiently for him to wrap things up. She took that opportunity to reply to some unread messages in her phone. She had seven from Marcus, most of them cursing her out and calling her all type of bitches. She shot him a text back letting him know what happened. Seconds later, he was blowing up her phone. She sent him another text telling him she'll call him right back, just as J.R. was wrapping up his call.

"Everything cool?" Lexi asked, shifting her body in the seat so she could face him.

"That was Donnie, I was telling him about the shit with your sister baby daddy."

"Ohhhh yeah, so about that?"

"What about it?" J.R. questioned.

"You really gon go through with that job, now that you know the connection between us?" she inquired.

"Look baby, this is business. A half of million-dollar job business. This shit ain't personal," he informed her.

"The fuck if it ain't. That's the father of my niece or nephew. Them growing up without a dad is more personal than you think," she snapped.

"I get what you are saying baby, but you gotta look at things from my perspective."

"Yo perspective? I could never view things from the eyes of a killer," she said, cutting him off.

"Killer? Oh, you judging a motherfucker now?" he asked, staring at her in the eyes.

"No, I am not judging you. I'm just stating facts."

"Look Alexis, the work gon get done either way it goes; one of them motherfuckers gon die. Imma be honest with you, I didn't know there was a twin until today. How me and Donnie see it as, we can knock either one of them off, get paid and be back in Atlanta before anyone notices. Because I love you, Imma let you decide who gon get this bullet, will it be D'Mani or D'Mari?"

Chapter 4

After Victoria and Andrea left the living room, Alyssa was lost in her own thoughts. A day that started off with laughter, cheer, and love, had taken a turn for the worse in the blink of an eye. The loss of their father had shaken the Holiday sisters' world, but the secret about their dad not being Andrea's biological father shocked the hell out of them all the most. It made Alyssa think about their childhood and why they pushed them so hard to live according to the word of the Lord. Alyssa knew that everyone had a past, but she never thought that her parents would have secrets that would hurt the family the way it did. Although they were all frustrated with the thirty-year-old family secret, Aunt Shirley's words hit home. They not only had to be there for their sister, but they needed to be there for their mother as well.

Besides the major issue, Alyssa couldn't shake the conversation that took place on the way home from the hospital. Not only was she nervous about D'Mani remembering her from the club, but Alyssa couldn't wrap her mind around the fact that the man she had been building a case against for the last few months had a damn twin brother and both of them were fucking her sisters! Alyssa thought that she was going to have to pull her damn truck over when he grabbed Anastasias' face, but when her sister eyed her letting her know that she was cool, she kept her focus on the road, but continued to listen to the conversation. When Anastasia told him that they would finish their discussion later, the way D'Mani looked at her made her a bit uneasy, but she didn't let it show. Alyssa wondered what she would do when the time came for her to decide between her family and her career and with one of her sisters being in love with the target and the other pregnant by his brother, there was no way she could turn D'Mani in.

"Alyssa, are you okay?" Stasia shook her lightly breaking her out of her thoughts.

"Huh? Oh, yeah. I'm good. I'm just...you know." She gave a weak smile.

"I figured as much, but you know everything is gonna be okay, right?"

"Yeah. I know."

"Damn. Y'all sure know how to pick some fine ass men," Aunt Shirley chuckled as she entered the room.

"Since Lexi don't wanna share J.R with me, I guess I'm gonna have to take one of y'all men." She took a sip from her flask as she eyed Alyssa and Anastasia.

"Aunt Shirley, you better go somewhere with the non-sense. I ain't in a joking mood right now," Stasia dismissed her aunt with a hand wave.

"Because y'all had a stressful day, I'ma let y'all live."

"You're so sweet, Auntie," Alyssa stated sarcastically.

Alyssa remained on the couch for a few more minutes before she walked upstairs to her bedroom, closing the door behind her. She flopped down on her bed and placed her hand behind her head as she stared at the ceiling. She felt like her life was slowly but surely falling apart as she thought back to the day she got laid off from the FBI. Alyssa began to regret her decision to stay with the FBI after her and Abraham fell out about her job. As far as career goals, she thought that she would retire as an agent, but being as though that was now longer the place for her, she needed to find another career path when she returned to New York.

As she let her mind wonder, someone knocked on her door minutes later before they entered the room. Corey closed the door behind him making his way over to the bed to join her. Alyssa lifted up so he could lay down and then she rested on his chest. He ran his fingers through her hair as they laid there in silence for a moment.

"How are you feelin', bae?"

"Not too good. I missed a lot of years with my dad and when I thought that I was going to be able to make up for the time we lost, he dies." She fought back her tears.

"You can't beat ya self up about the past. You ended things on a positive note with ya pops. Of course, he was in the hospital when you spoke with him on the phone this mornin', he was in good spirits and probably happy that all of his daughters were under the same roof with no drama. I know he's proud of y'all for buryin' the hatchet." He kissed her forehead.

"I guess you're right, love."

"So, what are we gonna do about this weddin'?" he questioned.

"We're just gonna have to wait. This is gonna be a long week, but we can talk about it when we go home. Plus, I think we need to take some time to figure out if this is something we really want to do. I know the situation with your fling was a scam, but we need to re-establish some trust, Corey. You travel a lot and I don't want to be worried about you fucking around on me," Alyssa answered with sincerity.

"I understand, Alyssa and believe me when I tell you that I'm gonna make shit right between us again. I'm not goin' nowhere and neither are you. You hear me?" He lifted her chin to look at her.

"I hear you." She smiled.

"I'm about to go hang with the fellas. Do you need anythin' before I go?"

"Naw. I'm good, bae."

They embraced in a passionate kiss before he got up from the bed and left the room. Alyssa couldn't help the smile that spread across her face. No matter the mistakes he made, she knew that without a doubt, Corey was the man for her. No woman liked when their man made a mistake; especially, when it came to infidelity. But, when a man was willing to correct his mistakes and prove his love to his woman, that was some sexy shit.

Alyssa pulled her phone out of her pocket to check it and was surprised that she had so many missed calls and texts from Kelly and Tara. Alyssa responded to Tara's text letting her know that she would call her as soon as she could, but decided to call her bestie to update her about her father and the rest of the family drama. After talking to Kelly for over an hour, she promised her friend that she would contact her when she returned to New York. Alyssa placed her phone on the nightstand before lying back down in her bed and taking a nap, which was something she was in need of.

Chapter 5

After a long and stressful week, Saturday had finally arrived. Although Andrea was dreading the funeral for her dad, it was needed so that everyone would get closure and be able to move forward. Neither of the sisters attended the wake the day before. Andrea couldn't bear the thought of looking at her dad in the casket two days in a row, and all of her sisters understood. Surprisingly, their mom even said that she understood, but she had to be in attendance so that someone from the immediate family would be there. Aunt Shirley and her flask were there to keep their mother from being alone, along with some more family members.

Most people always wore all black to funerals for some reason, but the Holiday Sisters decided to brighten it up just a little. They had all went to North Park Mall on County Line Road a few days before and Drea bought them all yellow dresses and black blazers form Belk. Since yellow was a color of comfort, she figured it would fit because they all needed comfort. Yellow also happened to be Abraham's favorite color, so it was definitely befitting. It was five minutes after ten and the funeral was scheduled to start at eleven. The family car would be there in fifteen minutes to pick them up. Andrea looked at herself in the mirror and she couldn't describe her feelings. She was still trying her best to be strong. Once the funeral was over, she felt like she would be better, she just prayed that she would be able to get through it.

"Sisteerrrr… you look so good," Lexi walked in and squealed.

"Thanks Baby Holiday… even though I know you only tryna make me feel good."

"Bitch, you fine… I know this week has been harder on you than any of us, besides mommy… but, I promise you we gonna get through this together. Since you took some time off work, we gon make the best of it… okay?" Lexi responded.

"I might not even go back to work," Drea admitted.

"Bitch, is you crazy? You love your job!"

"Maybe that didn't come out right… I've been silently working on building my own firm and I finally have enough clientele to open up Holiday at Law. I've been scared, but seeing how life changes in a heartbeat, this has made me want to move forward with my dreams."

"That's great, Drea… that would be so dope… and who knows, maybe I'll come work for ya," Lexi winked.

"Yeah right… yo lil hot ass ain't leaving Atlanta."

"You never know… if the price is right, I'll do anything," Lexi replied and did a little twerk.

"Hey y'all… mama sent me over here to see if y'all was ready," Alyssa peeked her head into the doorway and said.

"Yup… we coming that way now," Lexi said as she picked her phone up off the bed when it chimed.

"What you smiling at?" Drea quizzed.

"At this hard ass nigga tryna be sweet and shit," Lexi replied.

"He coming to the funeral?"

"Nawww… he don't really do funerals, but he'll be back by the time we get to the house."

The three of them made their way next door just in time to see the family car pull up. Knots formed in Drea's stomach, but she had no choice but to move forward. She knew that she had her sisters, but a small part of her wished that D was there with her. They had talked and texted all week and he promised to call her by the time he thought that everything would be over. She knew that everyone had lives to live and they couldn't stop living just because it felt like her world had stopped. When they made it inside, Anastasia and Kyler were sitting on the couch and Aunt Shirley was walking into the living room with her best friend in her hand, her flask.

"Where's mommy?" Lexi asked.

As soon as the question left her lips, their mom walked in and she had on black and yellow and they never told her what they were wearing.

"Wait a damn minute… why nobody didn't tell me we was wearing black and yellow? They say family be ya worst enemy," Aunt Shirley fussed.

"You got on black Auntie, dang," Stasia rolled her eyes.

"Yeah but not yellow," she continued fussing.

"I have a yellow scarf you can wear… I'll go get it," Drea shook her head and then headed back to her house to get it so that she could calm their aunt down.

By the time Drea walked back out of her house, she saw everyone walking towards the family car. She handed Aunt Shirley the scarf and then got in. The ride to New

Jerusalem was a quiet one. For the first time ever, even Aunt Shirley was quiet. Drea wished that she could take a swig from her flask, but that was out of the question in her condition. When the limo stopped, everyone sighed at the same time. The parking lot was packed to capacity and vehicles were lined all up and down the road. So many people were in attendance for the Home Going Celebration for Pastor Abraham Holiday. As soon as they got out, family and friends made their way to them and passed out hugs and gave their condolences.

"Family, come this way and line up in two's starting with the spouse, followed by children, and then other family members," the funeral director stated.

Victoria and Aunt Shirley were at the front of the line, followed by Drea and Lexi, Anastasia and Kyler, Alyssa and Corey and then other family filled in. Drea felt someone staring at her, so she looked to her right and saw some lady that she had never seen before. She was dressed like she was a widow, and Drea figured that she probably was. When Lexi nudged her, Drea looked up and saw that her mom and aunt were looking at the woman too. The pastor began reciting the 23 Psalms and brought their attention back to the service because it was time to walk in.

"The Lord is my shepherd, I shall not want. He maketh me to lie down in green pastures. He leadeth me beside the still waters; he restoreth my soul. He leadeth me in the path of righteousness for His name's sake. Yea though I walk through the valley of the shadow of death, I will fear no evil; for thou art with me; thy rod and thy staff, they comfort me."

Drea and Lexi were standing a few feet away from the white and gold casket by the time that scripture was halfway over. She heard people crying and one of them sounded like her mom, but Drea couldn't focus on anything, nor could she move her feet. Lexi must have pulled her forward because the next thing Drea knew, she was looking down at her dad's lifeless body. She leaned over the casket and broke down crying. The whole week had been hard, but nothing compared to that moment. A few minutes later, Drea was being pulled back and ended up on the front pew between Lexi and Aunt Shirley.

When Sis. Shannon got up and started singing 'Precious Lord Take My Hand,' Victoria broke down for the first time. Hearing her cry and show emotions made all of the girls cry. The ushers began fanning all of them. The rest of the service was a blur until it was time for remarks and expressions. The M.C. made it known that the family only wanted a few people and to limit the expressions to two minutes. A couple of church members got up along with Abraham's best friend who was the deacon and a couple of family members. Drea was enjoying the remarks, but she was also ready for things to speed along. When the lady got up who she had locked eyes with, Aunt Shirley stood up and Drea knew that something was wrong. Her mom had a scowl on her face, but she pulled Aunt Shirley back down and whispered something to her.

Andrea hurriedly got up and motioned for the M.C. to keep the microphone. As soon as she got there, she found courage that she didn't know that she had and began speaking.

"My dad was an awesome man and he was loved by many. We can tell that from the outpour of people amongst us today as well as all the acts of kindness that has been shown this past week. We know that plenty of people may have something that they want to say, but we must respect my mother's wishes and keep this short and sweet. If she's up for it, she may allow time for some of you to speak at the repast, but for now, we have to move forward."

Andrea made her way back to her seat, but she couldn't help but to feel that some shit was going to go down soon. She sat down and Lexi placed her arm around her and then leaned over and whispered.

"Girl, I thought you was bout to drop the secret up in this bitch."

"Hell naw… fuck these nosey ass people."

The eulogy was short and sweet just like they wanted and Drea was relieved that everything was almost over. She still had to get through what she considered was the hardest part, the cemetery, but once that was over they would all be able to get closure and move forward. A vacation with lots of drinks was needed, but just a vacation would suffice since she couldn't drink. Tears rolled down Drea's face as they rolled the casket out.

"It's almost over, Drea," Lexi comforted her and she nodded her head because no words would escape her lips.

When they made it outside, once again there were people waiting to hug them and give them their condolences. Hannah made her way to Drea first and then she saw a few of her colleagues.

"I know this bitch ain't…" she heard Lexi mumble and looked up to see Bre coming their way.

When Bre tried to reach in to give Lexi a hug, Lexi pushed her away before Drea could step in and do it. She wanted to say something, but her senses kicked in that it was not the time or place, so Drea pulled Lexi along so that they could get to the cemetery. Andrea hadn't saw Bre since the stunt she pulled at Thanksgiving and she hadn't heard anything about her since hearing that fight over the phone when she called Lexi that time. The look in Bre's eyes made Drea make a mental note to warn her baby sister because her ex friend was actually looking like a lunatic. She needed Lexi to be aware of her surroundings at all times.

They arrived at their father's final resting place a little while after and gathered under the tent. Drea vowed not to act a fool, so she closed her eyes and allowed her tears to flow freely down her cheeks. She rocked back and forth and felt several hands on her, but she didn't want to open her eyes until it was time to go. Once they were dismissed, all of the sisters grabbed a rose and placed it on the casket before it was lowered into the ground.

"Are y'all gonna need a ride from the church since y'all all rode in the limo?" Hannah asked as they made their way back to the limo.

"They agreed to make sure we all got back home, but I'll probably ride with you," Drea said.

On the way back to the church, she felt her phone vibrating and took it out and saw that it was D calling just like he promised.

"Hello."

"Drop your location… we planned on being back for the funeral, but our flight got delayed and we just left the airport," he told her.

"Okay… I'll send it now," she replied and hung up.

"Your man back?" Stasia queried.

"Yours too," Drea smiled for the first time that day as they made their way back to the church for the repast.

Chapter 6

Lexi looked in the mirror and shook her head at the sight before her. Her eyes were puffy, the massacre that once rested under her eyes was now smeared. The bone straight Brazilian weave that was sewn-in tight, was now in disarray and all over her head. Lexi went inside her Birkin bag and pulled out a brush. She began to stroke her hair lightly, making sure that everything was back in place before she washed her hands and headed out. She picked her bag up from the sink, but when she reached for the door handle, the door swung open and Drea walked in. Simultaneously, both sisters smiled at each other before Drea too began to look in the mirror. Lexi closed the door and decided to stay behind and wait for her sister.

"So, how you holding up? "Lexi asked, looking at her through the mirror.

"I guess, I'm ok. I still can't believe we just buried him," she replied, letting out a long sigh.

"Yeah, me either and you know what? I've been thinking, after graduation, I'm going to move back home to be with mommy. I can't imagine her being in that big ass house alone. And then you, with D'Mari living in New York, you are going to need all the help you can get with Thing 1 and Thing 2," Lexi laughed.

"Awwww look at Baby Holiday. I'm proud of you. You are truly growing up. I can't tell you the last time I've known for you to do an unselfish act," Drea replied, as she fixed her hair.

Just as Lexi was about to curse her out, the bathroom door opened again and in walked Anastasia and Alyssa.

"What the fuck y'all doing in here?" Stasia asked as she headed to an empty stall.

"Girl, stop cursing; we are still in a church," Drea scolded her.

"Aw, my bad!" Stasia apologized followed by the sound of the toilet flushing.

"You ok?" Lexi turned around and ask Lyssa who had been extremely quiet lately.

"Yeah sister, just a lot on my mind," she replied, after being in a daze for a few seconds.

"Well, regardless of what happens, there's nothing that we can't overcome together. I love y'all," Drea said, pulling all four sisters into a hug.

"Ok, now that all that mushy shit is over, let's get done with this repast so we can put this day behind us," Lexi said, breaking the circle first and leaving out of the restroom.

Mr. Holiday's repast was being held in one of the recreation rooms at the church. With the help of some of the church members, the room was decorated in yellow and black. Each round table had either a yellow or black table cloth laid across it. Five long square tables placed against the wall, housed the food. There were two huge speakers in each corner of the room, as well as some pictures of Abraham and the Holiday family flashing across a projector on the wall. Lexi scoped out everyone in attendance before a huge smiled crept across her face. She quickly parted ways from her sisters and made her way towards the door. Once she was close enough, she yelled out to him.

"Marrccuussss"

Marcus began to walk forward, meeting her halfway. Lexi jumped into his arms, it had been too long since the last time she'd seen her best friend.

"Thank you so much for coming!" she said to him once she released from their embrace.

"You know I'm coming rain, hail, sleet or snow for my best friend. How you holding up?" he asked.

"I'm ok, I guess. I'm just ready for all this shit to be over with, she admitted truthfully.

"Well, it will be soon," was all he said before Lexi pulled him away from the door and towards a table.

"Soooooo, where's bae at? I thought he was down here with you," Marcus questioned once he took a seat.

"He went back to Atlanta two days after Christmas, but he came back for the funeral, only to not come to the funeral," she replied, rolling her eyes.

"Well, since you brought it up. I saw how you dissed Bre after the funeral and before you go off on me, I told her ass not to come," Marcus confessed.

"With all the shit going on right now, Bre is the last of my worries, but I am going to fuck her up the first chance I get," Lexi admitted.

"I figured she was just coming to pay her respects."

"Pay respects my ass, that bitch is so grimy," Lexi snapped.

Lexi and Marcus talked about the last semester of school and what they planned on doing once they both touched back down in the A. She loved her sisters and even her man, but neither of them were Marcus. She couldn't wait to go out and act a damn fool with the gay male version of herself.

"I gotta confession," Marcus said out of the blue.

Lexi cocked her head to the side and waited for him to spill the beans.

"If I was into the fish, I'll be fucking all three of your sisters. Them bitches are fine honey."

Lexi let out a hearty laugh, her eyes followed Marcus's as he watched Alyssa, Andrea, and Anastasia walking over in their direction.

"They about to serve the food Lexi and they want us up there first," Alyssa stated.

"Ok, here I come," she informed her sister before standing to her feet.

"Come on and line up before all these hungry ass church folks eat all the food," Lexi said to Marcus before walking off.

Although Lexi wasn't hungry, all the food in front of her made her stomach growl. It had been a while since she had some good old southern cooking. She considered making her a plate now and eating it later, once she got high.

"Attention everyone, Mrs. Holiday will lead us in prayer as we bless this lovely food," Deacon Williams announced, getting everyone's attention in the room.

Victoria stood in the middle of the floor and said grace, "Father, praise you for friendship and family! Thank you for bringing us together today. The people in our lives bring us such joy, and we are grateful for time spent in fellowship together. Help us use this time to bond closer as a group, and learn to love each other more. Bless our appetites, both physical and spiritual, to honor you in all we do. In Jesus' Name, Amen."

Amen, sounded across the room as everyone prepared to fix their plates. Lexi stepped out of line and went over to where her mom was standing.

"Mommy, you want me to make you a plate?" she asked.

"Oh, no baby, I'm not hungry," Mrs. Holiday said forcing a smile.

"Mommy, you have to eat something."

"I know and I am going to eat. Just put me one up and I promise to eat it later, Alexis."

Mrs. Holiday kissed her daughter on the cheek before walking off to speak with other family members. Lexi spotted Marcus back at the table with his plate. She made her way over to him, walking up behind him.

"You fucking that rib up," she said, startling him a little.

Marcus looked over his head at her and smacked his lips before digging back into his plate. Lexi teased him a little more by massaging his shoulders as if she was prepping him for a big fight.

"There you go champ. Fuck them ribs up," she laughed.

Marcus chuckled, but didn't allow Lexi taunting him, stop him from feeding his face.

"Damn, I leave you alone for a few hours and you already entertaining other niggaz."

Lexi turned around and came face to face with J.R. A smile instantly spread across her face as he stood there wearing an all-black Gucci collar shirt, a pair of all black Balmain jeans, some black Timbs and a black scully. The yellow diamonds that danced off of his chain and Rolex, completed his look.

"Heyyy baby," she squirmed, standing on her tippy toes, stealing a kiss.

"So, fuck me, huh?" Marcus stood up and said before heading to the trash to throw his plate away.

Marcus and J.R. greeted each other with a dap before the three of them sat down at the table.

"How you holding up, baby?" J.R. asked.

"I'm good. You hungry?" she replied.

"Nah, I'm straight. How moms and your sisters doing?" he pondered.

"They good too. Surprisingly, there has been no drama, minus the fact that Bre showed up at the funeral.

"Damn, straight up? That lil bitch crazy," J.R. laughed.

"Yeah, and her crazy ass gon fuck around and...."

Lexi paused when she heard commotion coming from the hallway. She recognized one voice, that voice belonging to Aunt Shirley. It was like all four sisters' Spidey senses went off at the same time because all four of them headed towards the voices.

"Bitch, you got a lot of nerves showing up here," Aunt Shirley yelled into the face of the woman who Lexi recognized from the funeral.

"I just came to pay my respects, Shirley," the unknown woman responded calmly.

"Bitch, please. Since when did side chicks care about respect?" Shirley fumed.

"Auntie, what's going on?" Drea spoke up first and asked.

"Drea, this woman here is the reason why your mother and father damn near divorced," Shirley blurted out.

"Wait. What?" Alyssa asked.

"It's a long story," the woman stated, eyeing Drea.

"Well, you here. We here. I think we got the time," Anastasia stated, looking at her watch.

"No, this is not the time nor place. I just wanted to say my final goodbyes to you ladies' father," the unknown woman spoke up again, but Lexi noticed when she said the word "father" she looked at Drea again.

"Hoe please, you weren't worried about good timing when you called my sister on some---*"Hello Barbara this is Shirley, woman to woman"* type shit," Aunt Shirley snapped.

"Whoa. Whoa. Whoa. Who the fuck is Barbara? I'm lost," Lexi said, looking around at her sisters.

"Lord, this child is slow," Anastasia said, shaking her head while rubbing Lexi's back.

"I didn't come here for this. Y'all take care," the woman replied, walking off, leaving everyone especially Lexi in utter confusion.

"Auntie, what was that about? Who is that woman? I recognized her from the funeral," Drea loaded question after question.

"Drea, it's not my place to tell you," she replied.

"Since when you cared about something not being your place?" Alyssa mumbled, but they all heard her loud and clear.

Aunt Shirley stuck up her middle finger, but proceeded to tell the girls.

"Drea, that's your real father's wife."

"HOLD UP… WHAT?" Anastasia blurted out.

"Your dad had an affair with Lisa, the lady who just left, right after y'all parents got married. Victoria, before she got saved, got revenge by sleeping with her husband on some eye for an eye type shit. Except, she got pregnant with you when she did."

Aunt Shirley's words left all four sisters' speechless. Alexis couldn't believe what she just heard. She had no idea that her parents were both cheating. Her family secrets and lies were starting to spill out as the days went by.

"When all y'all secrets came out at Thanksgiving, I told all four of y'all not to feel bad because we all have secrets. I just never thought shit was going to hit the fan this soon," Shirley stated before walking off.

Andrea shook her head and followed their auntie back into the room.

"This shit crazy!" Anastasia said, walking off as well, with Alyssa behind her.

"Can somebody please tell me who the fuck is Barbara and Shirley" Lexi yelled out to her sisters, but nobody said a word, as they disappeared into the crowd.

Chapter 7

The whole day had been draining to Anastasia and she couldn't lie, after seeing her father for the last time and all of the emotions and drama that had kicked off at the funeral, she was happy as hell to see people beginning to leave the repast that they'd put together. Every time someone came up to her or her sisters to give their condolences, she wondered how long she would be able to keep it together before she spazzed out. Stiffly, she gave her attention to one of her distant relatives that came to pay their respects.

"Anastasia, honey, again I'm soooo sorry for you guy's loss. Your father was a great man and a wonderful leader," the lady whose name Stasia didn't know told her, as she juggled three plates wrapped in foil.

Anastasia raised a brow, but refrained from telling the lady exactly where she could stick every single one of those plates. She forced herself to nod at her hoping that she would move along, but she started talking again.

Anastasia looked for an escape as she half listened to her, when she spotted her son at the water fountain with Zyree, she didn't even excuse herself before she walked off while the lady was still talking because she didn't give not one fuck. As she approached the two who seemed to be having a conversation, she wondered when the hell he'd gotten there and why he felt the need to talk to her son. Aunt Shirley and her damn big mouth always started unnecessary shit. She had told her that Zyree wasn't Kyler's father, but her old ass felt the need to push the issue.

The last thing she needed on top of her divorce was that nigga trying to claim paternity. When she stopped in front of them, she caught the tail end of their conversation.

"Yeah, I love basketball too I try to go to every game I can," Zyree was explaining and Kyler was eating that shit up. Neither had noticed Anastasia as she stood there because they were so into the talk of basketball.

"Really? My dad never wants to go to games... my mom always takes me," Kyler explained sadly and Anastasia instantly felt a pang of sadness for her baby, but she quickly put that in the back of her mind, clearing her throat.

Kyler smiled up at her seemingly unaware of her frustration and Zyree held a cocky smirk.

"Hey ma!" Zyree said he likes basketball too!" he exclaimed happily.

Anastasia gave him a small smile and nodded how mothers do when they want to hide the way they really feel about a situation.

"That's great honey, but let me talk to Mr. Zyree for a second okay," she said through her teeth and grabbed ahold of Zyree's arm pulling him a short distance away.

"He got my same love of the game, Stasia," he started in excitement before she could even say anything.

"Zyree, I'm more than aware of the fact that he loves basketball, that does not determine paternity nigga! The question is what the fuck are you doin here trying to sneak and talk to my son no less?" she hissed angrily.

She could understand him thinking that Kyler was his due to the timeline, but the day of her father's funeral was not the time to be addressing the shit. The smile he was sporting instantly fell from his lips and his face marred in irritation.

"I knew your father, too, Anastasia…"

"Yeah and he ain't like yo ass," she interrupted, rolling her eyes.

"That doesn't change the fact that I came to pay my respects, but don't try and play me, Stasia. You know that's my son," he growled, grabbing her arm tightly.

"I haven't seen you in over five fucking years and as soon as you come back around its some damn drama. I don't know how else you want me to say this, but Kyler is not yours!" she let him know for what felt like the hundredth time.

It may have looked a little shady to everyone who knew their history, but she was sure that her son belonged to Richard's stupid ass. She was tired of having the same fight with that man. Back when she first was forced to marry Richard, she would have given anything to have been pregnant by Zyree, but the fact remained that he wasn't Kyler's father……all she had to do was get him and her family to understand that.

"Prove it! Why won't you just take a test and get it over with?" he asked, cocking his head to the side, but before she could say anything else, Richard appeared at her side like he was anymore welcome than the next man.

His eye was still pretty black from being hit at the hospital, making him look completely out of place. He was dressed in a dark suit as if he had attended the funeral, though she hadn't saw him there and she was sure no one else had or else there would have been a fight. She looked around quickly to see if anybody else had spotted his crazy ass, but nobody was looking their way.

"Anastasia, who the fuck is this guy? Every time I turn around you're in some other man's face," he scoffed, looking between her and Zyree with distain. One would think that he had gotten enough of getting his ass beat after the hospital, but apparently not, because there he was getting into another nigga's face over Anastasia like he had a right.

"Richard, first of all, what the fuck are you even doin here? And me talking to him ain't got shit to do with you!" She was so fed up with Richard acting a fool every time they came in contact with one another.

"Whatever you need to holla at Stasia about can wait my nigga, we was already in the middle of something," Zyree jumped in, putting his arm up in an attempt to make Richard back up.

"I don't give a damn what you're doing, this is my wife!" Richard roared, drawing the attention of a few people around them. He grabbed Anastasia's other arm and pulled her closer to him, while Zyree yanked her back.

"What the fuck is wrong with y'all?" she snapped angrily snatching away from them both as they stared each other down.

"This is my father's repast and y'all up in here acting crazy as hell!" She was happy to see that her sisters were on their way over even though the scene was embarrassing as hell. Since she'd come home it had been some type of bullshit surrounding her family and it was mostly involving her.

"Damnnnnn girl, every time I turn around you got some niggas acting a fool," Alexis said as soon as she was close enough.

"Shut up Lexi, you know she ain't fuckin' with them," Alyssa said with a roll of her eyes. "Now Richard, I don't know how you got in here or why you even came, but we just laid our daddy to rest and you need to get out of here with that crazy shit!"

"Yeah, nigga unless you want yo ass beat... again," Lexi threatened, clapping all in his face. Anastasia could see that he wanted to say something, but knew better once he saw J.R. come up behind her.

"Fine… I'll leave, but this ain't over, Anastasia," he grunted before walking off.

"Isn't nigga! This isn't over!" Alexis yelled after him.

"Really Lexi?" Anastasia asked shaking her head at her sister who merely shrugged.

"What? His ass the one who be goin around checking grammar and shit, I been dyin to correct his ass."

"Whatever Lexi." With, a frown, Anastasia turned to Zyree who was still standing within their circle as if he didn't need to excuse himself also.

"Ummm you can go, too," she let him know, feeling a little bit more in control now that her sisters were there. He smiled and lifted his hands in surrender.

"You got that, Stasia; but, we have unfinished business so be looking out for me."

"Nigga is that a threat?" Lexi fumed lunging for him, but J.R. held her little feisty ass back. Knowing that things weren't going to work in his favor either, Zyree backed away from the group.

"Nah, that's no threat. Stasia knows I don't make those," he said, staring her down not at all fearful of Anastasia's sister and her boyfriend, but they all knew that. While Richard was a corporate, scary man, Zyree was street through and through. The last thing he was scared of was a man or woman that bled the same as him. With one last nod, he walked away blending into the crowd of people that were leaving since the repast was finally coming to an end.

"Girl, calm yo lil ass down and stop tryin to fight all these niggas," J.R. chastised as soon as Zyree was out of eyesight. He released the hold he had on her and she stood next to him with an attitude, that Anastasia was sure came from not being able to hit anybody.

"You know how I do, boo; ain't not nan nigga gone come for my sisters." She let it be known and folded her arms across her chest.

"You got that, ma. But, you still need to turn down some; that's what I'm here for. Trust me, I got you," he said, causing her to smile and blush.

"Okay bae," she gushed happily and despite the craziness of the past few minutes, Anastasia was happy that her sister was in love.

"What was all that about, Stasia? Them niggas looked like they was bout to rip you apart," Alyssa questioned, looking at her sister with raised brows. It seemed as of late Anastasia had been having bad luck with the men in her life and the last thing that anybody wanted was for her to get hurt.

"Nothing girl. Richard on his fake tough guy shit and Zyree on this paternity thing," Anastasia explained nonchalantly.

"That nigga was here?" the sound of D'Mani's voice drew all eyes to him as he stopped where they were, looking as sexy as ever dressed in a black hoodie, black jeans, and Timbs. Instantly, Anastasia felt herself melt under his intense stare, she was so far gone that she almost didn't hear Alexis's messy ass mumble uh oh.

"I'll explain it later, let's just gone head to Drea's," Anastasia dismissed, ushering him towards the door and grabbing her son's hand who had surprisingly stayed exactly where she'd told him to. The day had been hell, and all she wanted to do was take off her heels and go to sleep. That was exactly what she planned to do once she made it to her sister's.

Chapter 8

Although Alyssa was drained from the funeral the day before, it didn't stop her from going to check on her sister that morning. She went next door to Drea's house and found her and Lexi in the kitchen. Alyssa asked them how they were doing and they were doing better than the day before. When Andrea hinted that she needed a vacation, Alyssa suggested that they come to New York. After agreeing to the idea, Andrea agreed to book their flight for later on in the day and she informed Alyssa that she would call when they landed.

Anastasia, Alyssa, and Corey booked their flights to return home that day and when they touched down in New York, they took cabs to their destinations. When Alyssa and Corey arrived at her Condo, she carried her luggage straight to her room dropping it in the middle of the floor. She flopped down on her bed before she kicked off her shoes and took a deep breath. The highs and lows of the week low key took a toll on Alyssa and she hoped that she would be in a better mood when Andrea and Alexis touched down in New York.

Corey entered the room and took a seat next to her on the bed. Alyssa placed her head on his shoulder as he wrapped his arm around her shoulder. They sat quietly for a few moments before she broke the silence.

"You got any plans for the night?"

"I'm gonna chill with my cousins tonight and watch the ball drop on the big screen and since ya ass gonna be out with ya sisters, I guess I gotta wait until you come home to get some pussy," he chuckled.

"Naw. I need that before I leave out and when I come home," she smirked.

"I got you, shawty." Corey kissed her forehead.

"So, what are you and ya sisters' getting' into tonight?"

"I'm going to meet them at Anastasia house and we'll eat and have drinks and shit there before we head out to Time's Square. I figured that would be a nice way to bring in the New Year despite the crowd."

"That'll be dope."

"Yup. I don't know what else we're going to do while they're here, but at least we'll be bringing the New Year in with a bang." She gave a small smile.

The couple chatted for a few more minutes before they got comfortable in the bed, cuddled up close to each other, and drifted off to sleep for a few hours. They woke up around three in the afternoon and a text came through on Alyssa's phone. Grabbing her cell phone, Corey handed it to her and she checked it. She read the thread from her sisters group chat and felt like she missed out on a whole day instead of few hours. The messages started around 10:30am and were still coming in as she tried to catch up. Drea and Lexi had just landed in New York and was on their way to Anastasia's house. Alyssa texted them the plans for the night and everyone was on board. Sitting up in bed, she grabbed a rubber band off her nightstand and put her hair in a ponytail before walking into the kitchen.

Alyssa grabbed two bags of wing dings from the freezer before grabbing the hot sauce from the cabinet along with a couple of tin pans. She prepared buffalo wings and macaroni salad for the pregame warm up at her sister's house. Noticing that she only had a half of bottle of Grey Goose left, Alyssa sent Corey on a liquor run. While she waited for the food to get finished cooking, she picked out her outfit for the evening and being as though it was going to be freezing outside that night, she decided on something cute and warm.

It was nearing six in the evening when Corey returned from the store and Alyssa had just finished making the macaroni salad. After covering both of her dishes with foil, Corey made good on his promise and filled her insides with his thick, long shaft before she got ready for her night out with her sisters. Dressed in a pair of light denim jeans, a pink long sleeve sweater, and a pair of pink knee boots, Alyssa put on her gold hoop earrings before fixing her ponytail. Grabbing her leather coat, keys, wallet, and cell phone, she grabbed the tin pan of wings while Corey grabbed the alcohol and the salad. After loading everything in her car, she kissed her fiancé good-bye before jumping behind the wheel of her car. Her Cadillac Escalade was being shipped to New York and she couldn't wait for it to arrive at the end of the week.

Alyssa arrived at Anastasia's house forty minutes later and parked in front of her house. She honked the horn and seconds later, Lexi and Stasia came out and helped her bring the food in while she carried the liquor. Placing the bag on the kitchen counter, Alexis removed the bottles from the bag and clutched the bottle of Henny.

"Yaass! Now, I can turn the fuck up!" Lexi poured shots for everyone except Drea.

"How are y'all going to drink right in front of my face like that knowing damn well I can't drink?" Drea questioned as she began to make her plate.

"Shit. Like this." Alyssa smiled as the sisters' tossed their shots back.

"Fuck y'all." Drea flipped them the bird.

The three of them laughed before joining her at the table and fixing their plates. Anastasia made meatballs and rolls to make meatball subs along with fried chicken wings. Alyssa filled her cup halfway with Henny before taking a bite out of her food.

"After everything that went down yesterday, I needed this get away," Andrea admitted.

"How long are y'all staying?" Stasia inquired.

"Until the end of the week. I got school next Monday," Lexi said, not looking up from her plate.

"The same for me."

Alyssa nodded her head. As the sisters finished their food and drinks, the doorbell chimed and Stasia answered the door. She introduced the woman as her baby sitter and told her that she could help herself to some food. Alyssa ordered an Uber for them and when it was nearby, they put their coats on and kissed Kyler good-bye. As they left out the house, the Uber was pulling up and they hopped inside the car.

Traffic was hectic as people tried to maneuver through the city to get to their party destinations that evening. As they reached Time Square, they jumped out the car and held hands as they made their way through the crowd finding the perfect spot to stand. It was 10:00 pm when they arrived and they seemed to be enjoying themselves as they watched the live performances and the highlights of 2017. Alyssa was checking her Instagram when Andrea nudged her and pointed in Alexis direction. She was flirting with some fine ass dude and instead of any of them cock blocking, they let her be great. She was on vacation and the point of a vacation was to enjoy yourself.

As the midnight hour approached, they all got their phones ready so they could record the ball dropping. When the timer reached the last ten seconds, everyone in the crowd began counting down. When they reached one, everyone blew their horns and put on their 2018 glasses and head bands. The sisters took selfies on snap chat as well as videos of the scene around them. There was nothing but good vibes floating around and Alyssa was glad that she was bringing in the New Year with her sisters. Now that they were in a new year, Alyssa still had an old problem lingering, which was her suspension and the case. Alyssa knew how she wanted to solve her problem. She just didn't know how.

Chapter 9

Drea hated that she couldn't drink, but she had to admit that the night before was still fun while being sober. It seemed like it had been forever since her and her sisters had been out and had a good time. It had been even longer since they brought a new year in together. Many people only dreamt about watching the ball drop in New York, but the Holiday Sisters had created another memory by doing it together. 2017 had been shitty to say the least, but 2018 was already looking up.

"You woke yet, hoe?" Lexi walked into the room and asked.

"Hoe? You the hoe. J.R. woulda snatched yo lil ass up if he woulda saw how you was dancing on ol' dude last night," Drea laughed.

"Sisterrr… that was just innocent fun. Ima be good tho. I actually love that nigga!" Lexi admitted.

"Awww… I'm still in shock that this man still has your attention."

"Shiiidddd me too," Lexi laughed.

Andrea got up out of the bed and grabbed her travel case. Her and Lexi were staying at Anastasia's for the week. If her and Richard would have still been together then they would have been at a hotel, but since that wasn't the case, they saved that money and were also able to spend more time together. Before Drea could walk out and head to the bathroom, her phone chimed and she smiled when she saw that it was D'Mari texting her.

D: Good morning beautiful. Happy New Year again!

Drea: Good morning handsome. Same to you.

D: Since I got ditched for your sisters last night, how bout y'all all come over for a lil kickback later on at the crib?

Drea: You didn't get ditched silly... lol! But that sounds good. What time?

D: Y'all can come around six or seven. We gon be here all day tho so feel free to come whenever.

Drea: Okay. I'll see you soon.

"What the hell is you smiling at?"

"D'Mari them having a kickback and said we should all come over later," Drea told Lexi.

"That's cool… but, what we gon do for yo birthday Friday? You ain't even mentioned it."

"Honestly, I haven't thought anything about it with everything that's been going on," Drea admitted.

"Well, Ima make sure we do something. We leaving Saturday, so we'll close out our vacation with a celebration for you."

"That's cool… but, why you looking so annoyed?"

"Cuz every time I call J.R. the shit rings one time and then goes to voicemail."

"That means he's ignoring you… but why tho? J.R. don't wanna get fucked up, do he?"

"I hope he don't…" Lexi started saying, but she stopped and smiled when her phone rang.

Drea proceeded on with getting her stuff together so that she could shower. It was a little after eleven and she was getting a little hungry.

"What the fuck?" Lexi blurted out and Drea stopped and turned her way.

She watched as her sister dialed who she assumed had to be J.R. back to back to back, but he didn't answer.

"What happened?" Drea quizzed.

"He got me fucked up is what happened. I'm being faithful to his ass but he out entertaining bitches," Lexi fumed.

"What happened, Alexis?" Drea quizzed going into lawyer mode.

"Evidently his phone called me by accident and I heard some bitch all in his ear."

Lexi's phone started ringing and she looked at it and rolled her eyes. Drea watched as she sent J.R. to voicemail each time that he called.

"Fuck him… Ima show his ass who Alexis Holiday really is!"

Drea sighed and headed to the bathroom because she knew that there was no talking Lexi down when her anger was elevated. She would give her some space and do it later. Almost forty-five minutes later, Drea was done with her bathroom routine and entering the living room where Kyler was sitting and watching TV.

"Heeyyy nephew! Whatcha watching?"

"Hi Auntie Drea… I'm watching a movie called *This Christmas*. It's on commercial. It reminds me of our Thanksgiving."

"Were we that bad nephew?"

Kyler shook his head yes and Drea really agreed. When the movie came back on, it was on the part where Chris Brown was about to sing, so she exited the living room without saying anything else. Drea couldn't help but to chuckle because it was a true saying that kids paid attention to every damn thing. Drea found Anastasia in the kitchen cooking something that was smelling scrumptious.

"I didn't' think yo ass was gon ever get up."

"We didn't get in until after two o'clock and remember your time is an hour ahead."

"Yeah yeah yeah… I'm almost done with brunch. Lyssa didn't answer, but hopefully she'll call or text back.

"Okay, I'm shol hungry," Drea replied as she went and sat back at the table.

While she waited, she decided to call and check on her mom. The phone rang three times before someone picked up, but it wasn't Victoria.

"Happy New Year Aunt Shirley!"

"Naw naw naw… don't Happy New Year me… y'all lil hussies didn't take me to New York wit y'all!"

"Auntie, someone had to stay with mommy."

"She got all them fake ass people from the church stopping by all the time. Most of em wanted Abraham, but don't tell her I told you."

"Lord Aunt Shirley, where's mommy at?"

"Hold on… but I be damn if I miss the next trip… Vicky pick up the phone!"

"Hello," her mom finally got on the phone.

"Happy New Year, mom! How are you?"

"Happy New Year, baby. I'm okay… are all of y'all good?"

"Yes ma'am. Stasia is making brunch right now. Lexi is upstairs and hopefully Lyssa is on her way."

Andrea talked to her mom for about five more minutes until Lexi walked in and took over the conversation. Once Lexi finally hung up, Anastasia had the table set with food. She had whipped up a breakfast casserole, waffles, and a spread of fruit. Anastasia called Kyler and then fixed him a plate. He carried it back to the living room and then the sisters dug in.

"Well, I guess Lyssa got other shit going on for now. What y'all wanna do tonight tho?" Stasia asked.

"Oh… D'Mari invited us to a kickback. Since you know where they live, you can drive," Drea said after she took a bite of the casserole.

"That'll work… I need to see D'Mani anyway.

"Make sure he got a cousin there for me," Lexi chimed in.

"Shut yo hot ass up playing. You know you stuck on J.R. nuts," Stasia joked.

"I'm serious shit… fuck J.R."

The three of them talked as they ate and then decided on what time they were going to leave and everything. Drea took time to respond to the million Happy New Year texts and then called Hannah. She didn't show her excitement, but she couldn't wait to get cute and see her baby daddy later that night.

Chapter 10

Anastasia was happy that her and her sisters had been getting along so well, and that Lexi and Drea had decided to make the trip to New York to spend some more time with her and Lyssa. It was crazy how the death of their father and all of their secrets being spilled had brought them all together, but she couldn't deny that she loved how close they were getting. They'd all just finished eating and were waiting on Alyssa to arrive so that they could go shopping for something to wear for the evening at D'Mani's house.

She definitely couldn't wait since it had been so long since D'Mani had laid the dick on her. After all of the drama back in Mississippi, she wasn't sure that they could get back on track. Him not telling her about D'Mari, or the fact that people were after them was something that she should have been aware of. With everything that had been going on, they hadn't had a chance to talk about either and she was looking forward to figuring things out between them. Besides that, she was ready to be rid of Richard's demanding ass. After all of the crazy behavior he had been displaying lately, there was no way that she wasn't going to win her case against him and be free. She almost couldn't contain how excited she felt knowing that soon she wouldn't have to deal with Richard at all, besides when it came to their son.

Anastasia made herself comfortable on the couch with Kyler and rubbed his head as they all sat around and watched Lifetime while he played on his tablet. She shook her head at the craziness that was unfolding across her screen. It didn't matter what movie it seemed to be on that channel, it was always involving a nutty ass ex. She couldn't help but equate the man on the TV with Richard.

If he kept up with the foolishness, she didn't doubt that she would be needing to get a restraining order on him. She chuckled at the thought, drawing Drea's eyes her way.

"Hoe, what you over there laughing about?" she asked with her faced frowned up in confusion as she cupped her container of ice cream closer to her body.

"Girl nothing, I was just thinking of how this man on here remind me of R-I-C-H-A-R-D with all this crazy shit he doin," Anastasia explained, making sure to spell his name out so that Kyler wouldn't know who she was talking about. So far, he had not been witness to his father's behavior and she would like to keep it that way.

"Oh," was Drea's reply as she relaxed her face and finally brought the spoon up to her mouth.

"Wasn't nobody thinking bout yo greedy butt." Anastasia couldn't help but to say once she realized that Drea thought she was laughing at her eating the whole thing of ice cream.

"I wish both y'all would shut up before I miss what they saying!" Lexi snapped from the reclining chair that she was curled up in. Both sisters looked, rolled their eyes at her, and Stasia threw one of her throw pillows her way hitting, her upside the head.

"That's what yo ass get Baby Holiday; stay out grown folks business," Drea teased while Anastasia laughed at the displeasure on her baby sister's face.

"Y'all the ones actin like babies," she whined, throwing the pillow right back and sticking her tongue out at Stasia who caught it and tucked it underneath her body. Her and Drea laughed at how upset Lexi looked while she ran a hand through her hair and grumbled about how immature they were.

"Okay, okay, we'll leave you alone," Andrea promised, stuffing another spoonful into her mouth.

"You just don't want me to throw a pillow at yo hungry ass."

"You're right, cause if I drop my ice cream its gone be problems," Drea said, giving a warning look to each of her sisters.

"Girl, I'll take that damn ice cream," Anastasia joked, making a move like she was about to get up and try.

"Don't come over here, Stasia. I promise you gone pull back a nub messin with me," Drea threatened and the look on her face was so serious that both Stasia and Lexi knew she wasn't playing, which made them laugh even harder.

"You better leave her pregnant ass alone, Stasia; she don't look like she joking," Lexi laughed as she looked between the two in amusement.

"Okay…okay, I'm done," Stasia giggled, lifting her hands in surrender and easing back into her seat. Drea watched her with slanted eyes like she was really ready to fight her over that ice cream, before turning her attention back to the TV.

No sooner than Anastasia got comfortable in her seat again, the sound of the doorbell ringing had her up and on her feet. She made sure to lunge in her sister's direction, causing Drea to pull her ice cream closer while Anastasia and Alexis laughed.

"Hardy har har," Drea snipped, rolling her eyes as Anastasia continued to the door. She looked through the peephole and frowned at the older white man that stood on the other side. Figuring that it was probably some more foolishness due to Richard, she swung the door open just as he went to reach for the bell again.

"Oh! Ummm, Anastasia Holiday?" he asked like he wasn't sure while eying her.

"Yes, may I ask why you're looking for me?"

"You've been served." He stiffly shoved an envelope into her hand and hurried off.

"Hey! What is this?" she shouted at his back, but he refused to turn around. She watched him until he disappeared into the car parked in front of her house and drove off. "Asshole."

Without moving to go back into the house, she stood in the doorway and opened up the piece of mail that the guy had placed in her hand and frowned once she realized what it was. Zyree had served her with establishment of paternity papers. That was the shit that she had been trying to avoid with his slow ass. She'd told him on more than one occasion that Kyler wasn't his son and still he made it his mission to find out where she lived to serve her with a court order. Going to court to establish paternity of Kyler was the last thing she needed while she was going through this messy ass divorce with Richard. With a deep sigh, she moved to close the door when a foot stopped her and she looked up into the face of none other than Richard.

Anastasia rolled her eyes at the sight of her estranged husband and threw a hand on her hip. "What do you want, Richard?" she asked, not really caring, but ready to get rid of him as fast as possible.

"Ana, why do I have to keep chasing you down? Huh? You won't let me get Kyler and you won't let me get anywhere near you. What the fuck is your problem?" he growled angrily.

"You're damn right you can't get anywhere near me with yo crazy ass! And as far as Kyler goes, as soon as I'm no longer worried about his safety in your care the sooner I'll let you take him," she reasoned, taking in his disheveled appearance. It was obvious that he hadn't shaved and his clothes were wrinkled as hell. His eyes were red and he smelled like he'd bathed in vodka. She tried not to, but she couldn't help the look of disdain that crossed her face. It seemed like Richard was going downhill fast and she was hoping that he got his shit together and soon. She may have hated his guts, and no longer wanted to be with him, but she didn't want him to fall off the deep end.

"So, I'm crazy now? You don't think you have anything to do with that?" he asked with narrowed eyes. "Poor Anastasia, the shopping sprees, the money... the business, that wasn't enough for you. No, you had to go and find you some gutter rat ass nigga."

"Oh, hell no! I'm not about to have this conversation with you when you're clearly drunk as hell," Anastasia said and tried to move away from the door, but he put his arm in the way and grabbed at her with the other, snatching the paper out of her hand.

"Give me that back!" she barked, stepping fully outside. The last thing she needed was for him to see that paternity paper in the state that he was in. He didn't even realize that he had the paper until she had said something, but at that point his interest was piqued. Turning his body away from her, he shrugged off the weak blows she threw at his back as his eyes scanned the first few lines and he faced her in a rage.

"Kyler might not be mine bitch?!"

Anastasia's eyes widened in fear at the look of evil that covered his face as he stepped towards her, backing her into the closed door. If she thought he looked crazy before, he definitely had her shook now.

"Richard...I," she started to say, but he reached out and grabbed her by the throat making it impossible for her to speak.

"Oh, you ain't got shit to say now, huh? I should fucking kill you!" he said, barely moving his lips as he stared down at her with dark eyes. Anastasia tried to shake her head, but she couldn't move due to how tight his grip was on her. Tears sprang to her eyes as she frantically banged on the door with her hands and feet hoping that her sisters would hear her and come help. As if God was listening, the door came open and she fell back causing Richard to release her as Lexi's loudmouth ass came out cursing.

"You got my sister fucked up, bitch!" she shrieked, instantly punching and kicking Richard anywhere she could while Anastasia grabbed her throat and gulped in as much air as she could.

"What the hell going on out here?" Andrea asked finally making an appearance. She must have taken in the sight of Anastasia on the ground and Lexi chasing Richard down the street and realized exactly what was happening. Without waiting for her to say anything Drea dropped down to make sure Stasia was alright. She asked her a few questions and looked over her neck as Lexi walked back up looking out of breath and angry.

They both helped Anastasia up off of the ground and into the small hallway inside of her house. "Bitch, what the fuck? Richard done lost his got damn mind putting his hands on you!" Lexi fumed angrily as she paced in the small area. "Wait till I tell my nigga and wait till I tell D'Mani!"

"Lexi hush, you not telling nobody," Drea chastised, still looking over Anastasia who was trying to recover.

"The hell I ain't!" she grumbled and Stasia put up a hand to calm her down, shaking her head.

"No......don't... say nothin," she managed to get out while holding her throat. She didn't miss the crazy look her baby sister hit her with. "He's pissed about Zyree sending me papers for a paternity test." She let them know putting her head in her hands. She didn't know what she was feeling at the moment. To her it seemed like this was all Zyree's fault because she had told him too many times that Kyler was not his. Now Richard had come across the damn papers and that shit definitely wasn't gone look good in court.

"What the fuck?" Lexi said angrily shaking her head while Drea remained quiet and looked at her with sympathetic eyes.

"Well, I guess since I'm representing you I have to ask......" she finally said with her eyes still on Stasia.

"What? Richard is Kyler's daddy," Stasia told her firmly, if there was one thing she was sure about that was it.

"Unfortunately," Lexi mumbled to herself even though both sisters heard and looked in her direction with matching frowns. "What …hell y'all was thinking that shit, too."

"If Zyree's not Kyler's father, then you really don't even need to worry about this, but you probably should get a restraining order against Richard's nutty ass," Drea advised.

"I'm not worried, but I don't want no restraining order. I don't need any interaction with the police. I'll handle Richard on my own." Anastasia shook her head emphatically. She could see that Drea didn't agree with her, but the last thing she wanted to do was get Richard labeled a woman beater, when he was only reacting to recent events. No, she could handle Richard is what she told herself even though the look on Andrea and Lexi's faces said otherwise.

Chapter 11

Lexi threw on her black leather jacket with the fur around the collar, grabbed her black Chanel bag, and followed her sisters out of the house. She wasn't really in a partying mood, but she figured she would make best of the situation and try to at least enjoy herself. It was the first day of the New Year and shit was already starting off bad. Richard putting his hands on Stasia took the cake and on top of all that, she had been calling J.R.'s phone since last night, but he had yet to pick up. He pocket-dialed her and the first thing she heard was a female's voice in the background. She knew it wasn't good to jump to conclusions, but him not answering and then knowing he was in the presence of a bitch, made matters worse. Once he noticed he called her on accident, he had been blowing her phone up, only to get the voicemail each time.

"So how long is the ride to D'Mani's house?" Drea asked, getting in the front seat of Anastasia's ride.

"Girl, he like thirty minutes away, but with the New York traffic, that thirty minutes can turn into an hour," Stasia insured her.

"See, that's why, I could never move to a big ass city. I'll literally die in traffic," Drea replied, pulling down the sun visor and checking her makeup in the mirror.

"I felt the same way when I first moved here, but I got used to it."

"I see, so is Alyssa meeting us there or what? She already sent us off about going to the mall" Andrea looked over at Anastasia and asked.

"Yeah she supposed to. I texted her the address earlier, but she never replied. I don't know what's going on with that girl," Stasia stated.

"I personally think it's that job stressing her out. Maybe Daddy was right," Andrea reflected.

"Maybe, who knows, but I just want to enjoy myself today. New Year, new me, Imma make sure of that," Stasia said, turning onto the freeway.

Alexis didn't engage in the conversation with her sisters because she was too busy texting J.R. He had the nerve to send her a text stating that if she didn't answer her phone then he wasn't ever calling her again. She replied by saying,

Lexi: I don't give a fuck if you never call me again, nigga you can even block me. TF! You just went damn near 24 hours not answering me but now you wanna give ultimatums and shit…FUCK YOU BRO!

After sending that last message, she put her phone on Do Not Disturb and stuffed it in her bag. She laid her head back on the seat and closed her eyes.

"Baby Holiday, you quiet back there. You good?" Stasia asked, while looking back at her through the rearview mirror.

"Yeah sister, I'm good," she lied.

"You sure? I know J.R. been acting an ass, but it's nothing to fly back to Atlanta with you and handle him," Drea turned around and chimed in.

"He not even worth it, man," was all Lexi said.

Anastasia's timing was perfect. Traffic was a bitch, so they made it to D'Mani's crib in about an hour. The driveway was packed with about five cars, all of them foreign. Stasia had no choice but to park about two houses down.

"This nigga said small kickback, it looks like he having a party to me," Drea said as the three of them made their way down to the mini-mansion.

"Kickback or party, I don't give a damn. With Richard damn near killing me earlier, I need several drinks," Stasia stated, walking up first and ringing the doorbell.

The girls stood on the porch a few seconds before the door finally swung open. D'Mani or D'Mari, Lexi couldn't tell they ass apart, answered wearing a pair of gray Nike jogging pants, a white V-neck shirt, and some Gucci slides with socks, welcomed them in.

"Hey baby!" Stasia beamed and that's when Lexi knew that it was in fact D'Mani standing in from of her.

"What's up, baby?" he greeted her back, pulling her towards him, while gripping her ass.

Both Lexi and Drea looked at each other and smirked. Stasia was acting like a school girl all smitten and shit, but they both loved seeing their sister happy.

"Y'all come on in, Drea my bro in the back. Lexi where J.R.?" D'Mani asked.

"Fuck J.R.," was all Lexi said before following her sisters inside.

"That's too bad, I thought the lil nigga was cool, but if you say fuck em, then it's fuck em," D'Mani replied, closing the door behind them.

When Lexi walked in, she was pleasantly surprised. From the outside, the house looked nice, but the inside was amazing. The ceilings were high, the walls where pure white like cocaine. Beautiful paintings and structures decked out the living room, you definitely wouldn't have been able to guess that a man was the owner of the gorgeous estate.

D'Mani led them to the back of the house where the kitchen was located. Lexi was just as amazed at the way the kitchen was set up, as she was the rest of the house. She was starting to wonder why Stasia hadn't been left Richard ass alone if that was how her side nigga was living.

"Aye y'all, this my girl Stasia; this D'Mari's baby momma, Drea, and their little sister, Lexi," D'Mani said, introducing the ladies to the handful of people that were chilling in the kitchen.

"What up baby momma?" D'Mari came out of nowhere and said, rubbing Drea's growing belly as soon as he was in arms reach.

"What's up, baby daddy?" Drea replied, gushing back.

"So, this your girl, D'Mani, and this yo baby momma, D'Mari? I guess it's only right that I make you my wife then Lexi. Fuck it, let's keep it in the family," a guy said from behind.

Lexi turned around and looked at the man who spoke. He towered over her at about 6'3, he was dark, about as dark as Taye Diggs. He had a rough look about him, his dreads looked as if they needed to be twisted while his facial hair was lined up to perfection. Lexi noticed the tattoos on his neck and arms first. Her eyes then glanced down at the all red Retro 11's that were on his feet. There was no denying the fact that he was fine as hell.

"Aye Lexi, this our nephew, Rico," D'Mari said, laughing.

Lexi gave off a flirty smile and wave before taking a seat on one of the available stools by the island bar.

"Y'all want something to eat or something to drink?" D'Mani asked before walking off and heading to the ringing doorbell.

"I'm good, but I know Big Shirley over there hungry," Lexi said, pointing to Drea.

"Man, Lexi cool it out with all them hungry jokes. She is eating for three," D'Mari said, defending Drea.

"Thank you, baby and I'll take some chicken and lasagna," Drea added in, rolling her eyes playfully at Lexi.

"Look, y'all not finna gang up on my wife like that," Rico said, walking over to where Lexi was sitting.

"Thank you, hubby," Lexi replied, winking her eye at him.

Lexi took her purse off her shoulder, went inside and grabbed her phone. She had a missed call from Marcus and a few more unread text messages, none of them from J.R. When she went to see if he texted back, although he hadn't, he did read her last message and that pissed her off even more.

"What's up y'all?"

Lexi, Drea, and Stasia turned to the entrance of the kitchen and walking in came Alyssa and Corey. They all spoke to each other before Alyssa took a seat, joining her sisters.

"How long y'all been here?" Alyssa questioned.

"Not even thirty minutes," Stasia informed her.

"We ain't think yo ass was coming since you hadn't replied to our messages nor answered any of our calls today," Drea told her.

"My bad, I been taking care of business. What's up?" Alyssa asked.

"Shit, we chilling," Lexi finally added in.

The sisters sat around and talked a little more before D'Mani and D'Mari pulled them away. Lexi watched both of her sisters dip off in different directions. She silently prayed that the both of them got some dick and got a lot of it; enough for her too.

"You finna be cool right here by yourself, I'm about to go find Corey," Alyssa said, standing to her feet.

"Yeah, I'm straight. Go ahead," Lexi assured her.

"Yeah sis, she in good hands with me," Rico's handsome ass said to Alyssa who shook her head and walked away.

"I'm about to go smoke, you about to go with me?" Rico asked.

"Yeah, come on," Lexi replied.

All her sisters had left her and she didn't want to be sitting there alone; especially, since she deleted all her social sites for the new year. She would have definitely been bored. Rico extended his hand for her to grab and she accepted his invitation. He led her up the stairs to one of the bedrooms where he cut the TV on and sparked up a backwood. The two of them talked, laughed, joked, and before they knew it, they had smoked two backwoods. Lexi was as high as a giraffe's pussy, which wasn't a good thing because the higher she got, the hornier she became. She thought about how J.R. would fuck the shit out of her after their sessions and she instantly got wet.

"Lexi, you are beautiful," Rico said, moving closer to her on the bed as if he was reading her mind.

"Thank you. You not so bad yourself," she replied, feeling herself loosening up.

Without warning, Rico grabbed Lexi's face and kissed her. She found herself engulfed as their tongues intertwined. Alexis allowed her body to loosen up, laying back slowly on the bed. Rico was kissing her like she had never been kissed before. His kisses were so powerful, he might have had the ability to make her cum just from kissing, had he actually tried. Rico's hands roamed her body, causing chills to cover her skin. As soon as he went under her shirt, Lexi's cellphone rung. She silently cursed herself out for not putting it back on Do Not Disturb when she checked her messages downstairs in the kitchen.

"Let that muthafucker ring," Rico parted his lips and whispered and Lexi followed his orders, but once it stopped ringing, the phone chimed again, indicating that she had text messages pouring in.

"Hold on, let me just cut it off," she said to him before sitting up and going inside her purse, grabbing the phone.

Once she unlocked it, she noticed that the call was from Drea, as well as the text messages.

Drea: Where yo ass at?

Lexi: Upstairs

After Lexi replied, she put her phone on silent and walked back over the bed where Rico was laying down on his back. Alexis gave him a sexy grin before straddling him, picking up exactly where they left off. She felt herself getting wetter with each kiss, she knew right then and there that she was going to fuck the shit out of that New York nigga and have no regrets. She paused from their kissing session and pulled her shirt over her head, right when there was a knock on the door.

"Yo who is it?' Rico called out.

"It's Drea, Alexis Mariah Holiday, you better get yo ass out here right now!" Drea yelled from the other side of the door.

Lexi smacked her lips before getting off the bed and putting her shirt back on.

"My hating ass sisters not gon let us be great, but if you ever in Atlanta, hit me up," she said, giving him one last kiss before joining her sister on the other side of the door.

Chapter 12

Sleep didn't find Alyssa at all as she tossed and turn throughout the night. When Corey informed her that they were going to his cousin's house, Alyssa was excited to be meeting the people he chilled with the most. When they arrived at D'Mani and D'Mari's house, she damn near pissed herself. When she left Lexi to find Corey, Alyssa found him in a smoke session and that's where he dropped the bomb that the same twins that are with her sisters are the same twins he was related to. Alyssa tried her hardest to hide her discomfort while she was around his family and when it was time for them to leave, she quickly said her good-byes and darted out the house.

When the sun began to peek through the blinds, Alyssa sat up in her bed snatching her phone off the nightstand to see what time it was; it was 7:20 am. Noticing she had a text, she checked it. When she saw it was from Tara asking her could they meet up, Alyssa hesitated. If she linked up with Tara, Alyssa knew for a fact that she was going to try to convince her to help with the case that she wasn't supposed to be working on. As much as she wanted to ignore the message, she responded with a time and place for them to meet. Placing her phone back on the table, she headed towards the bathroom to take a shower.

As she finished up in the bathroom, Alyssa secured the towel around her before walking into her room where Corey was sitting on the edge of the bed glued to his phone. She let him be as she looked for an outfit to wear. Minutes after she finished putting on her lotion, she could feel Corey's eyes on her.

"Are you okay, Alyssa?" Corey quizzed.

"Mm hmm. Why you ask me that, bae?"

"You tossed and turned all night and that's the first time that's happened since we've been sleepin' together. Are you sure you're okay?"

"Baby, I'm fine." She smiled.

"Aight. What you about to get into tho?"

"I'm about to meet up with one of my coworkers. She has something to tell me about this case."

Corey nodded his head and Alyssa finished getting dressed. After she stuffed her feet into her wheat colored Timberland boots, she snatched her coat off the hook. Before she could leave the room, Corey blocked her path pulling her in for a hug and held her tightly causing her to melt in his embrace. They hugged for a few more seconds before he pecked her lips and released her. Alyssa felt better as she head out the front door with her keys and purse in hand. She unlocked the doors to her truck, climbed inside, and brought the car to life after slamming the door shut. She pulled off and headed to her location.

Arriving thirty minutes later at restaurant called Bubby's, Alyssa parked her car before throwing on her shades. She walked inside and immediately spotted Tara sitting at a booth in the back of the restaurant. Alyssa sat on the opposite side and grabbed the menu that was in front of her. She schemed to see if anything looked good and when her eyes landed on the French toast platter, she placed the menu back down. When Tara had her full attention, she spoke.

"I'm glad you agreed to meet with me, Alyssa because this case is getting out of hand."

"What do you mean?" she leaned forward folding her hands on the table.

"The agent that set you up is indeed one of our own, but what we didn't know is that he works for the owner of that club you went to. Not D'Mani. He's only a co-owner. The other man that owns the club, his real name is Pierre, but his street name is Blue." She pulled out a picture of him.

Alyssa's eye grew wide as she noticed the nigga in the picture was the same nigga that was flirting with her the day she went in there.

"I saw him at the club when I went there. That nigga is definitely a ladies' man," she chuckled.

"Blue and that snake, Quadree, the one who set you up, do a lot of business together. He got you out of the way because you he was afraid that you would expose him, but that's not all. A reliable source informed me that Blue was the target they were going after, but when bodies began to surface, someone called with an anymous tip that D'Mani was responsible for the murders and that's how the investigation got started. I'm not sure, but I think that Blue and Quadree are trying to frame D'Mani.

"Tara, why are you sharing this with me? You got a whole team that can help you with this."

"For two reasons. One because I don't trust anyone else and two because I'm trying to help you get your suspension lifted. I know you miss being on the team and this would be a good look if we brought them sons of bitches down. To be honest, I don't even want D'Mani to go to jail. My focus is on Blue and that pussy ass nigga, Quadree," Tara spoke through gritted teeth.

Alyssa looked at her with confusion.

"It's personal."

Alyssa nodded her head and before she could speak, the waiter appeared to take their food and drink order then disappeared as quickly as he came. With her hands still folded on the table, she began to think about the information Tara just gave her. Alyssa told herself that she was done with the FBI back in Mississippi and she meant it. The fact that D'Mani was being framed didn't sit well with her, but if she was spotted by anyone that was close to D'Mani and D'Mari, that could cause problems for her and divide their family again. As much as she wanted to help Tara, she just couldn't.

"I would love to help you but I can't. I'm done with the FBI and as much as I enjoyed the short amount of time I was on the team, it's time for me to move on to something different."

"Aight," Tara sighed.

"But if you change your mind, let me know soon. A meeting is supposed to be taking place at the club in two weeks and everyone that's a part of their organization will be there. I don't know all the details, but that's when we're going to raid the place and arrest whoever is in the building."

The waiter returned with their food and juices and they didn't hesitate to dig in. They chatted while they ate their food about non-work-related issues that was going on in their live. Alyssa didn't do too much talking. She just nodded her head as she ate. After the bill was paid, they hugged each other good-bye and promised to keep in touch.

Alyssa jumped in her truck and drove back home where Corey was parked on the couch watching Sports Center. She flopped down next to him and when she tried to lay on him, he moved away from her. Confused by his action, she needed to know what was up.

"Corey, what's up with you?"

"You tell me, Amanda," he scowled at her

Hearing the name that she used at the club that day made her heart drop to her stomach. Alyssa was stuck for a few seconds, but when Corey got up from the couch, she followed him behind to the bedroom.

"Listen, Corey. I can explain," she began.

"Go head. I'm listenin'."

"When I first started on this case, I didn't know who your cousin was. I was just doing my job. I didn't know then what I know now. So, you can't blame me for that. I've been suspended from the FBI for about a month because someone on my team framed me and they thought I was involved with the case. My coworker just asked me to help her with the case and I told her I couldn't. I'm done with the FBI."

"Why didn't you tell me about this when we were in Mississippi?"

"Baby, I didn't know that D'Mani was involved with my sister until we were at the hospital. That's when I found out about D'Mari and I just found out yesterday that they were your cousins." Alyssa shook her head.

"Why didn't you tell me that you were involved in the street shit, Corey?"

"When I proposed to you, I wanted to make sure that we wouldn't want for nothin' when we got married. So, I saved my legal bread and splurged with the illegal. I made moves in the streets because I was thinkin' of our future, Ma."

Alyssa wanted to crack a smile but she managed to keep a straight face.

"So, all those trips you took out of town? Were those legal or illegal trips?"

"Both, Lyssa."

"Are you done with the street shit, Corey?"

"After this last move, yes."

"Is there anything else I should know?"

"As of right now? Naw. I couldn't tell you about what I was doin' in the streets because that was somethin' I felt you didn't need to know. You feel me?"

"Yeah."

"Come here."

Alyssa walked over to him and he held her in his arms. As they stood in the middle of the floor, Alyssa told him what Tara told her about the meeting that was taking place in two weeks and how Blue and Quadree was trying to frame D'Mani. Corey promised that he would take care of it and told her not to worry. Alyssa felt like a burden was lifted off her shoulders after she told Corey the truth about her case. She didn't like keeping secrets from her fiancé and being as though that they were trying to rebuild their trust, there was no room for secrets of any sort. Alyssa felt good about her decision to leave the FBI. She could finally focus on planning her wedding and finding a new career in the process.

Chapter 13

"I know you gotta be having a good ass time because you haven't complained about that cold ass weather up there not once," Hannah said.

"Girl... it's cold as fuck, but I have been enjoying myself. It's been all love."

"You mean to tell me the Holiday sisters are still getting along?"

"Yes," Drea laughed.

"And it feels so good being together."

Oh lord... yo ass gon be tryna move to New York soon. You got your baby daddy and your sisters there already."

"Nah... I don't wanna raise my babies in the city, but I don't mind visiting as much as possible."

"Speaking of babies... I gotta start planning your baby shower. You know you not gonna make it to July 30th because twins always come early."

"I don't think I've fully grasped the idea that I'm having twins... two babies."

"Well, you better get it in your head. Yeah you going from zero to two, but it's all good. I can't wait to see what we having!" Hannah exclaimed.

Drea talked to Hannah for a few more minutes and then finally hung up. They were all going out in just a few to hang out. Andrea was dressed in some jeans, her brown

Ugg boots, a white sweater and she had her red pea coat laid out to put on. Lexi walked in the room dressed and it shocked the shit out of Drea because Lexi's ass was always slow as Christmas.

"Why you looking at me like that?" Lexi cocked her head to the side.

"Just shocked that Baby Holiday is dressed and ready," Drea shrugged,

"Shut the hell up and come on. Lyssa was just pulling up and Stasia ready too," Lexi rolled her eyes.

"I'll be glad when you get back to Atlanta and you and J.R. make up because you need some dick," Drea teased.

"Look at you… bitch start getting some on the regular and wanna talk shit."

"Well…" Drea stuck her tongue out.

They made their way to the living room still laughing and talking shit to each other and found Anastasia letting the baby sitter in. After Anastasia had everything set, the sisters gathered up their coats and purses and headed out. When they walked outside, Drea noticed Alyssa was in her new truck.

"Lyssa, you might as well drive since your truck is already warmed up," Stasia suggested taking the thoughts right out of Drea's head.

They piled into Alyssa's truck and the heated seats didn't take any time coming to life. After Alyssa finished texting someone, she backed out and headed towards the Wax Museum. They had tossed out several ideas on what they were going to do. They collectively decided on the museum first and then said that they would just wing it. It was Wednesday and traffic was still hell. That was one of the main reasons Drea didn't want to live in a big city. Visiting was just fine to her. It was crazy how a person could live twenty minutes from work, but it could easily be an hour commute because of traffic, and don't even mention if the weather was bad.

Almost an hour later, they arrived at their destination. The ride didn't really seem that long because they sang and talked shit to each other the entire ride. Alyssa's mind seemed to be elsewhere at times, and Drea figured that it had to do with her job situation. She made a mental note to talk to her later to make sure that she was mentally okay. They went inside, paid, and took pictures with every damn statue in the place. It was crazy how most of them looked so fucking real. The next stop was going to be at the Guinness Book of World Records, but Drea had gotten hungry.

"What you want to eat?" Alyssa asked when they got back in the truck.

"It really doesn't matter. Just pick somewhere," Drea replied.

"Okay, let's go to Grand Central Station and find something then. It'll be a variety there and we can mix and match."
"Sounds good to me."

That was where they made their way to. The various aromas of food made Drea's stomach growl. She had skipped breakfast and it was a little after twelve, so it was time to eat. When they passed by Danish Dogs, Lexi stopped and placed an order. Drea had a sudden taste for pizza and saw a sign for Prova Pizza and decided to head that way, but not before telling Lexi to order her a hot dog too.

"Damn bitch… you taking this eating for three shit real ain't ya," Lexi joked.

After Drea got her food, she told herself that she was going to stop by Zaro's Family Bakery on the way out to get a cupcake. She knew that she wouldn't be alone because her sisters were greedy as fuck. At least she had an excuse.

Thirty minutes later, they were all sitting down eating and enjoying their food. Anastasia brought up Lexi's Christmas gift to them and they started planning for their Valentine's trip.

"Y'all wanna see if the men wanna go… or just keep it for us?" Stasia inquired.

"I ain't got no man, bitch!" Lexi stated.

"Ughhh Lexi chill out… you know you gon make up wit that nigga. He seems to be the only person that can keep yo hot ass on a leash," Lyssa chimed in.

"I'm cool with it either way. Having the men there will only add more excitement," Drea said.

"I ain't buying their tickets," Lexi made known.

"They can buy their own tickets crazy ass," Stasia rolled her eyes.

Andrea noticed that Lexi had a look on her face that told her that she wanted to say something else, but she didn't. She knew that Lexi would reveal whatever was on her mind sooner or later.

"We can decide on that later," Drea ended the discussion and they all agreed.

Once they were done eating, they got up and threw their trash away. Just as she told herself moments before, Drea headed towards the bakery.

"Oooh I want a cupcake too," Lexi said.

"Wait a minute… is that… yeah that's that bitch!" Lexi said and took off running.

"Lexi!" Drea yelled out, but it was too late because she was gone.

"That's Lizz!" Stasia confirmed and they all took off running behind their baby sister.

By the time they made it to Lexi, she had punched Lizz in the face and slung her to the floor. Lexi wasted no time pouncing down on her. The lady that was with Lizz didn't even try to help. She just stood there and screamed. They reached their sister at the same time as security and Drea screamed for them to let her sister go.

"Arrest her! Arrest her right now!" Lizz screamed from the floor with blood running from her nose and visible scars on her face.

"Shut the fuck up!" Stasia yelled at her ex friend.

She made a move towards her, but Drea and Lyssa grabbed her at the same time.

Lexi was handcuffed right before their eyes and taken away.

"I'll be right there to get you, Lexi!" Drea yelled and then pulled her phone out.

She called Felix and he answered after the phone rang three times.

"Andrea Holiday… to what do I owe the pleasure of this call?"

"Felix… my sister just got arrested at Grand Central Station for jumping on my other sister's husband's mistress," she explained.

"Gotta be Lexi."

"You know it!"

"I'll take care of everything."

"She's about to graduate, Felix… I really don't want this on her record if you can make it happen," Drea pleaded.

"I'm on it… I'll text you where to meet me. We'll have her taken care of before they can even process anything. I'm gonna send you the address now."

"Thank you so much… I owe you!"

"Don't mention it."

As promised, Felix saved the day and Drea hugged him and thanked him for ten minutes straight while they waited on Lexi to walk out. The entire process had taken a little over an hour, but that was good timing in Drea's eyes.

"I'm freeeee!!!!" Lexi screamed to the top of her lungs a few minutes and caused all of them to laugh.

"This lil bitch act like she just did eighteen years or some shit," Drea shook her head.

They all thanked Felix again and decided to call it a day.

Chapter 14

After they picked Lexi's ass up from jail, Alyssa dropped them off at Anastasia's house and headed on home. After taking a hot bath, she threw on tank top, a pair of sweat pants and some ankles socks before getting comfortable in her bed with her laptop. Alyssa thought it would be a good time to go wedding dress shopping since her sisters were in town. She didn't have a clue of what type of wedding dress she wanted and Alyssa knew that her sisters would be happy to help her make a selection.

She googled bridal boutiques in the area and being as though New York was one of the most popular cities to shop for wedding dresses, Alyssa had more than enough stores to choose from. Alyssa clicked on the websites of the boutiques to see who carried the best dresses and she was torn between three shops. Choosing the one closest to her, she set up an appointment for the next day at two in the afternoon. When everything was a go, Alyssa grabbed her phone and went to the group message with her sisters.

Lyssa: I scheduled an appointment at bridal boutique tomorrow so be ready by 12:30

Drea: Cool

Stasia: Kk

Lexi: Aight hoe

"This hoe." She shook her head at Lexi's response.

Before Alyssa could stuff her phone in her pocket, a text came through. She checked it and it was from Corey telling her not to wait up for him. She replied be safe before placing her phone on the nightstand. Placing her laptop on the bed, she tossed the cover off her and headed to the kitchen to make something to eat for Corey. She couldn't help but to worry about him while he was out running the streets, but Alyssa had to let him do his thing. Even if she didn't agree with it.

When she was finished preparing his food, she wrapped his plate up and placed it in the microwave. Alyssa left a note for him on the kitchen counter letting him know where his food was before walking back to her room and dozing off to sleep.

The next morning, Alyssa was happy that she woke up in Corey's arms. Easing out of his embrace, she straightened up her condo before getting ready for the day ahead. She kissed Corey on his forehead before she left the condo to pick up her sisters. Alyssa couldn't hide her happiness as she drove to Stasia's house. She thought about the feelings she had when Corey first proposed to her and even with the problems they had, she was still doubt free. Even though they didn't have a set date for the wedding, just knowing that it was going to happen filled her heart with joy.

Pulling up to her sister's house, she honked the horn twice and waited for them to come out. Seconds later, they all came out of the house and piled into the car. They greeted each other as Alyssa headed towards the boutique.

"Aye Lyssa, do you know what type of dress you want?" Lexi inquired from the back seat.

"I don't have a clue, sis. I looked at the dresses they had online and I really couldn't make up my mind. I figured since all of us were together, y'all would help me decide."

"You know we got you," Drea chimed in.

"Are you sure you're ready to get married? I remember you telling me that you weren't sure at one point in time," Stasia mentioned.

"I'm not gonna lie. I wasn't at first, but out of everything that's happened between me and Corey, at the end of the day, I don't want anyone else but him." She smiled

"No man is perfect, but I feel like he's perfect for me."

"As long as you're happy, we're happy," Lexi stated.

"Any of y'all thinking about jumping the broom?" Alyssa questioned looking at them through her mirror.

"It would be nice to come home to D'Mari every night, but that's not something I would jump into. I feel like some men are either great fathers or great husbands. Not all of them can be both," Drea spoke up.

"You got that right," Stasia mumbled.

"I think I would like to get married but the to whom is yet to be decided," Lexi commented.

"J.R. ain't an option?" Lyssa questioned.

"Not at the moment." She folded her arms against her chest.

Alyssa looked over at Drea who just shook her head. Alyssa took that as a sign to leave the situation alone. So, she did. Alyssa arrived at the bridal boutique twenty minutes earl,y parking in the first spot she saw. Entering the boutique, they were greeted by a female that was dressed in a black pants suit. Alyssa gave her name and the woman introduced herself to them. She was the manager. After telling the woman that she didn't know exactly what she was looking for, she escorted them to the back of the boutique where there were a few couches and a lot of floor to ceiling mirrors. The four of them waited for the manager to return with a few dresses for her to try on. She returned a few minutes later with her assistant carrying all different styles of wedding dresses. Filled with excitement, Alyssa grabbed one of the dresses and hurried into the fitting room.

Alyssa tried on an assortment of dresses. Long dresses, short, dresses, dresses with mermaid skirts and ball gown dresses. Alyssa decided that she liked the long dresses better than the short one and after two hours of trying on dresses, Alyssa narrowed it down to two dresses that fitted her perfectly to the point that she could walk right out the store with. After her sisters told her that she couldn't go wrong with either dress, Alyssa decided to get a ballroom style dress with a train. After getting dressed in her regular clothes, the manager informed her that she ordered the dress in her size and that it would take a couple of weeks to arrive. Alyssa didn't have a problem with that. Her dress was $4200 and Alyssa handed over Corey's credit card with a smile on her face.

The ladies thanked the manager and her assistant for their help as they left the store. Everyone hopped into Alyssa's truck and when Andrea said her favorite line, "I'm hungry", Alyssa drove to a nearby restaurant. The Holiday sisters were seated immediately and they looked over the menu. After they were done looking over the menu, they ordered everything at once when the waiter came. Alyssa was having such a good time with her sisters that she became sad at the thought of them leaving. Going wedding dress shopping with her sisters made the experience of picking a wedding dress that much better. Alyssa hated that they wasted so many years not liking each other, but the past was the past. She thought about how her father wouldn't be able to walk her down the aisle on her wedding day, but she knew that he would smiling down on her when her special day came just like he was smiling at the sight of all his girls getting along.

Chapter 15

"I'm here to pick up an order for Alexis Holiday."

"No problem ma'am, give me a second."

Lexi watched the friendly baker headed to the back of the bakery to retrieve the cake that she ordered for Andrea's birthday. When she returned, she opened the box that contained a red velvet cake with fresh strawberries on top. The base of the cake was white with "Happy Birthday Big Mama" written in cursive red across it. After paying for the cake, Lexi headed to the nearest grocery store and got a tub of Neapolitan ice cream. She wasn't sure which one her sister wanted so Anastasia suggested she get a variety since Drea takes her ice cream serious. Once she was done there, he headed to the Sheraton New York Times Square Hotel where she booked two rooms. One room was for the party and the second room was for D'Mari and Drea, when the party was over. Lexi reached out to him about Drea's birthday and how her and her sisters wanted to throw her a small surprise party. It turned out that D'Mari had the hook up. In fact, he paid for both rooms, which was fine by Lexi's pockets.

Lexi exited Alyssa's truck and headed inside the hotel. She stopped at the front door and stomped off the snow that was clinging onto her Uggs before walking in. Once she made it to the reservations desk, an elderly Caucasian couple was wrapping things up. She waited patiently for them to get their keys and belongings, when her phone rang. She pulled the iPhone out of her pocket and rolled her eyes at the sight of J. R's name. Lexi slid the bar across, answering the call just as the hotel receptionist was ready to assist her.

"Good evening, I'm here to check in, I have a reservation under Alexis Holiday."

The reservationist asked for Lexi's ID and then keyed a few things into the system, all the while, J.R. was in her ear hollering.

"Why the fuck you checking into a hotel? Where you at?" he roared into the phone.

Lexi ignored him and thanked the lady once she handed her the key cards to the rooms. She listened to J.R. make idle threats as she headed to the elevator and up to the fifth floor.

"Jeremy, I don't know who the fuck you think you talking to, but you need to chill," she warned as she exited on her designated floor and headed to the first room.

"Lexi, on some real shit, we need to talk," he replied, much calmer than a few minutes before.

"How you wanna talk when you ain't been answering your phone and then when I do hear from you, it's not technically from you, it's from a bitch," she snapped.

"First of all, that was my cousin and if yo hot head ass would have answered your phone, then you would have known that," he shot back.

"Cousin my ass J.R., what do you want?" she asked.

"I wanna know when you are coming home," he quickly replied.

"I'll be back in Atlanta tomorrow, but I'm going to stay with Marcus until I find me a place."

"WHY THE FUCK YOU STAYING WITH HIM?" he yelled into the phone.

"Because I'm grown and I can do what I want to do and besides, I can't be with a nigga who has plans on killing my people," she advised him.

"Yo people? You ain't even know them niggaz last month, but fuck it. Hit me up when you touchdown and I'll drop yo shit off to you," he said before hanging up.

Lexi flopped down on the bed and let out a long sigh of frustration. She didn't want to end things because she really did love him, but she was stuck between a rock and a hard place. She could deal with a heartbreak before she could deal with another death that'll hurt her sisters. Lexi forced herself up and headed back downstairs to get the cake, ice cream, and decorations out of the car. When she got back inside the room, she texted Alyssa and Anastasia to let them know she'll be done in about an hour. Drea thought Lexi was out on a date with Rico, but she hadn't talked to him since Drea came cock-blocking at D'Mani's house on New Year's Day.

Lexi grabbed the bag that contained her clothes and took everything out. She laid a pair of ripped up jeans she got from Fashion Nova across the bed along with an off the shoulder sweater. She slipped out of her Uggs and headed to the bathroom. She grabbed a towel off the rack, cut the water on as hot as she could stand and got it. After making the best love ever to the water, she hopped out, grabbed a fluffy white towel to dry off with and headed back to the bedroom. After snatching the lotion out of her purse, she took a seat on the bed, at the same time her phone chimed. She had a few unread messages from the group chat with Anastasia and Alyssa.

Stasia: We on our way and D'Mani just texted me and said that they'll be there in twenty minutes so we all should pull up at the same time.

Lexi: Aight lil bitch

After replying, she quickly applied the lotion and threw on her clothes. She went back into the bathroom and fixed the high ponytail she was wearing before applying light makeup. Once she was completely done, she grabbed the bag she got from Wal-Mart that contained the Bluetooth speaker she recently brought, connected it to her phone and put on Meek Mill radio on Pandora. Lexi blew up a few pink and gold balloons and laid them throughout the hotel room. The bouquet of balloons that she got made, was placed in each corner. After checking her phone and receiving the confirmation that the food she ordered was downstairs, she grabbed the room key off the table and went to get the food. As soon as Lexi made it to the delivery van, a Porsche truck pulled up, she began to grab the food, but stopped when she heard a male's voice say, "I got it, lil sis."

She was relieved to see that D'Mani and D'Mari had finally arrived and could carry all those bags up for her. She was even more pleased at the fact that they bought Rico's fine ass along with them.

"I hope you ain't think you was getting away from me that easily," he said, grabbing the plastic bag that contained the sodas.

"Boy, shut up and take this shit upstairs," was all she said before turning and walking off, making sure she put a little twist in her walk.

The four of them took the elevator back up to the room. Once inside, she had the guys sit everything on the table while she went through the bags and pulled each item out, one by one. Lexi made sure to order a variety of food and made sure to get enough. She got three pizzas, hot/BBQ wings, cheese sticks, fried pickles, jalapeno poopers and some more shit.

"Aye Lexi, you wanna hit this?" D'Mani asked, walking over to where she was holding a blunt in his hand.

"Y'all black ugly asses bet not ruin my sister's birthday by getting us kicked out of here…. But yeah, let me hit that," she replied, taking a hard pull from the backwood.

"We good, I already slid the manager on duty a few extra bucks so we could smoke this bitch out," D'Mani replied.

The blunt went in rotation a few more times before there was a knock on the door. Lexi got up to answer, thinking it was her sisters, but it was Corey. She welcomed him in and he joined the four of them in the smoke session. Lexi's phone chimed and it was Alyssa this time, asking for the room number.

"Aye y'all, my sister's here," she said, standing to her feet, heading to open the door.

About two minutes later, Andrea, Anastasia, and Alyssa walked in, carrying more bags full of liquor.

"HAPPY BIRTHDAY SISSSSTTEEERRRR!" Lexi yelled, while Drea smiled and eyed everyone in the room.

"Awww thanks Baby Holiday," she replied, hugging her younger sister.

"Lexi, you did a good job setting this up," Stasia stated while she examined the room and its contents.

"Yeah you did sister. I ain't think you was going to be able to pull it off," Lyssa laughed as she took a seat on Corey's lap.

"Fuck you. Let's turn up," she replied, grabbing her phone and going to Apple Music.

Lexi searched Tupac's name and stopped once she came across his diss record to Biggie "Hit Em Up". That was her favorite Tupac song and it made her feel some type of way after she listened to it. The entire room bobbed their heads up and down and rapped along. When that song was over, she then turned to N.W. A's song, "Fuck the Police" and cut the volume up to the max. Her sisters, including the guys looked at her and laughed.

"Baby you good, what's up with your music selection?" Rico asked.

Lexi cocked her head to the side before replying, "Nigga, I just got out, this how I'm feeling."

Drea, Stasia, and Lyssa, curled over in laughter while the guys looked at them confused.

"She did like fifteen minutes in jail the other day for beating up somebody, now she thinks she's an outlaw," Stasia turned to D'Mani and said.

"I am an outlaw, I should go get THUG LIFE tatt'd across my chest," Lexi replied as she sparked up another blunt.

The room looked at her and shook their head before they got up and started making their plates. Lexi felt good seeing everyone enjoy themselves especially her sisters. Lexi noticed how D'Mari had Drea in the corner smiling so she walked over and intervened. Once she reached them, she went inside her pocket and pulled out the key card for the extra room she got.

"Happy Birthday, sister. I love you. Now, D'Mari let's turn them twins into triplets and fuck the shit out of my sister," Lexi said sticking out her tongue before handing them the keycard.

Chapter 16

"Damn, you hookin' it up ain't you, ma?"

Anastasia turned around at the sound of D'Mani's voice and couldn't help but bite her lip in appreciation. He stood before her bare chested with a pair of black basketball shorts hanging loosely around his waist.

"Naw, don't look at me like that... fuck around and be feastin' on you and not this food you got laid out," he said licking his lips and giving her a sexy grin.

Ever since her sisters had returned to their respective homes D'Mani had been at her house, fucking her on damn near every surface. After Richard had come over on his Ike shit she knew that she wouldn't be too comfortable staying there alone. She took Kyler to Juanita and called D'Mani over to "talk" and that turned into a whole lot of other stuff. Luckily, Lexi had agreed not to say anything although she was pissed, and despite her light complexion the redness had gone down, because D'Mani definitely would have been on a rampage had he saw it. Regardless of the circumstances, she was happy that he was there and could get used to waking up to him every morning and going to bed with him at night. Tucking her finger between her teeth she let her eyes travel the length of his body.

"As tempting as that sounds, I really don't want all this food to go to waste." She gave him a fake pout knowing fully what she was doing as she gestured towards the kitchen table that was covered with bacon, sausage, eggs, pancakes, grits, biscuits, fresh fruit, and orange juice. The dick definitely had her going overboard.

His eyes followed the movement, before he swaggered over and pulled her body closer to his. Anastasia shuddered under his touch as he buried his face in her neck and squeezed her softness.

"Too late," he mumbled between kisses. "I'ma get you right real quick, and we can heat this shit up later."

As bad as she wanted to tell him that eggs tasted terrible when they were reheated, his tongue entering her mouth stopped any words from escaping her lips. D'Mani lifted her off her feet and she wrapped her legs around his waist as he carried her over to the counter, sitting her down gently on top of it. Her short, silk robe came open revealing her nakedness underneath. A soft moan escaped her as he broke their kiss and latched onto her hardened nipple. She could feel a puddle of her nectar underneath her from nothing more than his kisses.

He blazed a hot trail to her left breast, taking a moment to give it some attention, before running his tongue down her flat stomach, past her belly button and stopping just at her mound. Her clit throbbed as she felt him lean closer and breathe deeply, inhaling her essence.

" You wet as fuck girl." His voice came out in a whisper like he was talking to himself and Anastasia slid her body closer, prompting him to continue the tongue lashing he had started. He let out a cocky laugh and pushed her legs farther apart before snaking his tongue up her center, causing her back to arch and she threw her head back.

"What I tell you, huh?" he asked and her neck snapped straight up to see his hard glare on her. "Keep yo fuckin eyes on me, ayite."

Wrapping his arms around her thighs he pulled her even closer so that her upper body was supported by her elbows and her legs rested on each of her shoulders. With his eyes still on her, he stuck his tongue right back between her slit, sucking her clit into his mouth and letting out a sound that was a mix of a growl and a moan. The way his eyes closed briefly, like her pussy was the best thing he'd ever had on his taste buds, made Anastasia's mouth drop open, but she couldn't even make a sound as a hard orgasm shook her body surprising both her and him. She honestly thought that her pussy needed a break after the hurting he'd put on her throughout the last twenty-four hours, but it seemed like it never got tired of D'Mani's dick… or his tongue.

Before she could recover from the climatic high she was on, he went right back to French kissing her sensitive nub, this time inserting two fingers inside of her and making a come here motion with them. Her leg fell off of his shoulder and without missing a beat he propped it up on the counter, with a look in his eyes that dared her to lower it.

"Fuuuck D'mani!" she shrieked as her knees shook and she tried to scoot away.

"Don't run, Stasia," he stopped his assault and demanded, lifting up just enough to display the glaze around his mouth. He didn't even make an attempt to wipe it away as he stared at her for another second, and then slowly easing his face back between her legs. The interruption must have pissed him off because he went even harder, alternating between sucking and then flicking her nub relentlessly.

By the time he finally released her, Anastasia felt like she would melt right off of the counter and on the floor, because she literally had no feeling in either of her legs. D'mani gave her a triumphant grin, wiped his mouth and then licked his hand from the wrist up to his fingertips, cleaning them of all her honey. In the next second he had her bent over the same counter she'd just been sitting on with his thick dick playing at her center. He ran the length of it along her wetness before entering her swiftly and making her let out a loud moan. The slow deep strokes he delivered to her body had her creaming as she moaned his name over and over.

"D'mani…. shit….D'mani."

"This pussy so fuckin good ma, fuck!" he grunted, smacking her on the ass and quickening his pace. "Come on this dick…. I know you ready." She shook her head no, unable to cum any more than she already had.

"Mmmmm I caaaan't," she whined, frowning at the impossible task.

"Oh, you can't… maybe I should stop then." He pulled himself out of her, instantly making her empty.

"No!"

"So, you gone cream on my shit like I told you?" he teased as he got against her body again, but not entering her.

"Yessss……Ssssss," she hissed as he placed his stiffness back in her center, he made sure to get a firm grip on her hair with one hand while the other applied pressure to her clit. There was no more making love to her body now, he had a point to prove and that's exactly what he did. He pulled almost all the way out and then slammed into her repeatedly hitting her g-spot. Anastasia could feel her stomach get tight as her orgasm began to peak.

"You ready to wet my dick up now?" he questioned never missing a stroke. Still unable to speak she nodded her head as much as she could with the hold he had on her. "Good......let that shit go." And as if her body had been waiting on his permission she came long and hard, feeling it all the way down to her toes. D'mani didn't miss getting his. Instead, he held her waist firmly with one hand and the back of her neck with the other until she felt him throbbing inside of her, filling her with his kids. Anastasia couldn't do anything but lay out on the counter barely holding on because her legs felt like noodles. Her breathing was heavy and her heart was racing even though she hadn't done any of the work. Unfazed ,D'mani planted a soft kiss on her neck, and murmured about how good it was before helping her into a chair at the table.

"Now we can eat," he said with a satisfied smirk on his face.

****

After filling up on the feast that she'd prepared, Anastasia and D'mani took a much-needed nap and were now getting dressed to go and pick up her son. Anastasia couldn't lie, she was feeling so good and refreshed that she'd forgotten all about the drama with Richard and Zyree. In her eyes, regardless of all of the cons, she was still with the man that she had wanted all along and she didn't plan on letting him go anytime soon. She wasn't even worried about D'mani meeting Kyler because she knew that they would get along just great.

"Why you over there lookin' at me like that? You ain't had enough yet?" he asked when he noticed her eyes on him. A smile instantly spread across her face and she dropped down and leaned across the bed to give him a kiss.

"I could never get enough of you." She knew the look in her eyes was dreamy, but she didn't care how drunk in love she seemed, D'mani was it for her. He let out a chuckle and shook his head at her.

"Yo, you gone have to stop talkin all white and shit, you ain't with that suit and tie nigga no more," he said planting kisses on her lips, as she frowned.

"I don't talk white."

"Yeah you do… and a lil country too, but I'ma give you some slang classes," he joked and they both laughed.

"Don't nobody need no slang classes." She waved him off with an eyeroll.

"Nah you don't… I like you being all surburbian and shit… Let's gone head get lil man so we can get back here and get shit figured out." He gave her one last kiss and moved his arm from around her waist.

Anastasia knew that she had the heart eyes looking at him right then, the only thing they needed to do now was see if Kyler liked him and she knew that he would, so she wasn't even worried. She sent her sisters a quick text in the group chat to see how everyone was doing and then slid her phone into her purse as D'mani headed out of the door to go pick up her baby. She couldn't wait to see how good things would go. It seemed like everything was coming together for her. Now, all she had to do was divorce Richard and prove to Zyree's dumb ass that he wasn't her baby daddy. Seriously, how hard could that be? Right…

Chapter 17

New York was all that and more and Drea missed it already, but she was happy to be back in the comfort of her own home. She had been lounging ever since she made it back Saturday night, and when Monday morning rolled around she was doing the same thing. Drea had taken an FMLA leave when their dad got sick. She was really at liberty to take off however much time she needed, but she was only going to use one more week and return to work the next week. After scrolling through Facebook and Snap Chat for a little while, Drea finally decided to be productive since it was almost noon. She went and retrieved her MacBook Pro and decided to get going on Anastasia's case.

Richard had been acting a plum fool and she couldn't wait until her sister could get rid of his controlling ass for good. There was always something about his ass, but Stasia put up a front about him so everyone kept their thoughts to themselves just to keep the peace and allow her to handle her own marriage. Honestly, Anastasia's marriage was probably the reason none of the Holiday sisters took relationships serious. Andrea hoped that Corey and Alyssa's would be different. She thought about how beautiful Alyssa looked in her wedding dress and smiled. It was great that Alyssa changed her plans and let them help her pick out a dress instead of Kelly. The last week had been full of wonderful memories.

Felix had helped Drea on so many occasions and she was beyond grateful. She knew he wouldn't want it, but she was going to send him something to show her appreciation. After reading through the information that he had sent her on Richard, she knew that she had the case in the bag. To add to that, Felix was able to back date the paperwork for Anastasia's store and add her name to it. It was unethical, but he was even able to gain access to his accounts and add Anastasia's name back on them. Andrea was sure that Richard wouldn't check them since he had already removed her sister's name. After finalizing all of the necessary documents, Drea saved them and stored them into a file and emailed herself a copy. She picked up the phone and called Anastasia to let her know that the nightmare was almost over.

"Hey Drea!"

"Hey Stasia… What you doing?"

"Just finished cleaning a little. Dusting was long overdue… What about you?"

"I actually just finished with everything for your divorce. I'm going to have Felix submit the documents this week. You won't have to do anything until it's time to show up for court because I'm handling it."

"How long will everything take?"

"Shouldn't be longer than ninety days. He won't contest once he reads all of the documents with the proof we have on him for multiple affairs."

"Multiple?? The fuck??" Stasia shrieked.

Drea hated to break the news to her sister, but she needed to know. Even though she had moved on, she knew that it would still hurt her because she had shared a life with that man and had a family.

"Yeah… I just finished going through all of the shit that Felix found and that lame ass nigga has been cheating for a long ass time. Sorry son of a bitch!" Drea fumed.

"You know what… I'm just ready for all this shit to be over wit."

"I know you are sister… and it'll be over soon," Drea comforted her.

They talked for a few more minutes until Drea got a beep.

"This mommy calling, let me see what she wants I'll talk to you later," Drea said and hung up.

"Hey mommy… you okay?"

"Yes baby… I don't know how I ran outta yellow corn meal… you got any?"

"Let me check… if I do I'll bring it, but if not, I'll just run to the store," Drea replied as she got up to go and check.

"You don't have to do all that…"

"It's no problem mom… I don't have any, but I'll go to the store and bring you some back. You need anything else?"

"I think that's all, but if I think of anything else, I'll call you."

Drea hung up and then grabbed her keys and hit the button so that the car could warm up. After a few minutes, she went to her room and put on her maroon Hurrache's and grabbed her grey North Face jacket. She was glad that she had actually got up and showered and got dressed early because it was still cold outside. Winter had really come to Mississippi and reared its ugly ass face. The temperatures there was matching the weather in Chicago and that was ridiculous. When Drea looked at the upcoming forecast the night before, it showed that there was a chance for snow the next week.

The wind knocked Drea in the face as soon as she stepped outside and she almost regretted offering to go to the store, but she was so used to running errands for her parents that it really didn't bother her.

"Thank you, Jesus for remote start," Drea said as she put on her seatbelt.

After a couple more minutes, Drea backed out of the driveway and then headed to the store. She decided that she would just go to Walmart so that she could pick up a few household items for herself. A few minutes into her trip, Hannah called and started talking about baby shower ideas and asking when her next appointment was. Her friend was really excited for her. Drea put on a good front, but she really was nervous as hell. Going from no babies to two, and then she would technically be a single parent and that thought alone scared her. She knew that women, and some men were successful at it, but truth be told, that wasn't anything that she ever wanted. She knew that D'Mari would be a big financial help, but she really wanted more and had no idea how to make that happen. It was all a consequence of a one night stand, so she just had to deal with everything as it came.

Walmart was packed as usual, but Drea made it in and out in about thirty minutes and that was a shock. It would have been way less time if they would have had more than one cash register open and if the self-checkout machines would have been working.

"Hey Drea... what's up?" she heard someone call out to her just as she was about to walk out.

Drea turned around and stared back at Zyree.

"Hey Zyree… what's going on?"

"Nothing… I just saw you and wanted to speak to my sister-in-law," he smiled.

"That's sweet and all… but let me ask you a question. Do you REALLY think Kyler is your son?"

She watched him sigh before he responded.

"Well… when Stasia said something about the timing… I gotta admit that it was off by a month or so, but I kinda just want a test to ease my nerves. I was wrong for coming at her like that, and I apologize, but I would hate to have a son out there and not be a part of his life," Zyree confessed.

"I understand all that, but you know there are ways to handle things. My sister has enough going on and she doesn't need the extra stress. If she decides to give you a test, then cool, but if not… you just have to roll with that. She never lied to you before, so why would she lie now?"

"To keep her family looking perfect."

"She's over that fuck boy… but, I suggest you approach her like an adult and see where it goes."

"You right… thank you, Miss Lawyer," he smiled and walked away.

Since she was out, she went through Dairy Queen and got some ice cream and then headed back home. She couldn't wait to get back so that she could FaceTime her baby daddy and see what he was up to. Just the thought alone caused Drea to smile.

Chapter 18

Lexi walked into Blue Flame Monday morning before class to speak with Rick, one of the owners. He agreed to meet her there since he was already in the area. She knew that Rick's old perverted ass had a thing for her and would have met her if he was on the other side of the town. The club was fully lit, which was unusual because shit was usually dim when she danced at night. She spotted Rick over by the bar with a shot glass in his hands and an extra one next to him on the counter.

"Hey Rick, what's up?" Lexi said, flopping down on the stool next to him in a pair of black Nike leggings with the hoodie to match.

"Sexy Lexi, what a pleasure," he replied, smiling showing the gold fronts that was in his mouth.

"Shit. Chilling how I be chilling. What's good?" she asked.

"You what's good. We been missing you around here. Tell me you called this meeting to tell me that you coming back."

"Well, that's the plan, but only if you welcome me back," she stated, winking her eye.

"You know damn well, you'll always have a home here at Blue Flame. Talk to me, what I gotta do to make that happen?" he asked, sliding the small glass that housed a shot of Henny towards her.

Before replying, Lexi downed the drink and then got straight down to business. Her and Rick rapped about a few things including a new business venture over three more shots of Henny. Him and her agreed that she'd be back on the schedule next weekend before they departed ways. Lexi left the club and arrived at her next destination fifteen minutes before schedule. She grabbed her phone from the cup holder and texted Kim, the realtor that Marcus's sister told her about. After letting her know that she had arrived, Kim texted back and told her to come inside.

The townhouse was beautiful. Three bedrooms and two full baths. It was much more space than Lexi needed, but for eleven hundred a month, she couldn't pass on that. The icing on the cake was, there was a month to month lease she was signing. Lexi had made up her mind about returning back to Mississippi and attending Graduate School there. The place was located in Gwinnett County, one of the best counties in Georgia. Everything she needed as far as shopping and eats were all in arms reach. After taking the tour, she headed towards campus. It was twenty minutes after noon, her Accounting class started at one o'clock which meant she had time to stop and get something to eat since she skipped breakfast that morning. She swung by Chick-fil-a and grabbed a spicy chicken sandwich along with a lemonade. As soon as the friendly drive-thru worker handed her the meal, she dug in. Traffic was slightly backed up as she headed to Clark, but since she's seen worse, she decided not to complain. Instead, she hooked up her phone to the aux cord and turned to Beyoncé's "Lemonade" album. She went directly to her favorite song on the album and turned it up to the max.

Ten times out of nine, I know you're lying
But nine times outta ten, I know you're trying
So I'm trying to be fair
And you're trying to be there and to care
And you're caught up in your permanent emotions

All the loving I've been giving goes unnoticed
It's just floating in the air, lookie there
Are you aware you're my lifeline, are you tryna kill me
If I wasn't me, would you still feel me?
Like on my worst day?
Or am I not thirsty, enough?
I don't care about the lights or the beams
Spend my life in the dark for the sake of you and me
Only way to go is up, skin thick, too tough

The lyrics to "Love Drought" spoke to her heart, causing her to think about J.R. Lexi couldn't front, she was missing him like crazy. She was truly in love with him, but she knew things wasn't going to work out. She had contacted him three times since her plane landed, but her calls and messages went unanswered. She thought about popping up and paying him a visit, but her pride would never allow her to do that, so she went to the mall and grabbed her a few things to get her through the week. Alexis pulled into one of the parking spots on campus and sat there literally until two minutes before the class started. She scrolled through Facebook and Snapchat while nipping on some waffle fries to pass time. After reading the lies and seeing all those ugly bitches with pretty filters, she grabbed her North Face book bag from the backseat and got out. She walked across the well-manicured lawn and into the South West building. Lexi piled into class with everyone else and from the looks on their faces, they rather be anywhere but there. Deciding on a seat up front, she popped a squat and got the needed material out of her bag, just as Professor Logan walked in.

Since it was the first day, they went over the syllabus while the Professor made it clear on what he expected out of them the semester. Lexi knew that meant that they were most likely going to be dismissed early that day, but her hopes faded away when she looked at the clock on the wall. Dr. Logan was still talking and there was only six minutes left in class. She rolled her eyes at the clock and then at him before she began to pack up her book bag. Once he officially dismissed them, she headed back to her car while texting Marcus to see if he wanted her to grab something while she was out. Alexis replaced her phone with her car keys inside the pocket of her hoodie. She thought her eyes were playing tricks on her because walking up, it looked like somebody was sitting on the hood of her car. She figured it was Bre, so she grabbed the mace from the front pouch of her bag, shook it up, and lifted the safety latch. The closer she got, the clearer she could see that it wasn't Bre, but J.R. Lexi opted out of putting the mace away, just in case that nigga decided to act up. Alexis, looked at him as he sat on the hood of her car wearing an olive-green Nike jogging suit, with a pair of wheat Timbs. There was no denying that he was a fine ass creature, but Lexi knew that now was not the time to be on some weak shit, so she hit the unlock button on the remote control and hopped in. She started up the car with him still on the hood and put it in reverse before he hopped down. As she was shifting gears, he appeared at her window, knocking on it lightly. Lexi cracked the window and stared at him momentarily.

"Move the fuck out my way or get ran over," she warned sternly.

"Watch yo mouth! You ain't gon do shit, so put the car in park," he replied, completely unfazed by her threats.

Lexi sucked her teeth before rolling down the window completely.

"Where's my shit, J.R.?" she asked.

"It's at home waiting on you," he replied, smiling ear from ear, but Lexi didn't budge.

"I called you like you requested when I landed, but you ain't answer my calls or text message. Why are popping up at my school?" she questioned.

"I was out of town handing business, my bad. But, I just got back today. I hollered at Marcus and he told me you were here and what time you got out. Alexis, we need to talk. I straight up love you ma, but...."

"But what? But what Jeremy? But you can't do one little ass thing that I asked you to do?" she said, cutting him off.

"That one little thing will cause me to lose out on a half a mil?" he shot back.

"Nigga, why the fuck does everything revolve around money? Clearly money is more important than me and you willing to risk it all. I love you too J.R., but I can't do this. I can't lay with a man that's causing my sisters pain. I love you, but I will not, I cannot be a part of this bullshit. You can keep the clothes, shoes and all the other shit I have at your house. Please don't reach out to me again until you are ready to bring me my MacBook Pro. If my senior project wasn't on there, you could have kept that motherfucker, too... Watch out!" she said before shifting gears into drive and pulling off, leaving the only man she ever loved.

Chapter 19

Things had been going great for Anastasia. Kyler had taken to D'Mani, just like she knew he would and D'Mani had fit right into their lives like he was meant to be there. He'd been spending so much time at her house that it was like he lived there. Every day, almost for the last week they'd spent together, going out and taking Kyler with them, and every night they'd been making love for hours. Things were so good that Anastasia felt stupid for hanging on to Richard's cheating ass for so long when things could have been like they were way sooner. She had wasted time trying to make things work with the man she called her husband. Putting up with his attitude and his pessimistic ways just for the appearance of "perfection". She had been so worried about what people might think that she'd deprived herself of happiness, but that was over with.

Anastasia smiled as she watched the two men in her life play D'Mani's Xbox 1 on the fifty-inch flat screen in her living room while she sat reading a book. They had an array of chips, pop, and other snacks spread out on the coffee table in front of them, which was usually a no-no in their house when Richard was there trying to control things. They really didn't use the living room for much of anything besides when they had company, before she kicked him out. The sound of them cheering brought her out of her thoughts as Kyler excitedly asked D'Mani how he had done something. He watched attentively while D'Mani explained which buttons he'd used to dunk the ball, and then he mimicked it himself smiling widely when he got it down. D'Mani turned around and looked at her with a smirk and winked causing Anastasia to blush under his intense stare.

That must have been what he'd been trying to get her to see all that time that he'd wanted her to leave

Richard's bitch ass. He rubbed her thigh discreetly, warming her center before he turned his attention back to the game. Anastasia liked to have melted from his stare alone, but the connection she felt when he touched her, was beyond words. She knew she was in love with D'Mani...either that or she was obsessed. There was a small voice in the back of her mind telling her that things wouldn't be like that forever, but she tried to ignore it. If you really loved somebody why couldn't it be perfect forever? The last week was a glimpse into their future for her. Them going out to eat, or to museums, arcades, they'd been doing some variation of each and she knew that it wasn't just because D'Mani wanted to get in good with her and her son. He honestly wanted to spend time with them, and on every occasion, he'd had as much fun if not more than the both of them.

Having a man around that actually wanted to do things with them was refreshing and Anastasia couldn't wait to see where things went. She tried to focus on her book, but she couldn't help but to look up every now and again just to get another glimpse of the two of them sitting there. Without another thought, she pulled her phone from her back pocket and snapped a quick picture of them before either could notice. Though she barely got a side profile of them it still was a nice picture.

"What you back there doin, ma?" D'Mani asked catching her as she was returning her phone to her pocket. She was caught red handed and she couldn't do nothing but blush with a shrug trying to play it off like she wasn't on some creep shit.

"You can't call her ma, she's my mama," Kyler expressed with his brows drawn together as he looked at D'Mani. They both let out a chuckle at his confusion.

"My bad lil man. Ma is just another way to address a woman, like shorty or sweetheart. It's just a nickname of sorts," D'Mani explained with a shrug. Kyler cocked his head to the side looking to Anastasia for confirmation. She nodded to let him know that what D'Mani was saying was true, but that didn't stop the confusion on his round face.

"But, my dad never calls you that," he mused and Anastasia couldn't help but think that the reason Richard didn't have a pet name for her was because he was saving them or whatever bitches he was fucking. She knew she couldn't tell her son that, but she also couldn't tell him that Richard was a stiff asshole either, so instead she opted to just tell him that his father wasn't the type to use nicknames. It was easy for him to accept that for an answer considering that he could see that there were many differences between D'Mani and his father. He had to know that whereas Richard never really cared about his interest or basketball and never let him chill in the living room, that D'Mani was the complete opposite.

He immediately wanted to shoot hoops, or watch the game, he talked to him and let him give opinions, almost everything Richard didn't do. Anastasia realized that it had only been a week, but it was still more attention than the boy had seen his entire life from a man, so she wasn't going to get in between that. The fear she'd once felt over her son getting attached was still there, but she was going to see how things went. Kyler was already turned back around and playing the game again, while D'Mani kept his eyes on her with a playful glint in them. She rolled her eyes at the silly look on his face, and that only made him wet his lips and hit her with a cocky grin. D'Mani knew what he did to her; just him licking his damn lips and then flashing his white teeth had her ready for the day to end so she could take him to bed. He winked at her and then turned back around to finish the game with Kyler and Stasia nudged him in the back of the head with her knee.

He was lucky that Kyler was right there or she would have taken his sexy ass upstairs. They really didn't have time for that anyway, since they were supposed to be taking Kyler out to dinner. She was tired of cooking, so they'd decided to go out for burgers. Kyler wanted Burger King and that's where they planned on going, even though D'Mani hated fast food. He chuckled, but kept his eyes forward because he knew she didn't really want them problems.

After another couple of hours of lounging around they all got ready to head out to the restaurant. The drive was a short one and they all chattered about different things. As soon as they pulled into the lot, D'Mani shut the car off and came around to open the door for her. She smiled bashfully at him being a gentleman since it had been so long. Next, he helped Kyler out of the car and grabbed ahold of her hand as Kyler ran ahead.

The restaurant wasn't crowded at all and they got their food pretty quickly, with Anastasia ordering the bacon king meal, while Kyler only wanted a kids chicken nugget meal with a milkshake instead of a pop, and D'Mani's old, picky ass surprisingly ordered the same thing as Stasia. As soon as they sat down at the table she received a call from a Mississippi number and it wasn't Drea, so she ignored it quickly, only for her alerts to go off letting her know that she had a text. With D'Mani and Kyler busy in their own conversation she glanced at the text to see that Richard had messaged her. He was asking if he could pick Kyler up for school on Friday. For a minute, she didn't know if she wanted to let him get anywhere near her so soon after the situation that happened on her porch, but she also didn't want to keep him away from his son. She frowned and thought about whether or not she should let him, when calling Drea came to mind. She quickly dismissed it though because she already knew that she would come at her about giving Kyler to Richard after the drama. Still, like Anastasia had said, she didn't want to keep Kyler away from his father because he was upset with her. She was positive that Richard wouldn't hurt their son. So, before she could change her mind she hurried to send him a reply saying that he could get him. He thanked her and she shoved her phone in her purse as she started to eat her food thoughtfully.

"You cool, ma?" D'Mani asked with his dark eyes on her.

"I'm fine, D'Mani... just enjoying the moment," she sighed and he bit his lip with mischief dancing in his eyes.

"Word? We ain't even doin shit but eatin. You must love a nigga, huh?" he cheesed, reaching across the table to grab ahold of her hand. Anastasia twisted her lips up and snatched her hand back using it to pick up a fry, and stuffing it in her mouth.

"Something like that."

"Oh yeah? That ain't what you was sayin last night," he said leaning closer. "We gone see if you poppin all that hot shit later." He winked, and Anastasia quivered at the threat. She was more than willing to take him up on that offer, it almost had her ready to cut dinner short just to see what he had in mind.

"We'll see," she teased, ignoring the buzzing of her phone inside of her purse. Anastasia knew that it was yet again Zyree blowing her up. She did need to talk to him about the paternity, but right then was not the time. Making a mental note to call him the next day, she continued to enjoy their dinner knowing that she was in store for some good loving later on.

Chapter 20

Since she went wedding dress shopping with her sisters, Alyssa's week was filled with job hunting, wedding planning, and worrying about Corey. Alyssa searched for new jobs daily, but nothing seemed to catch her eye. All the jobs that matched her resume were either some type of boring desk job or proof reading articles for a magazine company or the New York Times. Alyssa obtained a degree in Communications and even though the New York Times seemed like a promising opportunity, she wasn't sure if she wanted to live in New York for the rest of her life. Since the passing of their father, Alyssa had been heavily considering moving back to Mississippi. The bond that she had built with her sisters, being closer to their mother, and being a constant part of her twin nieces or nephews lives all played a part in her wanting to move back home. If anyone would've asked Alyssa to move back home a few months ago, she would've proudly said hell to the nah, nah, nah, but the thought of moving back home actually made her excited.

Alyssa was floating on cloud nine every time she thought about her wedding. She searched for bridesmaids' dresses for her sisters and which color she wanted them to be. Her favorite colors were purple and green so, she found the dresses she liked for her sisters in pastel colors and saved the dresses to her computer. Alyssa also searched for flower arrangements and wedding venues and saved them so she could discuss them with Corey whenever he wasn't moving and shaking. She couldn't deny how happy she was with how well things were coming along with her wedding, but for every happy moment she had wedding planning, the more she worried about her fiancé and the thought of him not returning home.

Between sports commentating and his illegal activity, Corey was barely home. Although he FaceTimed her throughout the day and texted her when he couldn't talk; when he didn't have to travel, he was busy running the streets. Alyssa wanted to tell Corey how she felt about his recent activities and how she worried about him, but the last thing she wanted to do was stress him or nag him. As much as she tried to keep her thoughts and feelings to herself, Alyssa didn't know how much longer she was going to be able to keep quiet.

Alyssa woke up Saturday morning to the smell of bacon and 'Picture Me Rollin' by Tupac blasting and wondered what the hell was going on. She didn't know what time Corey managed to drag his ass in the house, but she was confused as to why he was up before her when he normally slept until early in the afternoon after a night of running the streets. Tossing the covers off of her, she slid her feet into her slippers and headed to the kitchen where she saw two bouquets of red and peach roses and a big basket fruit bouquet from Edible Arrangements. Trying to contain her smile, she flopped down on a stool at the counter as she watched Corey at the stove. A few minutes later, he turned the music down and reached into the cabinet for a couple of plates and glasses.

"Good Mornin', Beautiful," Corey spoke with his back still to her.

"Good Mornin', Sexy. How did you know I was here?"

"Your scent and your breathin'." He turned around and smiled at her.

He walked over to the counter, leaning over it and kissed her passionately. When the kiss was over, they stared at each other for a minutes, biting their lips before Corey walked back to the stove to make their plates.

"I wasn't expecting you to be here this morning. I thought you might've had a flight to catch or an out of town trip to take." Alyssa tried to hide her attitude but failed.

"I cancelled everythin' I had planned for this weekend and won't be returnin' to work until Tuesday." He placed her plate and a glass of orange juice in front of her along with eating utensils.

"Oh really?" she asked surprised.

"Yeah," he chuckled.

"I had a feelin' my lady was getting' fed up with my late nights and me never being home. So, I figured I would spend the next few days with her to make up for my absence." He placed his food and glass on the counter before sitting down.

"I never said anything about you coming home late, bae."

"You didn't have to. It's my job to know my woman and even though you didn't say anythin', I know when you're about to get fed up with somethin'. So, this weekend, just like every day of the week, it's all about you," he smirked, which made her smile.

Alyssa took a few bites of her food and her mouth was in heaven. She was unaware of his talent in the kitchen and she was very impressed. Corey had prepared Veggie omelets, French toast with strawberries, turkey bacon with cheese grits. Alyssa was so focused on eating that she didn't hear anything Corey was saying.

"I know I can throw down in the kitchen, baby, but do you mind takin' a break so I can talk to you," he laughed.

"I'm sorry, Love. What were you saying?"

"I was sayin' how would you like to move back home after our weddin'?"

"You want to move to Mississippi?" she questioned.

"I mean it's not my first choice for a place to settle down, but it is a choice nonetheless."

"I have been thinking about moving back home. I just didn't know how you would feel about it, though."

"Wherever you want to move is cool with me. It takes nothin' for me to hop on a plane and visit my fam. I think it'll be dope for us to move down there so you can be with ya fam and help Drea with them babies. Ya mom needs you now."

Alyssa nodded her head in agreement.

"We can start lookin' at houses today if you want to."

"That sounds like a plan and then you can help me pick a venue for our wedding."

"Speaking of the wedding, you bought a $4200 weddin' dress, Lyssa?"

"Yeah. Is it a problem?"

"Not at all. I'm just not used to you spendin' that much on one thing alone."

"Well baby, it's a special occasion and I wanted a special dress. The price didn't matter to me."

"Shit, I can tell." He made her laugh.

"I'm just fuckin' with you. As long as you're happy, I'm happy and I know you're gonna look beautiful in that dress."

As they continued to talk, they finished their breakfast and put their dishes in the sink to be washed. The couple sat on the couch and Corey found a movie for them to watch on TV. 'Paid In Full' was his movie choice. Pulling out their phones, they downloaded the Zillow and Realtor.com apps and began their search for their new home. Alyssa searched for houses close to her parents' home and the next town over. She wanted to be close to her family so she wouldn't have far to travel in case of an emergency. They spent hours showing each other the houses they found and neither of them could decide on the one the liked best. So, they saved their top choices and decided to continue their search another day.

As they continued to watch movies, Alyssa rested her head on Corey's shoulder as he held her close to him. Alyssa was still in shock that he canceled his plans for her just to spend time with her for the weekend. She didn't know just how in tune Corey was with her until he read her that morning. Alyssa was very close to her breaking point, but she was glad that he knew her as well as he did and nipped it in the bud.

"Have you heard anything else from your co-worker about them raidin' the club next week?"

"Nah. The plan that she told me about is still in motion and she's not my co-worker anymore. I'm done with the FBI."

"I never thought that you would give up your job. I mean, I know you were suspended and everythin', but you had the opportunity to say fuck everyone and get ya job back."

"Yeah. I could've, but my family is more important than my job. Anyway, I've been lookin' for another one, but I haven't found anything I like," she sighed.

"You know you don't have to work, right? I make enough money for the both of us, bae. You know I don't mind takin' care of you."

She couldn't help but smile.

"I guess I can look for a job when we move," she shrugged.

"Like I said. I got you." He kissed her lips.

Alyssa's pussy got wet from the kiss and it wasn't long before Corey had her naked on the couch. Corey left a trail of kisses from her neck to her thighs and when he reached her center, he flicked his tongue over her clit causing her to squirm and moan. As he feasted on her pussy like it was his favorite snack, Alyssa grabbed his head holding him in place. As her eyes rolled to the back of her head, she thought about how lucky she was. Not having a job really bothered Alyssa because she wasn't the type of chick that was comfortable with sitting in the house all day spending up her nigga's money. Corey telling her that working was a choice for her further let her know that he was more than ready to get married. Corey sucking and slurping on her juices brought her back to reality as she exploded all over his mouth and tongue seconds later.

Chapter 21

As pro black as Andrea was, she didn't know how in the hell she had forgotten that it was Dr. Martin Luther King Jr.'s birthday. She had been so excited to return to the office that she never even looked at the calendar within the last few days. When she arrived at work at a quarter until eight, she wondered why the place was empty. Security was nowhere to be found, and it didn't hit that it was a holiday until she sat down at her desk and looked at the huge calendar. Since she was already at the office, she decided that she would go ahead and work on a couple of things before heading back home. Before doing any official work, Drea logged onto Facebook and posted one of her favorite quotes from Dr. King. She had several, but she decided on one of her top five.

"If you can't fly then run, if you can't run then walk, if you can't walk then crawl, but whatever you do you have to keep moving forward."

To Drea that meant that anybody can do anything and excuses are just that, excuses. You may not be able to do things how the next person does them, but you have to make do with what you have and never stop moving. At that very moment, she decided that she would definitely move forward with her plans of opening her own firm. She made over six figures currently, so it wasn't about the money. She was just never a person who was complacent and she always wanted more. Drea would be able to create a more solid foundation for her family as well and nothing else would make her prouder.

She spent the next few hours going through the list of properties that she had previously saved months ago that she was interested in for her firm to see which ones were still available. Drea sent some emails to request visits and then she sent an email to Felix. She knew that he was going to be happy that she was finally going through with something that she said she would do before they even graduated. If everything went as she had it outlined, Holiday At Law would be open before the year was out.

Drea had been so busy with planning out details that the time got away from her. When she looked up, it was almost twelve o'clock. Had it not been for her stomach growling, she never would have picked her phone up to check the time. Before she left, she took about thirty more minutes to outline her work plans for the week. At least she would be able to say that she didn't spend the entire time working on her own shit. She gathered up her things and prepared to exit her office. Drea didn't know exactly what she wanted to eat, but she knew she was hungry as hell and she was about to hit somebody's drive thru up because it was too cold to get back out anywhere.

"I'm so over this winter," she mumbled as she tightened her scarf up and exited the building.

When Drea made it to her car, there was a note on the windshield. She looked around to see if anyone was nearby before she grabbed it and got inside. After cranking up, Drea unfolded the note and then she became uneasy and locked her doors.

I didn't get you the last time, but you best believe that ass is mine!! Soon and very soon!!

She had forgotten all about the day she went to the hospital and someone was chasing her until that very moment. Actually, Drea had chunked it up to it being a case of mistaken identity because she had only had that one incident, but now she knew that it had to be her they were after. The reason, she had no idea. Drea took a picture of the note and sent it to the Holiday Sisters group chat. After a few minutes, they all started texting nonstop as she finally pulled away.

Lexi: What the fuck is that?

Drea: Someone left it on my car while I was at the office.

Stasia. What the hell? Have you left?

Lyssa: Have you called the police??

Lexi: Ain't you the police bitch?

Lexi: But wait tho... Drea why yo ass at work on Dr. King birthday? You been off twelve months and decide to go back on a holiday!!

Stasia: Shut up Lexi... that means that whoever left that note is really watching her because no one woulda expected her to be at work on a holiday.

Lyssa: Shut up Lexi

Instead of texting back while she was driving, Drea sent a voice memo cussing Lexi out and then defending her all in the first ten seconds of the message. She then told them not to worry, but deep down, she had an eerie feeling that had come upon her, so instead of going to get anything to eat, she headed home.

Lexi: You want J.R. to come fuck somebody up?

Stasia: You gon tell D'Mari?

Drea: No y'all… it's cool. If anything else happens, I'll be worried, but I'm not gonna sweat this right now. It's all good sisters!!

Her phone chimed a few more times with texts, but Drea put it down and began checking her mirrors constantly to see if she was being followed. She didn't see anything out of the norm. Twenty minutes later, she turned into her driveway and sighed. Her phone was still chiming with texts, but Drea ignored them because she didn't want to become stressed. Her doctor had already told her that twin pregnancies were high risk, so she calmed her nerves and then got out and headed to visit with her mom. The door was normally always unlocked during the day time, but ever since their dad passed, Victoria kept it locked. Drea used her key and let herself in.

"Moommm!"

"I'm in the kitchen baby," her mom answered and Drea made her way.

She had forgotten all about being hungry until she smelled the aroma of the food. Her mom was frying some pork chops, had cabbage and candy yams on the other eyes, and she could smell cornbread and knew that it was in the oven.

"Where's Aunt Shirley?"

"She went to check on her house yesterday, but she'll be back in a little while," her mom replied as she flipped the pork chops.

"You done fed them babies? You been to work today?" her mom finally looked up.

That question alone made Drea's heart flutter. Her mom had finally come to terms with her pregnancy and it made her happy as her sister's and Hannah about the twins.

"Actually, I haven't eaten and I'm starving... I forgot all about the holiday, but I stayed and did a little work since I was out."

"Well I'm almost done... you look like you done lost weight instead of gaining so Imma fix your plate myself," Victoria fussed.

"Trust me, I be eating mom."

"Yeah, probably junk."

Drea had no rebuttal for that because her mom was absolutely right, so she just chuckled.

"You know it's supposed to snow tomorrow... and any snow in Mississippi the whole state gon shut down... don't you go to work if it's snowing in the morning," her mom warned.

"I'm so ready for Spring... who told mother nature we needed cold weather."

Victoria fixed two plates and went and sat them on the table. Drea's mouth watered. Whoever had left the note had done Drea a favor because she would definitely grab something from a fast food restaurant. She said grace when her mom sat down, and then they dug in.

"Henry Mitchell,' Victoria said outta the blue.

"Huh?"

"Henry Mitchell... that's your real daddy's name.

"Mom... Abraham Holiday is my real daddy. I really don't care what happened back then. I can't lie and say that I wasn't hurt in the beginning, but I've had time to think about it. It was wrong to keep the secret, but what's done is done now. Abraham is the only man I've known, and there's no sense in meeting someone else after thirty years."

"I just wanted you to know his name. He died a few years back, and I never thought I would even have to face it, but secrets have a way of rearing their ugly heads."

"That's true... and I appreciate you mom, but we both can bury it," Drea got up and gave her mom a hug and a kiss on the cheek.

They talked about memories as that made them laugh and cry as they ate. When her mom asked to go to the next doctor's appointment, Drea's day had really been made, nothing else mattered at that moment.

Chapter 22

Anastasia sat alone in her quiet house pondering over the conversation she'd had with her sisters earlier that day. She couldn't lie, it worried her that Andrea was receiving threatening notes on her car, and she really wanted to tell D'Mani so that he could let his brother know. Even though Drea said she wouldn't stress about I,t she found herself nervous and for some reason she couldn't shake the feeling. It was hours later and she still felt like something wasn't right, especially since she had yet to hear from her sister.

Anastasia found herself wondering who would threaten Drea of all people. Her older sister had to be the definition of a southern bell when it came to the way she carried herself had treated others. Hell, the most adventurous thing she'd ever done was having sex with D'Mari and getting pregnant. She wondered briefly if that nigga had a girlfriend or baby mama out there somewhere that was capable of tracking her sister down, but quickly dismissed the thought. D'Mari loved Drea, that much was obvious. There was no way that he was going around doing her dirty. Other than the disgruntled spouse of one of her clients, Anastasia didn't know who would threaten Drea. Bre crossed her mind, that bitch was crazy, but she wasn't crazy, crazy. She'd known them for a long time so she had to know that regardless of her reputation, Drea would beat her down. Watching all those Lifetime movies had Anastasia paranoid as hell and trying to play detective in her living room. She shook her head and went to grab her something to drink from the kitchen, and a light snack. Maybe if she got some food in her, she could calm down and stop worrying. Besides Drea said she wasn't worried so she knew she needed to chill out and wait to make a move, just like she'd told her to.

After grabbing a bottle of water and a premade fruit salad from the refrigerator she made her way back into the living room and her spot on the couch. She was stressing herself out when she should have been relaxing and enjoying the peace and quiet, before Kyler came back. The week before Richard had called and apologized about the way he'd acted and asked if he could see Kyler that weekend. Anastasia knew that he had been in his feelings about the paternity, and already had figured that's why he went crazy. Despite his recent antics he had always been a great father and she knew that the possibility of Kyler not being his had to be a hard pill to swallow. So, instead of punishing him, she figured she would let him take Kyler over the weekend and maybe getting close to his son would tame the wild beast that had emerged.

She glanced at the time and saw that it was after three and Kyler had been out of school for the last half hour. Even though she knew that the calm in the house was about to be over, she couldn't wait to see her baby. All the time he'd spent with D'Mani had started to make her a little jealous, so she planned on having at least an hour or so alone with him before D'Mani came in and stole him away.

Her phone ringing brought her out of her thoughts and she let out a heavy sigh once she saw the school's number flash across the screen. The only time they called was if somebody was late to pick up their kid, and she hoped she didn't have to curse Richard's ass out for forgetting her baby.

"Hello," she answered, grabbing her keys and getting prepared to walk out the door.

"Hi, Anastasia, this is Miss Gibson, I was calling because…"

"I need to pick up Kyler. His father was supposed to pick him up today, and I don't know why he's not there, but I'll be down shortly," Anastasia cut her off rudely even though she didn't blame the woman for Richard's fuck up. She couldn't wait to see his cross-eyed ass, she was going to curse him out and she might even go upside his head.

"Oh no, Kyler wasn't in school today... he was called out sick... by his father. I was only calling to check on him," she explained, causing Anastasia to stop her movement towards the door.

"Kyler didn't go to school?" Anastasia asked with her eyes squinted in confusion. Richard hadn't said a damn thing about her baby being sick. He was perfectly fine before she handed him off to Richard and if at some point over the weekend he came down with something, she should have been the first call he made.

"Umm no ma'am, the secretary filled out a slip for him explaining his absence," Anastasia didn't need to hear anything else, she hung up on the lady and speed dialed Richard's number.

"I knew you'd call, bitch! I just didn't think it'd be this soon," he picked up on the first ring and spoke harshly before she could even say anything. Surprised at his tone and what he was saying Anastasia was stuck for a second. *What the hell is his problem?* She wondered to herself with a frown.

"Richard, what the fuck are you even talking about? Why didn't you tell me that Kyler was sick?" She wanted to know, putting a hand on her hip. "This is the crazy shit that stops me from letting you see him."

"Crazy! I'm gonna show you crazy you tramp! He's not sick, but I am about to keep him indefinitely because you can't seem to control yourself!"

"What the fuck do you mean indefinitely nigga, I will…"

"What? Tell that thug that you can't stop associating yourself with trash! You turning into a ghetto slut is one thing, but I refuse to let my son be around that type of shit, Ana!" he barked in her ear not letting her get a word in edgewise. She put a hand to her head thinking about how stupid it was to send Kyler to his father without prepping him to not say anything about D'Mani. The man was already unhinged because of Zyree and now there was more shit. The best thing that she could think to do was lie to try and calm him down.

"Richard, look I don't know what Kyler told you, but the only man he's been around is Lexi's boyfriend J.R.," she tried to explain and he let out an evil laugh.

"You must think I'm stupid, huh? Not only did he tell me that your sisters have been gone, but he made sure to mention that his whore of a mother's boyfriend, D'Mani, had been playing the game with him and taking you two out to have fun! And he also said that nigga has been sleeping there! So, don't try and lie bitch! Just know that I'm taking Kyler and he's not coming back!" he fumed. The silence on the other end of the phone let Anastasia know that he had hung up the phone. With tears streaming down her face she tried to call him back repeatedly, but kept getting the voicemail. The last thing she wanted to do was lose her son to Richard's nutty ass because she was moving on with her life. There was no way to even call the police since he was Kyler's father and she had not made any attempt to get a restraining order for all of the crazy shit he'd been doing as of late.

With her heart beating rapidly in her chest she called D'Mani hoping that maybe he could try and find them. He had to have a squad of goons at his disposal that he could put to use to find Richard and fuck him up. She hurriedly dialed his number and waited as the phone rang in her ear.

"Wassup bae?" he answered and she could hear the loudness in the background.

"Oh my God D'Mani! Richard took Kyler!"

"Hold on ma... Aye y'all niggas shut the fuck up!" he shouted to the guys he was with and then he brought his attention back to her. "Now, what you say?" he asked all the noise suddenly gone.

"I... I said Richard took Kyler! He was talkin about how Kyler told him that you been over here spending time with him and he said he's not bringing him back!" she howled in a full on ugly cry. She didn't know what she would do without her baby, there was no way she could continue to let Richard get away with the shit he'd been doing at that point.

"What! Stay there I'ma be right over... and don't call the police." He told her gruffly while she nodded like he could see her.

The next call she made was to Alyssa, even though D'Mani told her not to call the police she figured her sister could at least use some of her resources to help her find her son. All she had to say when Alyssa answered the phone was that Richard had Kyler and she told her that she would make some calls and be over immediately.

After hanging up with Lyssa, she made sure to call Andrea, but she didn't answer so Anastasia figured she was busy and left her a message. She hoped that she would return her call soon, because she needed all hands on deck so that she could get Kyler back. Of course, Lexi's thug ass was the next person she made a call to, she knew that her and J.R. may have been far, but all of her sisters loved Kyler and would easily hop a flight to come and make sure he was okay. She paced the living room with her shoes and coat on while the phone rang. When Lexi finally answered the phone she broke down into a fresh set of tears.

"Lexi! Richard took Kyler!"

Chapter 23

"You sholl beating the shit outta yo face just to walk yo ass outside to get a laptop," Marcus said over Lexi's shoulder as she applied the concealer over her eyes, fixing her eyebrows.

"Mind yo business bruh and let me be great," she replied, looking at him through the mirror in his bathroom.

"Oh, I am letting you be great and I can't lie, Imma miss yo ass when you move out next week," he confessed.

"Awwwww babbbyyy." Lexi said, placing her hand over her heart.

"Come here and give me a kiss," she said, standing to her feet, getting closer to him.

"Bitch, you better move; you know I don't play those games," Marcus screamed as he playfully ran away.

"Come on friend. Just one kiss. I might have what it takes to turn you straight," Lexi joked as she chased him around the bedroom.

"Chile, the Lord himself don't have what it takes. I am NOT delivert, bitch."

Lexi stopped running and fell out on the bed laughing at her best friend. She was going to miss him, too. The two weeks she had been staying with him was nothing but fun times. Growing up with all girls, Marcus was the closest thing to having a brother. Yet, he was just as feminine as she was. Lexi got up from the bed, went inside the closest and pulled out the latest pair of Mikes she had just purchased that morning and threw them on. She went over to the dresser and got her phone off of the charger just in time to read an incoming text message from J.R.

404-526-2133: I'm outside

Lexi: K

"Girl, did you really delete that man number like you don't know it by heart?" Marcus asked, standing over her shoulder with his nose in her phone.

"Yes, the fuck I did. The first step in getting over a nigga is deleting that number and the text message thread," Lexi said, flipping her hair, hitting Marcus in the mouth.

Marcus quickly snatched her phone and scrolled through it.

"Bitch stopppppp! I see messages in here from three months ago. You ain't delete shit," he busted her out.

"Don't fuck'n worry about what I be doing," she snapped, snatching the phone out of his hands before grabbing her coat and leaving out of the house.

The best thing about living in Atlanta was their winters. Here it was almost the end of January and it was seventy degrees. Outside of smiling about the weather, Lexi spotted J.R.'s car and it boosted her grin. Regardless of them ending things, he still had the ability to make her feel like no other. Lexi walked downstairs and towards his car. She went straight to the driver's side where his window was already down.

"I'll take my belongings please," she said, extending her arm inside the car.

"Man, get yo cho ass in," he replied, before looking her up and down.

Lexi didn't bother to contest. Instead, she did as she was told and got in. The car was full of smoke, she could tell that he just put the blunt out. Part of her wanted to curse him out about not waiting til he linked up with her before smoking, but she had to play the mad and "I don't care" role. The both of them sat in the car in silence until he finally spoke.

"My homie said that you back dancing and before you can say anything, I want you to know this....\. Alexis, I will shoot that motherfucking club up and make sure they have to shut that bitch down and yo ass will be out of a job. If you think I'm playing, take yo ass to work tonight and see."

Lexi rolled her eyes, but truth be told, she believed him and knew that he would make good on his word. Sure, she could risk it all and just work at another club, but knowing him, he'd do the same thing to the new club.

"I just want my shit," she finally said.

J.R. reached in the backseat and grabbed the MCM laptop bag before handing it to her and quickly pulling it back.

"Alexis, I love you," he said, looking at her in the eyes.

"I love you, too, Jeremy. but..."

Before Lexi could finish her sentence, her phone rang and it was Stasia's name flashing across. She held her index finger up towards him before answering the call.

"Calm down. Calm down. Stop crying. What's wrong?" she asked her hysterical sister.

"Richard kidnapped Kyler," Stasia said through tears and screams.

Lexi knew for a fact that she must have misheard her sister. She wanted to tell her to repeat herself, but she couldn't bear hearing those words again.

"What happened?" Lexi yelled.

As Anastasia told the story, tears began to escape Lexi's eyes. The thought of that bitch ass nigga harming her nephew hurt her heart.

"This Alyssa, let me call you back," Stasia said, ending the call.

Before Lexi could register her thoughts, J.R. was hollering.

"WHAT THE FUCK HAPPENED? WHY YOU CRYING?" he asked frantically.

"That was Stasia, she said that Richard kidnapped Kyler," Lexi filled him in.

Alexis watched the jaw bones tighten under J.R.'s skin.

"Not my lil homie, man," he replied, shaking his head.

"What part of New York that nigga stay in?" he asked.

"I'm not sure, I think Manhattan, but I'm not sure. Why?" she looked over at him and asked curiously.

"Don't worry about, it just stop crying," was all he said before pulling her over to his side and hugging her tight.

Chapter 24

Alyssa was pissed when her sister called her telling her that Richard had Kyler and by the tone of her voice, she knew that couldn't have been a good thing. She made a call to Tara who connected her with the computer analyst at the FBI headquarters. Alyssa gave him Richard's first and last name and had him send her an email of everything he could find on that son of bitch. Alyssa didn't hesitate to jump in her truck to be by her sister's side. Anastasia gave her the run down about what happened and Alyssa did her best to convince her sister that she was going to get her son back. Alyssa sent the file she had on Richard to Stasia's phone and she couldn't believe at how long his file was. It contained properties that she didn't know he had along with bank statements, insurance policies, cars he owned, and other secrets that Anastasia didn't know about her husband.

Alyssa stayed with Anastasia until D'Mani arrived that evening. Once her sister gave her the okay, Alyssa left and returned to her empty home. When she arrived home that night, Alyssa poured herself a couple of shots of Henny. With someone stalking her sister and the shit that just went down with Richard, Alyssa was ready to fill some motherfuckers up with some hot shit. Richard was on everyone's shit list, so she was positive that no one would miss his bitch ass. Andrea's situation had her stuck. She knew her sister had to be a little shaken up by the note she received, but Alyssa didn't understand how she could play it off like it was nothing. Was Andrea hiding something? Even though her sister down played her situation, she couldn't help but to pray for Andrea's safety.

The following day, Alyssa woke up and hopped in the shower. She had a lunch date that she didn't want to be late for. Alyssa hadn't seen her bestie in a while and it gave her an excuse to get out of the house. As much as she hated being unemployed, Alyssa told herself to just enjoy it because when she did start working again, she was going to be all in. After finding an outfit to wear for the day, Alyssa admired herself in the mirror to make sure she was straight before filling her purse with everything she needed and headed out the door.

Alyssa called Stasia as she maneuvered through the New York streets to her destination. She knew that Stasia was in good hands with D'Mani, but she still needed to check on her sister. Anastasia informed her that they have been looking for Richard at the locations listed in the file and they came up empty. There wasn't really anything that anyone could say or do to make Stasia feel better. After the call ended, Alyssa said a prayer that her nephew was found very soon, safe and unharmed. She had a feeling that Richard was going to have to pay drastically for the damage that he caused.

She arrived at the restaurant minutes later, finding a parking spot on the street. When Alyssa walked inside, she instantly spotted Kelly sitting at table in the middle of the restaurant and walked over to her.

"Hey Kels," Alyssa sang.

"Bitch! It feels like I haven't seen you in forever!" They hugged each other before they sat down.

"I know. The last time we talked was on Christmas when I told you about my dad."

"How are you and the family holding up?"

"We're doing better. We're closer."

"You and your sisters or you and your mom?"

"All of us." Alyssa smiled.

"My sisters stayed here for a week and we had a ball. They help me pick out my wedding dress, too."

"Oh, my goodness! I know that dress is nothing less than gorgeous."

"Kels, it is all that and then some."

"Well, it seems like I've been replaced." She playfully pouted.

"Girl, if you don't hush with that bullshit. Now, why are we here?"

"Your girl got a promotion. You are looking at the COO of one of the biggest media companies in New York."

"Go best friend. That's my best friend," Alyssa sang in a low tone as they laughed.

The waitress came over to their table and took their drink and food order before she disappeared. Alyssa's phone began to ring and when she saw it was Tara calling, she silenced the call. Alyssa didn't know what Tara was calling for, but she would be sure to call her later. Alyssa filled Kelly in on the wedding details and how she was dealing with being unemployed. Kelly suggested that she should start her own business or find a way to earn money from home and Alyssa took her friend's advice into consideration. Working from home or starting her own business was something Alyssa never considered, but the thought intrigued her.

Their food and margaritas arrived and they toasted to Kelly's new job and Alyssa's wedding. The ladies had a good time reminiscing about their college days and the goals they had set for their lives. The laughter and alcohol took Alyssa's mind off the bullshit her sisters were going through; even if it was just for the moment. By the time the bill came, Alyssa was finishing up her drink and the waitress handed her a to-go box for her food. After the bill was paid, the ladies went their separate ways and promised to call each other just to check in.

Unlocking the doors to her truck, she hopped inside, slamming the door shut. Before she could put her key in the ignition, her phone started to ring. Alyssa reached inside her purse, grabbed her phone, and checked it before she answered. Tara was calling her again and she figured it had to be important, so she answered.

"Hey Tara."

"Hey, Lyssa. I was just calling to let you know that Blue and Quadree are now in custody. When we raided the meeting last night, we caught both of them in the act of exchanging drugs for money and we discovered illegal weapons. We shut down their entire operation. Trap houses included and since neither of them are giving up any additional info other than what we have, the two of them and their workers will be doing a lot of jail time. D'Mani was nowhere to be found. Somebody probably tipped him off but that's okay," she beamed.

"You seem happy?" Alyssa chuckled.

"Seem happy? Girl, I am happy. I've spent too many years being disrespected by that man. I'm ready to live my life the way I want to. I'm glad I helped put that bastard away. I already got a new place and as far as my clothes, I can always replace that. I just wanted to let you know the good news."

"I'm glad you were able to catch him and good luck with your new life."

"Thanks, Alyssa. Are you sure you don't want to rejoin the team?"

"I'm sure. I'll talk to you later."

Alyssa ended the call, put the key in the ignition, and started the car. As she drove home, a sense of relief washed over her. Knowing that the case was over, Alyssa felt like her problems were over. She was tired of keeping this secret from her family, but she wasn't going to tell them unless she had to. The more she thought about it, she became excited because that meant that Corey was on the straight and narrow for good.

Arriving at her house, she was surprised when she saw Corey's car parked in front of her condo. Alyssa locked up her car before entering the house where she saw Corey carrying their suitcases.

"Corey baby, what's going on?" she asked confused.

"Put these in the trunk, start the car, and get in the passenger seat. We gotta go."

"Where are we going?"

"To Mississippi. I'll explain on the way."

Without asking any more questions, Alyssa grabbed the luggage and rushed out the door. She popped the trunk, placed the bags inside, and started the car form the passenger seat. Seconds later, Corey came out carrying the rest of their things and placed them in the trunk. He hopped in the driver seat and pulled off. Alyssa wanted to ask what was going on, but she figured she would wait until he was ready to talk. Alyssa pulled her phone out of her purse and sent a text to her sisters.

Lyssa: OMW to Mississippi

Chapter 25

Anastasia thought that getting everyone involved in the manhunt for Richard would help, but it was days later, and no one had a clue where he was. Even though the possibility of never seeing her son again was in the back of her mind, she was keeping it together enough not to lash out at those who were being there for her. Besides, it was all Richard's doing, and she regretted trusting him with their son after all of the erratic behaviors he'd been displaying lately. That was a mistake that caused her more and more grief every day that passed and she didn't see her son. She wondered if her baby was hungry, or cold. If he'd been sleeping okay, or taking baths. What if he was hurt, and crying?

There was just no telling what Richard had done to him and it was driving her crazy. She drove around for hours every day to any of the places that Richard used to frequent, parks that he may have taken Kyler to. She even went to Richard's job and found out that he had quit almost a whole month before. His crazy ass had his boss and everyone else in the office thinking that they were still together. Anastasia had called him so much that after ignoring over one hundred calls he'd finally blocked her number and that only made her more paranoid.

D'Mani was trying to help as much as he could, and so did her sisters, but still there was no Kyler. With dread filling her chest Anastasia pulled into her driveway after another day of looking for her husband and son. She'd gotten the address to an apartment he had begun renting and tried there, but it was empty. It didn't even look like he had taken Kyler there. She put her head on the steering wheel and let out a deep breath as tears of anger, and frustration fell from her eyes. How was she supposed to live with herself if something happened to her son because of decisions that she'd made? There was no way that she could and she knew that. Pulling down the visor, she wiped her face quickly so that D'Mani wouldn't know that she'd been crying.

After making sure that she looked presentable, Anastasia made her way into the house to learn that D'Mani wasn't even there. She threw her purse on the couch and headed to the kitchen to grab a glass or two of wine. It was beginning to be normal for her to finish out an entire bottle for the last few days. She couldn't help herself, it was the only thing that helped her feel a little numb to the pain. Of course, D'Mani didn't approve, and let her know how he felt about her starting on the road to addiction, but he would have to worry about way more than that if her son wasn't returned to her. She was fully prepared to go on the downward spiral she knew was waiting for her.

She was in the middle of pouring her second glass when her phone rang alerting her that Lizz was calling. Anastasia quickly hit ignore and took a huge gulp of her drink. She had half a mind to call her back talking shit and threatening her life, but she didn't want the bitch in her business. When she hung up and called right back, Anastasia just couldn't hold back any more and she answered gruffly.

"Bitch, why are you callin my phone? Huh? You tryna ruin my day or you want yo ass kicked again?" she fumed.

"Ana?" Lizz asked, sounding confused.

"Duh bitch! Ain't this my number!"

"Look Ana I'm not calling to start any trouble, but I have Kyler here..." she continued in that annoying voice. Anastasia didn't even let her finish though. She immediately hung up and grabbed her purse and headed to Lizz's house.

She should have known that was where Richard's stupid ass would take him. Out of all of the places that she'd checked, Lizz's secret apartment was the last place she thought to look. Anastasia ignored damn near every traffic law known to man as she sped through the streets until she was pulling up to the address. She barely cut the car off before she stormed her way through the lobby and into the elevator to that bitch's apartment. It was crazy to her that the last time she was there, her and Lizz were friends, and now after finding out that she'd been sleeping with Richard and beating her ass twice, she was back on a mission to fuck her up if need be.

The dinging of the bell inside of the elevator brought her out of her thoughts and she stepped through the sliding doors damn near knocking over an elderly white woman. Anastasia could hear her ranting about respect, but she didn't have time for that shit right then. She was trying to get her son back. As soon as she stopped in front of her door, she banged on it heavily. It didn't take long for Lizz to answer looking a hot ass mess and still sporting a bruised face from the last time they'd come in contact.

"Where is my son, bitch?" Anastasia didn't waste any time getting straight to the point. Nervousness was written all over Lizz's face as she stuck her head back inside of the apartment and called out for Kyler. A second later Anastasia could hear him running from somewhere inside. Lizz opened the door wider and out came Kyler. He was dressed in some different clothes than the ones she'd sent him in and Anastasia was grateful that he appeared well fed and taken care of. She dropped down to her knees and pulled him into her arms, hugging his small frame lightly as she planted kisses all over his face.

"Mama! You getting spit all on me!" he complained with a smile and wiped his cheek.

"My bad little man... I just missed you so much."

He rolled his eyes and gave his head a small shake before saying, "I was just with dad." She was glad to know that Richard hadn't said anything to him, and that he thought he was merely visiting his father. That was more noble than she'd taken him, but she still wanted his head on a silver platter.

"I'm so sorry about this, Ana. Richard brought him by like two days ago and said he'd be back. I haven't seen him since and that's when I called you. I swear if I had known..." she started, but Anastasia stopped her by holding her hand up.

"No need to apologize, I'm just glad I got him back." By this time, Anastasia was back on her feet with Kyler in one arm and clenching the fist of the other. Without warning she punched Lizz right in the nose causing her to fall backwards into her apartment and on the floor. Anastasia stood over her and pointed a finger in her face.

"Bitch, you had to know that was comin! I don't give a fuck if Richard left him here! Stay the fuck away from my family!" she growled, making sure to block Kyler's eyes from Lizz.

They made it down to the car in record time and Anastasia made sure to buckle him in. Once she got around to the driver's side she slid behind the wheel and pulled out her phone to send a quick text to her sisters that she had gotten Kyler back. After sending the text, she pulled away from the curb and kept looking at Kyler in the backseat.

"You hungry, baby?" she asked, jumping right into full mother mode. Sure, Kyler didn't look like he'd been starved or mistreated, but she felt extremely guilty for how things had gone down.

"Yeah... I can eat," he mumbled quietly with a shrug. Anastasia could only nod as she headed to the McDonald's closest to her, she found a spot fairly easy and pulled right in. She checked her messages to see if her sisters had returned her text, but none of them had yet. Just as she was about to throw her phone into her purse and go inside of the restaurant, she saw a tall man, dressed in all black leaving out. It looked just like J.R. She shook her head and leaned closer to the window to get a better look, thinking that maybe it was just someone who looked like him, but it was definitely J.R. Anastasia found herself wondering what the fuck he was doing in New York, and started to call out to him, but thought better of it. They were cool on the strength of Alexis, but they really didn't talk like that. She just hoped that he wasn't in town on some cheating shit, because she would hate to have to beat another hoe down, but that's what they were gone do. Picking up her phone, she went to call her sister to find out why J.R. would be in New York, but her phone rang displaying an unknown number. Anastasia swiped the call and answered as her eyes scanned the parking lot for J.R. again.

"Hello, Mrs. Nelson, my name is Defective Andrews." The voice on the other line filled her ears and she wondered what in the hell could a detective want with her.

Chapter 26

The work week flew by pretty fast and Andrea was happy about it. She had been in court two entire days and they were draining as hell. What should have been cut and dry cases turned into full days. But there it was, Friday at noon and she was off and headed out. After going back home to check on her mom and grabbing her bags, Drea headed to the gas station. Alyssa and Corey had been back in Mississippi for almost a week and Drea still didn't know the real reason. Her and Alyssa were able to eat dinner at Cheddar's one night and they talked about their upcoming trip, but nothing of real importance. Drea was about to head to Atlanta to help Lexi move into her new place. She thought about asking Alyssa to ride out with her for the weekend, but decided against it because she knew that her sister wouldn't want to leave Corey in Mississippi alone for the whole weekend.

After gassing up, Andrea hopped on 20 East and set her cruise control on seventy-five. Even though she had several connects that could get tickets thrown out, she always tried her best to do right and only pull out her wild cards when she really needed them. Drea grabbed a bag full of snacks while she was at the store, and the first thing that she opened was a pack of sour cream and cheddar ruffles. As much as she snacked, she hadn't picked up as much weight as she thought. At least she couldn't tell, but she would know in a couple of weeks when it was time for her next doctor's appointment. Drea was excited about D'Mari flying in to accompany her to her appointment. She couldn't wait.

Pandora was set on her thumbprint radio station. The music went from 'Confessions' by Usher to 'Made A Way' by Travis Greene to 'Hit Em Up' by Tupac all in a twenty-minute time frame. Drea didn't complain because she loved all types of music. Before the next song could play, her phone rang and Drea let it connect to the Bluetooth and then answered.

"Hello."

"Heeyyy baby mama!" Hannah sang.

"Girl, you so damn crazy," Drea laughed.

"Have you left yet?"

"Yes ma'am… I'm about thirty minutes in now."

"You never did say why you didn't wanna fly though," Hannah probed.

"The real reason is because I'm trying to wait and see how this situation turns out with my nephew. Stasia seems to think that he is okay, and I think so, too; but, I know her nerves are shot like ours. I don't think Richard's punk ass would really hurt Kyler, but I might book me and Lexi flights out of Atlanta to New York if nothing changes by tomorrow night after we get her settled in," Drea explained.

"Okay… that makes sense. And I thought all of the Holiday sisters had found love and here Lexi is moving on already."

"Baby Holiday is just scared. I'm doing this because it's what I'm supposed to do, but please believe Ima cuss her ass out once she moves back in with J.R. in another month. Brother-in-law only letting her feisty ass think she doing something, but I know he ain't letting her go."

Drea and Hannah talked for over an hour and Drea didn't mind at all. By the time she hung up with her best friend, she was way past Meridian. Even though Drea didn't like the fact that Lexi was wasting time and money, she was happy to be going to visit her in Atlanta because she hadn't been since last summer. After three more stops, several phone calls, and hours later, Andrea arrived at the address that Lexi had sent her. The neighborhood was nice, which was a plus. As Drea looked around, she couldn't find anything to fuss about. Lexi had picked a great location and it was even better that she had negotiated a month to month lease. Drea parked, picked up her phone, and then commanded Siri to FaceTime Lexi. A few moments later, Lexi picked up.

"Heeyyyy hoe!"

"Heeyyyy slut… where you at?"

"I'm pulling in right now."

Drea hung up and looked in the rearview mirror and spotted her sisters Midnight Blue Benz. Lexi blew the horn and Drea shifted into gear and then followed her to another building. As she followed Lexi, Drea couldn't help but to laugh out loud that she didn't realize before that stunt Bre pulled that Lexi was a stripper. It never ever crossed her mind. There she was a college student pushing the same kind of car as her, as well as rocking nothing but designer shit. Drea still found herself laughing after she parked beside Lexi.

"What the hell you laughing at? Lexi quizzed after they both exited their vehicles.

"Just thinking bout how I was dumb as hell and never put two and two together that yo ass was over here dancing and shit."

"Had all y'all asses fooled… and I'm bout to make me some more money shit. J.R. fucked up my shit for a minute, but I'm back on now."

Drea rolled her eyes and bit her tongue. She knew that Lexi's ass was just acting out because of the little breakup or whatever. Drea knew just like Lexi knew that J.R. wasn't going. Drea switched the conversation to Lexi's schooling and upcoming graduation as they made their way to her apartment. Lexi unlocked the door and they went inside. The place was very spacious and Drea approved.

"Told you I got this," Lexi playfully rolled her eyes.

"Okay… let's go to Bed, Bath, & Beyond so we can get your bedroom and bathroom stuff. Tomorrow we can pick out some furniture for the living room and get a few kitchen appliances. You don't need much since you don't cook."

"I don't cook because I don't have time, hoe."

"Whatever… what time is the stuff from storage gonna arrive?"

As soon as those words left Drea's mouth, Lexi's phone rang and she could tell by the conversation that someone was pulling up.

"Right now," Lexi said after she hung up.

A few minutes later, the door flew open and Marcus pranced in.

"Oh, I'm moving in this biitttcchhh… all this room," he emphasized.

"Hey Marcus. I was wondering why she needed so much room too, but Ima just let her do her."

"You two hoes know I love space so shut up," Lexi rolled her eyes.

"Drea, you looking mighty sexy... I told Lexi if I was straight I would definitely swoop you up," Marcus cooed and Drea couldn't help but to laugh at his ass.

"D gonna fuck you up Marcus," Lexi chimed in.

"I said "if"... D got it though."

The movers that Lexi hired brought her bed and clothes in and they were in and out within forty-five minutes. As soon as they were done, they all made their way out so that they could do a little shopping and then get something to eat.

"I normally ride shotgun, but I'll let you make it this time," Marcus said after Lexi unlocked the doors to her car.

After Lexi crunk up, Drea put on her seatbelt and then watched as Lexi reached into the ashtray.

"Oh no the hell you ain't," Drea stated as she slapped Lexi's hand.

"Daammmnnnn... you lucky you pregnant or you would be smelling this smoke today," Lexi rolled her eyes.

Two hours and almost twelve hundred dollars later, they were sitting at a booth in the Cheesecake Factory eating and chopping it up. Drea could see why Lexi loved Marcus so much. His ass was crazy and kept them laughing. While they ate, his ass sat there and pointed out men that were married who he said were on the down low. When Lexi asked him how he knew, he told her that he knew every damn thang and she better not question him.

Drea's phone rang and she saw that it was Alyssa calling, so she told them to hold on.

"Hey Lyssa."

"Hey Drea… it's actually Corey. Lyssa is in the shower and this was the only opportunity I've had to call and talk to you and since you're with Lexi, I can kill two birds with one stone."

Drea put the phone on speaker and told Lexi to listen.

"Okay, what's going on Corey?"

"I want y'all to help me plan a surprise wedding for Alyssa. Like a destination wedding or something. I fucked up kinda bad, but I want her to know that I love her and I wanna pull it off without her knowing."

"Oooh we can plan it for our Valentine's trip in Jamaica. That'll be so dope," Lexi chimed in.

"That's a great idea… we can definitely pull it off," Drea agreed.

"Yup… we got out tickets. We would only have to get one for mommy and Aunt Shirley… and whatever guys these hoes bring. I'll be solo," Lexi clarified.

"Okay… Ima gonna save y'all numbers and I'll hit y'all up. Spare no expenses," Corey said.

"Sounds good," Lexi and Drea said in unison.

"Oh… one more thing. Drea…" Corey began and Drea took the phone off of speaker because it had gotten louder in the restaurant.

"What's up?" she asked.

"Umm… somebody shot up D'Mani's car and D'Mari was with him. One of our cousins called me, but I haven't talked to them yet."

Drea hung up without saying goodbye and called D'Mari's phone about five times, but he never picked up. It was then that she began to panic.

Chapter 27

Lexi watched her sister's facial expression change in a matter of seconds. They went from planning a surprise wedding for Lyssa to her eyes being filled with worry. Alexis couldn't wait to jump down her throat to see what was wrong as soon as she ended the call.

"What happened?" Marcus asked, beating her to the punch.

"Corey said that D'Mani car was shot up and D'Mari was in there with him," she replied, shaken up.

"GET THE FUCK OUTTA HERE! WHEN?" Lexi yelled.

"He didn't give me an exact time, him and Lyssa is in Mississippi," she informed her.

Lexi didn't know what to do or what to say. She was stressed the fuck out and all the shit she was dealing with wasn't created by her own drama. Drea's stalker situation was still on her mind and the fact that she hadn't heard anything from Stasia regarding Kyler in a couple days was eating away at her, too. And then the news that both of her sister's men had been involved in a shoot-out was chipping away at her nerves. Unable to take anymore, she grabbed her phone off of the table and called Stasia. Surprisingly her big sister answered on the first ring and she could tell by her tone of voice, that she either received the news about D'Mani or Kyler was still missing.

"Are you ok? Where is Kyler?" Lexi panicked.

"Kyler is fine, but ……"

"I know already. Are you on your way to the hospital to be with D'Mani now?" Lexi asked, cutting her sister off.

"D'Mani? What are you talking about? Hospital? What Lexi?"

Alexis paused and wondered why her sister sounded like she was crying if she got Kyler back and she didn't know about D'Mani yet.

"What's wrong then? Why are you crying?" Lexi finally asked.

"I was just about to call you and tell you about seeing J.R. when I got a call from a detective," she paused.

"You seen J.R. where? And why the fuck is a detective reaching out to you?" Lexi questioned.

"I seen J.R. yesterday here in New York but a detective just called me to me that Richard is dead," she said, followed by light sobs.

Lexi's mouth flew open, causing Drea to snatch the phone from her.

"What the hell happened?" Drea asked.

Anastasia delivered the same news to Andrea, causing her mouth to fly open as well.

"Put it on speaker," Marcus requested and Andrea did so.

"They called it a robbery gon' bad. The detective told me that whoever did it, followed him home after a trip to the bank. They must have caught him going into the garage because that's where the neighbors found him with a gunshot wound to the head. They took his money, car, and jewelry. They later found the car in a ditch."

"Oh, my God, sister! I'm sorry to hear that. Me and Lexi will be on the next flight out," Drea informed her.

"Hell nah, Lexi won't be on the next shit. Y'all can mourn, but I'm feeling like Dorothy in the Wizard of Oz.... ha ha the wicked witch is dead," she said, taking a sip from her lemon water.

Marcus elbowed her while Drea shot her a look.

"What? I didn't like that motherfucker alive, why act like I'm hurt that he dead?" she said, shrugging her shoulders.

"I don't need you guys to come now, wait until the funeral. But, what was Alexis ignorant ass saying about D'Mani?" Stasia asked.

"Nothing, you have enough shit to worry about," Drea replied.

"What happened, Drea?" Stasia hissed.

"Corey called and said that their car was shot up…"

"OH, MY GOD!! WHAT?" she screamed.

"Yeah, he said that they are cool, but I'm trying to get in touch with them now," Drea informed her.

The two of them talked while Lexi zoned out. What was the odds of Richard getting killed and D'Mani getting shot at, all while J.R. was in New York? Most importantly, why was that nigga there? Tired of playing Inspector Gadget, Lexi waited for her sisters to wrap up the call so she could get to the bottom of the shit. Once Dre handed her the phone back, she FaceTimed J.R. She waited impatiently for the phone to connect, all of sudden she lost her appetite.

"What's up, baby?" he said, smiling into the phone.

"Where you at?" she asked, getting straight to the point.

"I'm walking to the parking garbage, about to head home," he replied.

"Looks like you at the airport to me."

"Yeah, I had to take a little trip," he said, smirking.

"A little trip my ass. How long until you make it home?" she inquired.

"About thirty minutes. Why what's up? You about to come give me some pussy?"

Both Drea and Marcus's eyes bucked at his response, but Lexi didn't pay them no mind.

"Yeah, I'm finna give you sum alright. I'll meet you there," she said before ending the call.

Lexi dropped a hundred-dollar bill on the table before scooting her chair back and standing to her feet. Marcus followed without any questions being asked, while Drea sat there looking crazy.

"Let's go, Andrea," Lexi ordered.

"Bitch, I ain't finish my food yet," she replied, stuffing a fry in her mouth.

"We can get yo fat ass something on the way, but right now, I need you to keep up," she told her big sister before walking towards the exit.

Once inside the car, Drea drilled her with questions, forcing her to come clean.

"Why are we rushing to J.R.'s house? Why was he in New York?" she asked.

Lexi took a deep breath and let her sister have it.

"J.R. is the one who killed Richard."

"WAIT, COME AGAIN!" she said, chocking on the to-go cup of Sprite that she just had to take with her.

"You heard me right."

"Alexis, how do you know? I know J.R. a thug, but got damn; what type of super thug is this nigga?" Drea asked, causing both Lexi and Marcus to laugh.

"Let's just say, this nigga is a super-duper thug, ok! And I'm pretty sure he is the one who shot at D'Mani," she confessed.

"ALEXIS! NOW, I'M OFFICALLY LOST!" Drea yelled.

"Look, J.R. is a hitman, that's what he do for a living. He told me about a hit he got out on some cats from New York. I didn't know the niggaz he was referring to was D'Mani and D'Mari. That's the real reason I ended things with him," Lexi explained, never taking her eyes off the road.

"What the fuck? What type of shit is that?" Marcus asked from the backseat.

"I know, it's crazy," she admitted.

"I'm speechless, I just don't know what to say," Drea replied, rubbing her belly.

"Me either and I'm sorry, sister," Alexis apologized.

"What are you sorry for? You ain't do shit, I feel sorry for you. You had to leave the man you loved because you didn't condone him doing some shit that'll hurt your sisters, but I promise, we gon' figure this shit out," Drea said, reaching over and rubbing Lexi's knee.

Lexi smiled to herself because she felt a sense of relief. She hadn't told a soul and the secrets were eating her up inside. She knew that there was nothing she could do to stop J.R. from harming the twins, but she had to find a way to resolve the issue or she was going to be fucked.

The rest of the car ride was quiet which was good for Lexi because she needed to get her words and thoughts together for when she confronted J.R. Luckily for her, she had perfect timing because she pulled in the driveway right behind him. Before the car could fully get into park, she hopped out.

"Nigga, is you fuckn crazy!" she yelled, walking up to him.

"Nah, but you must be... Who the fuck you think you talking to?" he asked sternly.

"J.R., what the fuck was you doing in New York?" she asked.

"I had to take care of some business," he replied nonchalantly.

"Was that business my brother-in-law?" she asked.

"Aw you mad cuz I killed that nigga?" he said with a screwed-up face.

"Hell nah, I don't give a fuck about him. I'm talking about you shooting at D'Mani and D'Mari."

"First of all, let me tell you something… when I shoot, I don't miss, so I don't know what the fuck you talking about now," he informed Lexi as he walked up on her.

Drea stepped in between the two of them and diffused the situation. Lexi stood there deep in thought and Drea must have been reading her mind because the next words that left her lips were exactly what she was thinking.

"Well, if he wasn't the one trying to kill them, then who was it?" Drea pondered.

Chapter 28

Alyssa was parked on the couch with her MacBook Pro on her lap. She had been in a funk for the past few days because of Corey and his situation. He was paranoid and ready to flee to Mississippi because of a shootout that happened when the FBI raided the meeting at the club. Corey explained to her that when he was leaving the club, two agents saw him getting into a car and opened fire and without even thinking, he fired back and shot one of the agents. When the shots slowed down, he hopped in the car and took off. The car he was driving wasn't his, but he wasn't sure if the agents got a good look at him due to the light in the back of the club. Corey didn't know if the agent was still alive but he didn't want to stick around to find out.

After listening to his story, Alyssa convinced him that they didn't need to leave New York. Being as though the car that he was driving wasn't his and he wasn't sure if they even recognized him, Alyssa thought that it was best to find out what the FBI knew about the situation and if the agents survived or not. She could tell that Corey still had his mind set on running, but he decided to listen to his woman and wait it out. When he agreed to stay in New York, Alyssa was relieved. She didn't want to up and leave her sister to handle the mess with Richard by herself. Alyssa tried to convince him that everything was going to be okay, but by the expression on his face, she knew that he felt otherwise.

Things seemed to go from bad to worse with Corey when he found out that D'Mani and D'Mari's car was shot up. The incident that happened with the twins was unrelated to the scene that went down at the club, but the fact that his family was almost killed behind some street shit had Corey re-evaluating his life. In a matter of days, what seemed like easy money and a glamorous lifestyle turned into the opposite for him. He knew the ins and outs of the streets because of his cousins, but Corey was never that guy. Like so many men, he got blinded by the money and how easily it came to him. He never stopped to think about when shit got real. Corey decide that he was going to leave that street shit alone and stick with being a full-time sports commentator.

Alyssa was on her laptop searching for jobs that would allow her to put her Communications degree to use. She went on indeed and searched for jobs in Mississippi. She didn't apply to any of them. She just wanted to see the variety of jobs that were available in her field of interest. After she saved the jobs that suited her, she checked her email and saw that the boutique had emailed her letting her know that her wedding dress was ready. Alyssa's frown turned into a smile. Seconds after closing her laptop, Corey kissed her on her cheek before sitting down next to her.

"Hey, bae. How are you feeling?"

"I'm aight. Just happy to be alive and that the twins are good. From what they told me, they don't know how they made it out alive."

"As long as they're alive, that's all that matters. I'm glad you decided to give that street shit up so I won't have to worry about you anymore." She turned back to the arm of the chair and Corey leaned back on her.

"Yeah. I'm done with that shit. My focus is you, work, and this weddin'."

"Speaking of the wedding, we still have to decide on a venue."

"You don't have to worry about nothin' else pertainin' to the weddin', I got that covered." He looked up at her smiling.

"What? When did you do all this?"

"I'm not givin' you no details, Alyssa. You're just gonna have to trust me." Corey winked.

"A surprise wedding, huh? Well, can I at least know the date?"

"Nah. That's a surprise to."

Alyssa grabbed a pillow off the couch and hit him with it.

"My wedding better not be fucked up, Corey." She giggled.

Corey snatched the remote off the table and turned to the news. They were both tuned into the TV when a story about an FBI agent surviving a shootout at a raid appeared on the screen. The news reporter stated that the man who shot one of the two FBI agents is still at large and neither of the agents could identify the shooter due to darkness. Other than the two agents, there were no witnesses and they are asking the public that if they knew anything that they would be rewarded if the information that was given lead to an arrest. The couple hugged each other tightly both relieved that Corey was in the clear. With no witnesses, they had no case. Alyssa silently thanked the Lord before breaking their embrace.

"Damn! I'm glad that shit is over with," Corey sighed as he leaned back on Alyssa.

"You ain't the only one, bae."

"So, what's our next move?" Corey looked up at her.

"Good question. I guess we could start looking for housing?" She shrugged.

"That's cool."

Before Alyssa could say anything else, her cell phone began to ring. Corey grabbed her phone off the table and handed it to her. When she saw that it was Stasia calling, she answered.

"Wassup Stasia? Is Kyler okay?"

"Kyler is fine, Lyssa. But, I'm calling to tell you that Richard is dead."

"WAIT! SAY WHAT NOW?!"

"The detective told me that is was a robbery gone wrong."

"Oh, my goodness! Are you okay? Do you need me to come over?"

"I just need you to help me get through this funeral, but if I need you sooner than that, I'll call you."

"Okay, sis."

When the call ended, she couldn't help but feel bad for her sister and the chain of events that she was going through. She had gotten Kyler back, but now she had to deal with the funeral of her husband. Even though they were going through a messy divorce, Alyssa knew that her sister was fucked up behind Richard's death. None of the sisters would miss his ass, but they knew Kyler would miss him dearly. Alyssa began to shed tears for her sister because she had a tough job ahead of her, which was telling her son that his father was gone.

Chapter 29

It seemed as if it was one thing after another with the Holiday sisters. Even though none of them cared for Richard, he was still their nephew's dad and their sister's husband, so they had to be there for them no matter what. Lexi was adamant about not going to Richard's funeral, but Drea shut that shit down with the quickness. She was sure that Lexi was going to act an ass, but it wasn't out of the question that they all wouldn't have, since there always seemed to be drama at funerals. Drea had initially booked her flight for Friday morning, but when Anastasia called upset about how Richard's mom had been treating her, she changed her flight to Wednesday night and arrived bright and early Thursday morning.

After Andrea retrieved her luggage from baggage claim, she clicked the Uber app and requested a car. Her phone rang a few minutes later letting her know that her ride had arrived and she exited the airport and was hit in the face by the disrespectful ass New York weather. She thought about having D'Mari pick her up, but Drea knew that her sister needed her so she decided to go to her house first. With the heavy traffic, it took the driver damn near an hour to get to Anastasia's house. When the driver pulled up at Stasia's house, he got out and retrieved her luggage from the trunk. Andrea thanked him again and then hurried towards the house. Since she texted Anastasia right while they were pulling up, she didn't even have to knock or wait in the cold because she opened the door.

"Hey Drea," Anastasia hugged her sister once they were inside.

"Hey sis... are you okay?" Drea asked when she saw the puffiness in her sister's eyes.

"I'm more pissed off than anything, Drea. That bitch ass mother of his is on one," Stasia replied as she made her way to the kitchen table where they both sat down.

"What else has she done?" Drea asked as she grabbed a couple of grapes that Stasia had on a fruit tray in the center of the table,

"I still have no idea where or what time the funeral is. Every time I call, she hangs up in my face and the last time she said she would let me know the day of," Stasia fussed.

"Oh, she think we can't find shit out without her? She got me fucked allll the way up," Drea said as she pulled her phone out and started texting Felix.

"Kyler is at school, right?"

"Yep... I didn't let him go Monday and Tuesday, but since he missed all last week I had no choice but to send him on back."

"How is he holding up?"

"He's been having his moments, but for the most part he's good. Kyler is a smart kid and he has been paying attention to everything that has been going on. I feel bad about the messy ass divorce and now this though," Stasia admitted.

"That's to be expected. Both of you are going to be just fine," Drea replied as she continued texting.

"When is Lexi arriving? I know she still pissed off that you making her come."

"Her flight arrives in the morning still. I know Lexi wasn't gonna come earlier than I already said, so I let her make it. Where's Lyssa?"

"I think she's at home. She came by yesterday, but I haven't talked to her today yet," Stasia replied.

"Oh okay… We gotta fill you in on what Corey asked us to do, but we'll do that later," Drea replied and then smiled as she read the last few text messages that Felix sent.

"What you skinning and grinning for?"

"Guess what we doing tomorrow?"

"What?" Stasia quizzed.

"We got an emergency hearing for Richard's estate and it's in the morning at ten. Since his mother wanna play games, we gon show her who she fuckin wit," Drea smirked.

"So, what's gonna happen?"

"What you mean? You get everything, Stasia," Drea looked at her like she was crazy.

"What about the funeral?"

"It's Saturday at noon… Felix is gonna send the address to the church in a minute."

"I'm ready to get this shit over wit, but I know it's gonna be a bunch of drama. His stupid ass family."

"Always some damn drama… you need to get some rest though. You gotta be flawless tomorrow when we step in the court room," Drea informed her sister.

"I think I do wanna take a nap... but, I hate to while you're here."

"Don't worry bout me. I'll be okay."

"Hmm I bet... ass probably bout to be all up under D'Mari," Stasia teased and then got up and walked out.

There was no need to reply because Drea knew that her sister already knew the deal. She had been texting D'Mari and Felix at the same time and he was already on his way. Andrea wasn't going to stay with him, but there was no way that she could be in New York and not see him. Drea ate some more of the fruit that Stasia had sitting out and then walked into the kitchen and grabbed a bottle of water. About thirty minutes later, Drea's phone rang and it was D telling her that he was outside. She grabbed her purse and then left out after locking the door. When she walked out, she saw a black Maserati and knew that it had to be him. As Drea made her way, D'Mari got out and then met her. He pulled her in for a hug, and before he let her go, his mouth covered hers and made Drea's knees weak.

"Damn... she found herself saying after the kiss ended.

"I don't know what you did to me, but I like it," D said as he opened the door for her and helped her in.

"You done fed my kids yet?" he asked after he hopped back in.

"I just ate some fruit that Stasia had, but surprisingly I'm not all that hungry."

"Well, Ima grab a pizza and some wings so you can eat when you get hungry... then we can do whatever you wanna do."

"Hmm... I like the sound of that," Drea smirked.

"Freak," D'Mari laughed and then reached over and grabbed Drea's leg.

As he maneuvered through the New York streets, Drea couldn't help but to smile at just how much joy D'Mari brought her. It felt like the two of them had known each other forever. He never judged her for the one night stand that resulted in them having twins on the way, and he was attentive to her wants and needs from miles and miles away. D'Mari checked on her every single day, multiple times and he made it known that he would always do whatever was necessary to keep her and the kids happy.

"What you over there thinking about?" he quizzed.

"You... I really can't believe how my life has changed so much, all because of you," she admitted.

"Change is good... I'm thinking bout making a few changes myself soon," he pondered.

The conversation between the two of them flowed with ease as D'Mari continued to drive. After he stopped and picked up the food, he made his way to a gated community where he had a condo. Drea couldn't resist eating a couple of slices of pizza and a few wings as D'Mari drove.

"This is one of the properties I was telling you about," he said as he parked.

"Wow... this is nice," Drea stated.

D'Mari had confessed to her that in the past, he did help his brother out with some illegal shit years ago, but he currently had several properties and businesses that he ran. He made it known to her that he would always have his brother's back if a situation occurred, but he wasn't out there like that. Drea respected his honesty as well as his drive. He could easily be getting his hands dirty daily, but the fact that he made investments spoke volumes. Drea wanted to ask him about the shooting from the week before, but she decided against it. They made their way inside and the place was immaculate. He gave her a tour and as soon as they made it to the bedroom, no more words were spoken.

Andrea had no plans on spending the night with D'Mari, but the shit just didn't go as planned. He didn't want her to leave and she didn't want to leave, so she called Anastasia to make sure that she was okay. When she gave her the green light, it was on for the rest of the night. D'Mari worked Drea over so good that she didn't wake up until the next morning.

"Oh my God… what time is it?" she panicked.

"Too damn early," D mumbled.

"I gotta go to court with Stasia at eleven," Drea said as she reached for her phone.

She was relieved when she saw that it was only fifteen minutes after seven, but she still needed to get going because her luggage was at her sister's crib.

"It's early babe, but Ima have to go soon. Lexi and Lyssa will be here soon, too… I don't even have a toothbrush with me," Drea rambled.

D'Mari got up from the bed and walked into the bathroom and walked back out with Walmart and Victoria Secret bags and handed them to her. The Walmart bag had a mini travel pack and the other one had a Pink outfit and a few pair of panties and bras.

"If I woulda known you was working, I woulda had you a suit here too," he told her.

"So, it was your plan for me to stay, huh?"

"Damn right," he laughed and Drea laughed with him.

Two hours and a love making session later, D'Mari pulled up to Anastasia's house. Drea kissed him before she got out and told him that she would call him later.

"Nah, I'll see you later," he told her and she giggled like a school girl.

When she made it to the door, she knocked and a few minutes later it opened.

"And just where the hell you been, hoe?" Lexi rolled her eyes.

"Don't start no shit... I gotta go get dressed."

Drea heard Lyssa and Stasia talking in the kitchen so she went and spoke to them. After giving both of them hugs, she went into work mode.

"I'll be ready in ten minutes... y'all need to be ready as well because we have to be on time. It's imperative," she turned on her heels and made her way to the guest room.

Drea was glad that she had packed a suit as well as a dress. Her skirt fit a little snug, but it wasn't enough to make her uncomfortable and she was happy about that. After she was done getting dressed, she sprayed on some perfume, stepped into her heels, and grabbed her portfolio that she always kept near her. When she walked back into the living room, her sisters were actually ready. Lexi's face was still screwed up, but she was ready as well.

"Let's go," Drea announced.

They made it to the courthouse thirty minutes early and walked inside.

"You little bitch! I can't believe you're doing this before we can even get my son into the ground," Richard's mother spat.

"Who the FUCK you calling a bitch? You ugly ass hoe," Lexi stepped to her, but Drea pulled her back.

It wasn't that she really wanted to, but she didn't want her sister to get arrested for the second time in New York.

"You started all…"

"Stasia… there's no need for a response. Let's go," Drea cut her off.

An hour later, the Holiday sisters walked out of the courtroom with just as much pride as they walked in with. Just as expected, Richard hadn't changed anything and everything that he owned went to Anastasia, his wife.

"This nigga did more for you dead than alive," Lexi said as they walked out.

Everyone knew Lexi's ass was crazy, and they couldn't help but to laugh at her as well as her statement. They hopped into Anastasia's car and before she could crank up, something hit the windshield. It was hard as hell, but it didn't break.

"What the fuck?" they all said in unison.

They opened their doors and got out to see what the hell had happened.

"That hoe," Anastasia said and Drea followed her eyes to one of the women that was with Richard's mom.

Before they could make their way towards them, two cops intervened and told them that they had saw everything. Lexi yelled out curse words, along with Lyssa and Stasia. A cop walked over and talked to them and then asked them to go ahead and leave. They finally agreed.

"Y'all see this shit? Now, can y'all imagine how tomorrow gonna go?" Stasia said when they were all back in the car.

Chapter 30

Anastasia braced herself for the fuckery that she knew was going to be on the other side of the church doors, as her and her sisters approached. She could barely hear the small chatter that they were making due to how loud the pounding of her heart was in her chest. Holding on to Kyler's small hand tightly, she stopped at the door and took a deep breath.

"You cool, Stasia?" Drea asked, bringing her out of her thoughts. All eyes were on her holding looks of concern.

"Yeah, you look like you bouta pass out," Alyssa noted, placing a hand on her shoulder.

"Girl, I don't know why?! Richard was making your life hell, so God sent him there," Lexi mumbled so that Kyler didn't hear and shrugged her shoulders. Anastasia's eyes bucked in surprise at her sister.

"You keep talking like that you gone be right there with him," Drea chuckled.

"Jesus knows my heart, hoe, and he loves me like I am."

"Yeah, keep believing that," Alyssa said under her breath.

"Look, let's just go in here and get this over with y'all," Anastasia finally spoke, meeting the eyes of each of her sisters.

She already had mixed emotions about even being there, the last thing she needed was them bantering around her and raising her anxiety. They all gave a single nod that they were ready except Alexis's stubborn self, she rolled her eyes further letting everyone know that she wasn't happy to be there. Releasing a deep breath, Anastasia pulled the huge brown door of the church open and they all filed inside.

Not wanting to cause a distraction they sat at the very back pew after each grabbing an obituary. Anastasia noticed that the casket was a very expensive silver one, with a beautiful array of flowers surrounding it. From where they sat she couldn't see the body, but they had two huge portraits of Richard on each side of the casket. It was the one that he'd taken for his company that he worked for, and she had to admit that he was very handsome in it. His eyes were full of pride at his new position. All of a sudden, a wave of sadness hit her and tears poured from Anastasia's eyes. True, her and Richard weren't on the best of terms, but even after he'd kidnapped Kyler she really didn't want him dead. She cried for how short his life was, and for how much he would miss of Kyler's life.

"Is you fuckin' cryin over this nigga, fool?" Lexie hissed angrily once she saw her sister's wet face.

"Watch yo mouth in church, girl," Drea chastised quickly while Anastasia nodded and tried to contain herself.

"Oh shit," Alyssa said with her eyes on the podium. Anastasia followed her gaze with a look of confusion until she realized that Richard's boss Harold and Lizz were walking towards the microphone to speak. The man seemed distraught as he boohoo'd about how Richard was like a son to him, and Lizz consoled him by rubbing his back. Anastasia's mouth dropped at the audacity of that hoe.

"I swear that bitch ain't shit!" Lexi spewed with a bitter look on her face. It seemed that all of the sisters were shocked at the presence of Lizz and her husband when Anastasia hadn't even been formally invited. She scanned the front row looking for his stuck-up ass mother, and saw her sitting right next to the aisle with a big, ass hat on. The two women who'd been with her at the hearing were sitting right next to her and Stasia just shook her head. That woman hated her so much that she invited the whole state of New York, but had left her and her son out in the cold. She heard Kyler sniffling beside her, and wrapped her arms around him. Anastasia knew that she needed to put her feelings to the side and be there for her son. Regardless of the things that Richard had done, he had always been a good father in his own right and she knew that Kyler would miss him. He clung to her as he cried his little heart out and it brought a fresh set of tears to her eyes.

"Did you see this?" Alyssa whispered pointing to a spot on the obituary.

Anastasia started to wave her off because she knew that it was no telling what Richard's mama had put on them, but she wiped her eyes and looked anyway. On the list of family members next to Kyler's name was Richard Jr. Anastasia's head snapped up to the front of the church to see his mother, and the woman who threw the shit at the car standing with a baby in her arms that looked to be at least 2. He was knocked out and had his face in his mother's chest, but Anastasia already knew that, that was Richard Jr. She could hear Alyssa saying something, she was honed in on the woman as her pew went up to view the body.

Before she could stop herself, she was on her feet pulling Kyler along with her. At that point, she was done being diplomatic about the situation. That bitch knew that Richard had a whole damn love child out in the world and didn't tell her anything. Her and Kyler made it to the front of the church just as his mother and the lady were turning to go back to their seats. As soon as her eyes landed on Anastasia she frowned and lifted her pointy ass nose in the air.

"What the hell are you doing here?" she demanded, looking between her and Kyler like they were shit on the bottom of her shoe. The woman stood behind her and held her son closer to her chest, with tears still coming down her face, over Richard's no-good ass.

"You know what? I asked myself that same thing Beverly. Stupid of me, to think that I should bring my son! Your Grandson to say good-bye to his father, but it's obvious he wasn't shit alive and he ain't shit now!" Anastasia roared drawing a chorus of gasps around the church. Beverly clutched her neck with one hand and slapped Anastasia with the other.

"Oh, hell naw!" Lexi who was right behind her sister shouted and tried to get to the old lady, but Drea held her back. Anastasia shook her head to let Lexi know that she could handle it and turned back to Richard's mother.

"You will not speak ill of my late son! You and that little hoodlum in training are no part of this family! This is Richard's heir!" Beverly spat pointing to the baby behind her who had woken up due to all of the yelling. Anastasia couldn't help but laugh at this crazy ass delusional woman in front of her.

"Fuck you, and that ugly baby, bitch!" Anastasia heard Lexi say from behind her.

"Girl, I'm bouta drag you up outta here, don't stoop to this old bitch's level," Drea told her, but Lexi just huffed in irritation. Alyssa came over to Stasia and put an arm around her.

"Come on, sis. You don't need this shit, and Kyler don't need this bitch in his life," she whispered in Stasia's ear, but everyone who was close enough could still hear.

"Damn right he don't cause he got a aunty that'll slap any hoe over him!" Lexi fumed still struggling to get around Drea who looked out of breath. Anastasia knew that they better get her hotheaded ass out of there before she really showed her ass. Turning back to Beverly she nodded.

"You're right, he is Richard's true heir, but all he's going to gain is a crazy ass grandma, and a side hoe of a mother while my little hoodlum will go to an ivy league school courtesy of your son. You have a shitty day, bitch... come on y'all," Anastasia told her and motioned for her sisters to come on as she walked away. She could hear Beverly spewing curse words and acting a damn fool behind her, but she continued to walk, only turning around at the sound of skin on skin contact.

"I'm not as nice as my sister! You got the right one! Now, hoodlum that bitch! Fuck you, that baby, and this side hoe... fuck all y'all in this church!" Lexi was standing nose to nose with Beverly who was holding her cheek, and Richard's secret baby mama was doing the same. She just knew that her sister hadn't just slapped both their asses. She charged back in her sister's direction as Harold and a few other men approached them like they were going to try and restrain them.

"Harold, you need to go find out why yo wife was fuckin' him while you was up there talkin' about how much you loved him!" Alyssa ranted as Anastasia made it back to them. Harold stopped right in his tracks and his pale skin turned bright red, as he looked at Lizz angrily and he went and started arguing with her.

"Lexi, let's go now! This bitch gone call the police!" Anastasia grunted, pulling her sister away from a shivering Beverly. That's what her ass got, talking all that shit. The way she saw it, that bitch deserved everything coming to her for how she had acted in front of her grandson.

When they finally got Lexi out of the church, she had walked ahead of them still going off like it was somebody out there. They let her get it off her chest though as she made it to the car and began pacing. Anastasia stopped and stooped down to her son's level and looked him in the eyes.

"Kyler, baby, I know that we don't usually act that way, and I discourage you from behaving like we did, but I don't want you to listen to anything that old bird said about us okay. You have a whole family of people who love you and with or without her, you're going to be just fine," she told him and he nodded.

"I didn't really like Grandma Beverly anyway, she couldn't even cook," he said with a shrug causing Anastasia to chuckle.

"I need a drink after that shit." Alyssa said, shaking her head as she zipped up her coat.

"Yeah me, too, bitch," Anastasia agreed. This past week had been extremely eventful for her, from Kyler being kidnapped, to Richard dying, to getting all his money and finding out he had a secret baby on her. Honestly, she was just glad that it was over and she could fully close the door on the whole situation.

They finally made it to the car where Lexi was still pacing angrily and Drea unlocked the door so that they all could climb inside. She didn't start the car right away just threw her head back on the seat and let out a breath.

"Leave it to the Holiday sisters to turn out a funeral," she mumbled, causing them all to fall out laughing.

Chapter 31

"So, let me get this straight, Richard's tight booty ass got another son and the bitch showed up at the funeral?" Aunt Shirley asked the same question over again.

"Yes Auntie." Lexi replied rolling her eyes as she placed the phone call on speaker to finish washing the dishes.

"Annnnndddd Richard's tight curl wig wearing ass momma was talking a gang of shit, huh?" Aunt Shirley rambled on.

"Yup!"

"Girl they asses lucky I wasn't there. I would have flipped that nigga casket over."

Lexi damn near dropped the wine glass she was rinsing. Her and her favorite auntie had been on the phone for an hour talking about all the drama and bullshit that was going on. Lexi even told her about her issues with J.R., leaving out the whole killing the twins part. Shirley damn near jumped through the phone. She was pissed off, according to her, she could have been fucked J.R. while he was in Mississippi had she known the two of them wouldn't last.

"So, after all those demons came out of the closet, then what happened?" Shirley questioned.

"Shit, I slapped Richard's mommy and his bitch in the face and we bounced," Alexis replayed the events over in her head as she filled her in.

"THAT'S WHAT I'M TALKING ABOUT CHILD! In the church and all. I know yo scary ass sisters wasn't gon do shit but you…. But you…. I knew you had it in you. I'm starting to think I'm yo real mother, hell Victoria just birthed you," Shirley yelled into the phone.

Lexi moved about the kitchen cleaning up while they chatted for about another ten minutes. Aunt Shirley's doorbell rang, she said it was one of her many men so she had to go. Lexi hung up with no questions being asked. She had her laugh for the day, she could always count on Shirley for that. After cleaning up and taking some chicken wings out of the freezer to cook for dinner, Lexi went to the bedroom to lay down. She needed to take a nap before she headed to work later on that night. As she laid in the bed, her thoughts drifted off to J.R. and how she missed him so much. She hadn't spoken with him since she confronted him about shooting at the twins. He denied it, but something told her that he was lying. Just as Lexi began to drift off, her phone rang and it was Marcus calling. She picked up the phone and heard her best friend crying.

"What the fuck wrong with you?" she asked in a panic voice, sitting up straight in her King size bed.

"Can you come over please, Alexis?" he begged.

"I'm on my way!" she replied, hopping up and getting dressed.

She threw on whatever was in arm's reach and ran out the door. She did the dash as she rushed to Marcus's house. Her heart was pounding, wondering what the issue could have been that had her best friend so upset. Whatever it was, Lexi was going to be there for him. Marcus stayed twenty minutes from her new townhouse, but it took her a hot ten minutes to get there that Sunday evening. When Lexi pulled up and parked, she noticed another car in the driveway, but she didn't pay it any mind. Instead, she jumped out and ran up the steps, ringing the doorbell nonstop. After the fifth ring, Marcus had yet to come to the door, so Lexi twisted the knob and to her surprise, it was open. Before walking in any further, she rambled through the contents in her purse and came up empty handed. She thought about going back to the car to see if she had a weapon in there, but she didn't want to waste any more time. She had seen too many movies where the person in her position never made it out alive.

"Fuck it," she mumbled to herself before slipping inside.

All the lights were on and there was sound coming from the TV. Alexis nerves calmed a little when she heard laughter. Letting her guard down just a smidge, she made her way to his bedroom. The door was wide open, she found Marcus sitting on the bed eating a bag of chips talking to some female whose back was towards Lexi.

"Nigga what the fuck is wrong with you?" Lexi roared.

Marcus jumped, causing his chips to fall on the floor and the woman to turn around.

"Bitch, you ever heard of knocking?" Marcus said, rolling his eyes while bending over picking up the bag.

"First of all, lil bitch, I rang the doorbell several times."

"Aw girl, that doorbell don't work," he said, waving her off.

"Why the fuck you call me crying like something was wrong and most importantly, why is this bitch here?" She snapped, pointing and directing her attention to Bre.

"Just listen, best friend," he began to speak.

"Listen my ass...." she said, holding up her hand interrupting him.

"See, I told you this was a bad idea," Bre whispered to Marcus.

"Ya think!" Lexi said, looking over at her frowning before turning to leave the room.

"Alexis, I'm sorry for everything I did to you. I need to right my wrongs before I leave this Earth," Bre screamed out.

"Shorty, I don't give two fucks about you. Stay the fuck away from me, right your wrongs that way," Lexi replied.

"But Lexi, she's dying," Marcus screamed out causing her to stop in her tracks.

"Just hear her out," Marcus continued as he placed his hand on Lexi's shoulder, turning her around to face Bre, who had tears running down her face.

"I have stage four breast cancer. I just found out two weeks ago. I rejected the chemotherapy because it's not going to do me any good at this point. I came over to tell Marcus and I asked him to get you over here so I can tell you, too; as well as apologize. Lexi, I've been a horrible friend, a horrible person and I am truly sorry. I admit that I fell in love with you, but went about it all the wrong way. I don't want to leave this Earth knowing that I never got a chance to say I'm sorry."

Alexis stared into the eyes of her former best friend and wondered where they went wrong. They had known each other since grade school, but were now sworn enemies. Lexi could be a cold-hearted bitch when she wanted to, but even after all the shit Bre had done to her in the past, her heart wouldn't allow her to not hurt right then and there.

"I'm so sorry to hear that, Bre," Lexi finally found the words to say.

"Don't be sorry, I'm the sorry one. I love you, Alexis, and now, I wish like hell I had not done the things I've done. Then maybe, just maybe, I'll have my best friend with me during my last days."

Marcus pulled Alexis and Bre into a group hug and the three of them cried until they couldn't cry anymore. Death had a funny way of bringing people together, first her father did it with her and her sisters and now her and Bre.

Chapter 32

It was a Tuesday when Alyssa walked out of the building from her job interview. A few employers had found her resume on Indeed and emailed her the details of the jobs they were hiring for. After finding the best offer, she set up an interview with a computer company for the position of a communication specialist. Alyssa jumped behind the wheel of her truck feeling good about her interview. Even though she felt positive about the job, if she was hired, Alyssa would have to stay in New York. She was looking forward to moving to Mississippi, but she began to second guess her decision. Alyssa pulled out her phone and sent a text to Kelly letting her know to meet her at the boutique before she put the key in the ignition and pulled off.

During the drive, Alyssa decided to call Drea and check on her and the babies. She placed the call and Drea answered after the phone rang twice.

"Hey Lyssa."

"Hey Drea… how are you and the babies?"

"Just fine… I have a doctor's appointment coming up soon that I'm excited and nervous about."

"I'm sure it will go just fine."

"I pray it does. How are you though?"

"I just left a job interview. It went pretty well and I'm a little excited about."

"That's great, sis… are you packed and ready for Jamaica?"

"Almost… I'm so ready to escape this cold ass weather in New York and have fun with y'all," Alyssa admitted.

"It's gonna be sooo much fun."

"While I have you on the phone… do you know any good realtors?" Lyssa inquired.

"Hmm… yeah, Felix has a cousin who is awesome. I actually ran into her a couple of months back at the store. Her name is Justice Balark. I'll text you her information."

"Cool cool… thanks sis. I'm bout to pull up at my next stop, so I'll talk to you later."

Alyssa hung up with her sister and arrived at the boutique around noon and parked in the nearest spot. Kelly tapped on the passenger side window. Alyssa jumped out the car running onto the pavement to hug her friend. Locking the doors to her truck, they walked into the boutique and was greeted by the manager with a smile. The manager remembered Alyssa and told them to follow her to the fitting area. While the manager went to the back to get her dress, the assistant didn't hesitate to ask questions.

"So, are you nervous about getting married?" The young, black girl asked with a smile.

"I'm not really nervous yet, but it's probably because I know it will be awhile before we jump the broom," Alyssa replied as she thought about all of the things that had been happening in her life. She was ready, but she wasn't in a hurry because it seemed as if something was always going wrong in the lives of the Holiday sisters.

"I'm sure those nerves will kick in soon," the girl chuckled.

"I'm sure," Alyssa agreed with a smile.

The manager walked into the fitting area with her dress in hand and Alyssa smiled from ear to ear. The manager suggested that she try it on and Alyssa didn't argue. She quickly changed into her wedding gown and almost cried at her reflection. The dress was even more beautiful than she remembered. Alyssa couldn't wait until the day that she could wear her dress for real, whenever that was. Kelly sobbed as she complimented her friend on her dress selection. After Alyssa changed backed to into her clothes, she thanked the ladies for all their help before leaving the boutique. She placed her dress in the back seat of her truck and they hopped inside heading over to the mall to pick out Alyssa's shoes and accessories.

They spent at least two hours at the mall trying on different shoes and jewelry. After Alyssa made her final selections, they grabbed a quick bite to eat before leaving the mall. On their way back to her car, Alyssa updated her bestie on what was going on with her family and fiancé. After telling Kelly what happened at the funeral and the mess Corey was involved in, her friend's mouth hit the floor.

"Damn. It seems like it's always some shit popping of at y'all funerals."

"Tell me about it, but that shit is water under the bridge now. The only reason why we came was to support our sister and nephew. Now that's it over, we can move on with our lives."

"I can't believe Corey got mixed up with some street shit. I know that shit was stressor." Kelly shook her head.

"Yeah, it was. I'm just glad that he learned his lesson because I don't know if I was going to be able to put up with that shit much longer," Alyssa huffed.

"I hear that. Do y'all have anything planned for Valentine's Day?"

"Me and my sisters were supposed to be going to Jamaica on a girl's trip, but it's now a couples' trip."

"I'm so jealous right now."

"Don't be, boo. We need some peacefulness in our lives," Alyssa laughed.

Alyssa dropped Kelly off at her car and hugged her before they went their separate ways. As she drove back home, Alyssa couldn't fight her excitement. Even though she didn't know the exact date of her special day, just knowing that day was coming was enough for her to get excited about. Alyssa thought about calling her sisters to find out if they knew anything about what Corey had planned, but being as though they had their own shit going on, she decided against it.

Parking in front of her condo, Alyssa grabbed her dress along with her shopping bags and walked inside. She heard Corey on the phone with someone, but he quickly ended the call when he heard Alyssa come in. She eyed him suspiciously as she made her way over to him and pecked his lips.

"Who the hell were you talking to?"

"Umm… uhh, that was just D'Mani,' he stuttered.

"Let me see the phone then," Alyssa held her hand out.

"This how we doin Lyssa? We can't get married with no trust and shit," he argued.

"Whatever Corey... you told me that you was gonna handle the wedding plans, but you haven't said shit. Do you really wanna get married or you having second thoughts?"

"Here you go wit this again... I would have never put that ring on your finger if I wasn't sure," Corey shook his head.

"You know what..."

"Save it Alyssa... don't even fuck up the mood with nonsense. You know I have a lot got on, so you gonna have to trust me. Just concentrate on enjoying this trip and since you don't like the way I'm handling shit, we'll make the wedding plans together when we return," he cut her off.

Alyssa wanted to cuss him the fuck out, but she bit her tongue. He only said one thing right since she had made it home and that was about enjoying the trip to Jamaica. She planned on doing just that and she would deal with him and the wedding shit, as he called it once she returned, if she decided to do so. Alyssa put away her dress and the stuff that she bought at the mall, and then she started pulling out things to pack for the trip. She needed to unwind because Corey had low key pissed her off, so she made her way towards the kitchen to get a glass of wine. She heard Corey talking in the bathroom and the words that left his lips made her stop dead in her tracks.

Chapter 33

It had been a little over a week since the last drama, and everything finally seemed to be smooth in Andrea and all of her sisters' lives. She was extremely excited about their upcoming trip and prayed that everything would be fine. They had all of the details for Alyssa's wedding mapped out, which was going to be on Valentine's Day, she had booked flights for her mom and Aunt Shirley to arrive that Tuesday, and she locked eyes with D'Mari in the rearview mirror and smiled as he drove her, her mom, and even Aunt Shirley to her doctor's appointment. D'Mari flew in the day before at the last minute just to be there. Drea's appointment wasn't supposed to be until the next week, but she had forgotten all about the trip when the receptionist handed her the card at her last visit. Her and her sisters would be leaving out on Sunday for Jamaica and would be there for a whole week.

"They gon be able to tell what we having at this appointment? It need to be some boys because we don't need no mo messy as women like y'all Holiday sisters," Aunt Shirley said out of the blue.

"If we messy, we got it from you, Aunt Shirley," Drea smirked.

"Don't listen to her, baby," Aunt Shirley directed her attention to D'Mari and everyone laughed at her ass.

"We just want healthy babies... we don't care if they boys or girls," Victoria chimed in.

"I agree," D'Mari spoke up and Drea agreed.

"Hmph... y'all can agree wit each other all y'all want... I know what I'm praying for."

"You pray?" Drea quizzed.

"Yeah smart ass, and if you don't hush Ima pray for them lil chaps to be just like me."

"Let me shut up then."

Andrea gave D'Mari the rest of the directions and they pulled up to the clinic about ten minutes later.

"Y'all sit tight," D'Mari instructed after he found a parking space.

Drea watched as he got out, walked around and opened the passenger door and helped her mom out, then he did the same for Aunt Shirley, and saved her for last.

"Whoo chile... he's a keeper. Ion think no man has ever opened a door for my ass," Aunt Shirley said.

They made their way inside and Drea signed in. she briefly thought back to how she felt so alone when she first found out that she was pregnant. Things had definitely changed for the better because her support system was phenomenal. Drea got a kick out of the Holiday sisters group chat with them going from talking about her being greedy to expressing their excitement about the twin's due date. Drea had a nine o'clock appointment and she was so happy that her doctor didn't overbook like most. It only took five minutes before her name was called and she completed the urine sample and got her vitals checked.

After all of the little stuff, which was the most important, Drea and the rest of the crew sat in the room while waiting on the doctor and the ultra sound tech to come in. It was confirmed that she was thirteen weeks pregnant, and out of the first trimester. That was exciting news, but the nurse still informed her to be careful and not overdue anything because being pregnant with twins was always considered to be high risk.

"Well, hello everyone. Drea, you have a whole fan club here today I see," Dr. Livingston stated after he walked through the door.

"Yes, sir I do," she smiled.

"Well let's get down to it… everything is going just fine, but I know this is the part that everyone has been waiting for, huh?" the doctor took a seat on the stool next to the table where Drea was laying.

Drea jumped as the cold gel was rubbed onto her stomach. D'Mari chuckled as he squeezed her hand.

A few seconds later, the heartbeats of the babies filled the room. The love in the atmosphere was contagious, as well as the tears that Victoria and Andrea shed.

"My baby is really having some babies."

"This shit is real… I mean… this is real," D'Mari corrected himself.

Drea looked up at his face and she could tell that he was genuinely happy. It made her heart smile. Even Aunt Shirley was smiling. Kyler was the only grandchild and with him being in New York, Victoria didn't get to spoil him how she wanted to. Drea knew that it was going to be different with her babies because she was so close by. She could honestly say that she was finally happy with the situation. She just wished that her dad was still living so that he could witness his first baby girl giving birth. No matter what, Abraham was her dad and no one could tell Drea any different.

"Can you tell what she having yet?" Aunt Shirley inquired.

"Not yet... the only thing we know is that they are identical," Dr. Livingston informed them.

"Well, how the hell you know that and you can't tell what they are?"

"They are in the same sac. Identical twins share the same sac, while fraternal twins are in different ones," he explained.

"Hmph... it's gon be two boys y'all. Anybody wanna bet?"

No one answered Aunt Shirley, they just laughed at her. Drea wrapped up her appointment and scheduled the next one for the next month. The doctor told them that it was a great chance to determine the sex by then because she would be past sixteen weeks and that was when most people found out.

Later that evening, Drea and D'Mari decided to go and spend some time together since he was scheduled to leave that next morning. She was already sad about him leaving, but she knew that she would see him in just a few days because he was going to Jamaica as well. What was supposed to be a sister's trip had turned into a family trip, but everyone was getting along, so it was all good. They were headed to Vicksburg to the casino so that they could eat and she was sure that D'Mari wouldn't mind playing the table games or something. As he drove, Drea got an eerie feeling and D'Mari must have sensed it because he asked her if she was okay. She sat there in silence wondering if she should tell him that someone had been following her.

"What's wrong, Drea?" he asked again as he made a turn that they shouldn't have been taking.

"Why you turn?" she ignored his question.

"Don't avoid my question... what's wrong?"

"Well... someone has been following me, and I have no idea who," she confessed.

"I see... and whoever it is must think you're alone now. You just stay calm... Ima handle this shit. I don't need you stressing."

Drea heard him, but what he was saying was easier said than done. Who in the hell could be following her? She peeked and looked in the side mirror and it looked like it was a Camry. She wrecked her brain trying to figure out who it could have been. Just when a person popped into her head, D'Mari stopped the car so fast and did a spin in the road and turned around. The way her car spun around, you would have thought that they were in a movie. To add to the dramatics, D'Mari cut the car off and jumped out with a gun that she didn't even know he had.

"Open the door!" D'Mari demanded.

As soon as the door to the Camry opened, Drea locked eyes with Deacon Jones soon and she felt a twinge of guilt. She had embarrassed the man at church and that must have been the reason that he had been following her. He looked like he was about to shit a brick as he stared at D'Mari. Drea didn't want him to die, so she got out of the car.

"Wait D'Mari... I know who he is."

"I'm so sorry for how everything played out at church. I was wrong. It was just that..."

"Nah, fuck that... you ain't gotta explain shit to him. Listen to me... this cat and mouse shit stops TODAY... I'm only letting you make it on the strength of her, but if she tells me that she even thinks you're following her again, you won't have to worry about anyone else," D'Mari calmly, but firmly got his point across.

No other words were spoken. Drea was glad that they were on a side street instead of the main highway or interstate. She felt relieved that she finally knew who was after her. Drea was thankful that D'Mari was with her and how he handled the situation was very impressive. They didn't let that small mishap ruin their day. The two of them went on to Vicksburg and enjoyed themselves. They made it back to Drea's house around eleven and ended the night by making love. Each time that they were together, Drea never wanted it to end and it was getting harder and harder not to be by D'Mari's side every day.

Chapter 34

Anastasia's head was still spinning from the events at the funeral when she, Alyssa, and Kyler boarded their flight for Mississippi. At this point, Richard's bullshit didn't even surprise her anymore, so finding out that he had a secret son out there only proved how selfish him and Beverly truly were. In their attempt to scheme, and lie, they'd denied Kyler a relationship with his baby brother. She looked over in his direction as he stared out of the window of the plane with his tablet in his hand and headphones covering his ears. He'd been pretty quiet since the funeral; probably trying to sort out his feelings after hearing all the hateful shit his Grandma had said about him. Now, she had to subject him to some more stupid shit, by allowing Zyree a paternity test. If she hadn't been forced by the courts she definitely, wouldn't have gone through with it because she knew he wasn't the father.

She could understand his point of view, considering the time frame and the fact that so many bitter women lied about who their child's father was out of spite, but Zyree knew her. That was probably one of the most troubling things about him pushing the issue. They'd known each other for a long time and she had never lied to him, even when her father first started forcing her to date Richard, she'd told him. So, for him to act as if she would lie about something so serious really irritated her, and she couldn't wait to prove his ass wrong so that he could move on with his life.

"Damn bitch, you look like you wanted to leave me the aisle seat," Alyssa quipped as she slid into her seat and rolled her eyes.

"You snooze, you lose, hoe." Anastasia stuck her tongue out at Alyssa childishly causing her to laugh. She was glad that her sister had flown in with her, so that she wouldn't have to deal with this on her own. Once, they finished with the test they were going to fly out to Jamaica to join their sisters and their men, for a baecation and Alyssa's surprise wedding. Anastasia couldn't wait to relax on the beach, and spend time with her family, after all of the stressful shit that had been happening. It seemed like the sisters were all getting their happy ending and she was excited.

"You're so annoying," Alyssa giggled and gave her sister a playful shove. "What you was over here thinking about anyway? You were in lala land when I walked up."

"I was thinking about how I can't wait to get this shit over with so I can see D'Mani sexy ass on the beach shirtless!" Anastasia sighed and looked off into space like she could really picture the sight. "That chocolate, skin with water dripping down those wash board abs, and…"

"Nah, kill the visual, hoe. I don't wanna think about bro without clothes!" Alyssa cut her off and they shared a laugh.

"Whateva… You know you're excited too."

Anastasia pretended to be offended as she got more comfortable in her seat. Talking about D'Mani had brought him to the front of her mind and she couldn't wait to be in his arms again. She was glad that him and D'Mari were okay, after that shit that had happened back in New York, and she couldn't wait to see him. At first, she was really scared about him being in a shootout, but she quickly realized that it was a part of the game. He'd promised that it was nothing he couldn't handle and that he would always make sure that her and Kyler were okay. She believed him too.

"I'm gonna make the best of it, but…" Alyssa said, but then cut her sentence short.

"But what?"

"Corey has been all secretive and shit lately… I'm beginning to think that he's cheating and I'm not putting up with any more bullshit," Lyssa confessed.

"Girl… you're just overthinking. Cut it out and get ready to enjoy this trip.

"No, I'm serious… I heard him planning to meet up with someone and he was whispering and shit. He shouldn't have shit to hide."

"Lyssa… I'm sure it's nothing. Let's just enjoy the trip and you can address that afterwards.

Alyssa never responded, she just simply sat back and put her seatbelt on. Anastasia knew that she was going to love the surprise that Corey had planned for her once they arrived in Jamaica. It was honestly, taking everything in her not to spill the beans about the wedding. She could never keep a secret from her sister for too long and she hated that she was feeling like Corey was cheating, but the sheer happiness that the surprise was going to give Alyssa made her bite her tongue because it would be worth it in the end.

Anastasia also couldn't wait to see her sisters in a more relaxed and chilled setting. It seemed like every time they were together some type of bullshit kicked off. Being able to just kick back stress free was just what they all needed.

It wasn't long before their flight was underway and Anastasia read a book on her Kindle while, Kyler slept on her shoulder, and Alyssa pulled out her laptop. She didn't even realize that she'd fallen asleep herself until Alyssa shook her awake and gave her the side-eye. "What grown lady fall asleep during a two-hour flight? Bitch, you getting old," she joked as Anastasia sat up and wiped the crust from her eyes.

"You got jokes, huh? Ain't nothing old about all this," Anastasia grumbled, pointing at herself. She woke up Kyler and got their things together so that they could get off the plane as people moved through the aisles and out of the door. Once they had their carry-ons they exited the plane and went to grab their luggage. Alyssa had scheduled to rent a car for the day and had gone to grab it while Anastasia grabbed one of those things to tote all of their suitcases on.

They met out front and loaded all of their things into the small SUV that Alyssa pulled up to the curb in. Considering that they each only had two suitcases it didn't take them, but five minutes to fill up the car and be on their way. Since they were only stopping through to take the test and drop off Kyler with their mother Anastasia had Alyssa drive straight to the DNA testing center. The sisters made small talk with each other and Kyler on the way and soon they were pulling up to the building. Anastasia took a deep breath and removed her seatbelt, so that she could talk directly to Kyler. She didn't think that he would be traumatized or anything by what they were about to do, but she knew that he would be curious as to why someone was going to swab his mouth. Thankfully, Zyree had already come in to give his sample and wouldn't be there today, further making the situation awkward. "Okay, Kyler you remember what we're here to do, right?" she asked, looking into his little face. He nodded and gave a slight shrug as he put his tablet into his bag.

"Yep, we're here to get tested for the flu before you go on your trip," he said, putting his back pack on his shoulder and reaching for the door.

"That's right. It's going to be really quick and then we'll go to Grandma's," Anastasia told him with a smile. She could feel Alyssa staring a hole into the side of her face the whole time, but she didn't acknowledge her until they were out of the car.

"You petty as hell. Why you tell him that shit?" Alyssa asked as they walked up the small walkway and into the building with Kyler a few steps ahead.

"Cause he already just lost his father, found out he got a brother, been introduced to a new man, and found out how his Grandma really felt about him. The last thing I need is to confuse him anymore, by telling him that we're here to find out if he got a different daddy; especially, when I know that nigga ain't his daddy," Anastasia explained.

To her it was simple, why tell him the truth about why they were there when Zyree wasn't going to be a part of his life? He'd already been through so much, so there was no reason to inform him and have him asking questions, and being even more confused. Alyssa rolled her eyes, obviously not satisfied with her answer, but she didn't care. She knew her sister probably wouldn't understand her reasoning, but once she had a child, she would see what lengths you would go through to protect them.

Anastasia checked in at the front desk and was given a small form to fill out while they waited. As soon as she sat down next to Alyssa, she started with the shit again. "So, you're absolutely sure that Zy isn't the d-a-d-d-y?" she whispered causing Anastasia to stop writing on the paper in front of her.

"What you tryna say, Lyssa?" she asked with narrowed eyes even though she knew exactly what her sister was getting at.

"I just want to know if you're sure, sure or if you're just wanting to be done with Zy."

"Listen, cause you sounding like Aunty Shirley right now. I am absolutely, positive that Zyree had no parts in that lil boy over there." Anastasia made sure to look her sister directly in the eyes as she said it. She was starting to get tired of people asking her if she was sure about Kyler's paternity. Nobody liked him which was probably the reason that they were all kinda leaning towards Zyree, but that didn't change the facts. Richard was Kyler's father. Alyssa held her hands up in surrender and mumbled an okay as she went back to looking through the magazine in her hands, while Anastasia went back to filling out the form.

When she finished she took it back up to the desk and waited on them to call her name, which didn't take too long. A short, chubby nurse eventually came out and had her and Kyler follow her to the back-testing area. She was asked a series of questions before they swabbed her mouth and then Kyler's. The whole time Anastasia felt as if the lady was judging her and she tried to hide her irritation.

"How soon can we get the results back?" she wanted to know as she watched the lady place labels on each of the samples.

"Within the week ma'am, as soon as we get them in you can set it up for us to call you and let you know or you can call yourself, plus a copy will be sent to you and the other party." Anastasia nodded her understanding and hoping that the results came sooner rather than later. As they were leaving, Kyler told her he was hungry, so she had

Alyssa stop through a McDonald's before heading to their mother's house.

As soon as they pulled into the driveway Kyler took off running into the house, leaving her to carry his bags inside, but she didn't mind. She grabbed the small duffle bag and suitcase out of the trunk and hurried up the sidewalk with Alyssa at her side, as Aunt Shirley came to the door.

"So, he finally got you down here to take that test, huh?" she asked, standing in the doorway with her signature flask in her hand. Anastasia couldn't help, but roll her eyes at her drunk ass Aunty, hoping that the disrespectful shit she wanted to say wouldn't slip out.

"Hey to you, too, Aunt Shirley," she mumbled instead as she moved past her and into the house to greet her mother. Ignoring the smart ass reply she knew was coming, she dropped his bags on the stairs and headed to the kitchen where she found her mama making Kyler a plate of what looked like chili and cornbread. "Hey mama," she greeted her with a hug once she set his plate down in front of him. Thoughts of the McDonalds he had right next to him were gone.

"Hey baby, where's your sister?"

"Oh, she's right behind me. Probably up there being held hostage by Aunt Shirley," Anastasia said, eyeing the pot of food.

"Gone head and get y'all some for the road, Stasia, I can tell you ain't had a home cooked meal in a while," her mama joked, nodding her head towards the stove with a smile. Anastasia wasted no time grabbing up a couple of the storage bowls and filling them up.

"You ain't gotta tell me twice, ma."

"I already know," she chuckled. "How have you been though, with everything going on?" she asked, her voice turning somber, letting Anastasia know that she was talking about things with Richard and Zyree.

"Happier than a pig in shit!" Aunt Shirley spat as she entered into the kitchen with Alyssa in tow.

"Shirley, watch your mouth around this baby, and stop talking like that," their mother scolded while Anastasia and Alyssa both hid a smile. Aunt Shirley was right on the money, she was definitely happy that she no longer had to deal with Richard's ass.

"Girl, please, we all happy that nigga gone, you just too sanctified to admit it, but I'll admit it for the both of us, and trust me all the shit he done heard in this house since Christmas, he'll be just fine." Aunt Shirley waved her sister off. Anastasia choked back a laugh and sat down at the table so that she could hurry up and finish her food. They still had a flight to catch and she didn't want her Aunt to accidentally let the surprise slip while she ran off at the mouth. Their mother smacked her lips, but didn't argue with Aunt Shirley; probably because she knew that she was right. They sat at the table together and caught up on things before the girls headed out to catch their flight.

Anastasia had been glad to see her mom and Aunt, but since she knew that they were coming along for the trip, she didn't feel too bad about leaving that day and excitement filled her once again as she got settled into her seat with another bowl of food in her lap while Alyssa drove them to the airport.

Chapter 35

Alyssa and Anastasia checked their luggage before they made their way through the Atlanta International Airport to meet their sisters at the gate. They walked side by side as they passed fellow travelers trying to make it to their destinations. Alyssa tried to put her thoughts about Corey to the back of her mind, but thoughts of him cheating kept creeping in. She tried to take the positive road and listen to her sisters' words about how much he loved her and that he wouldn't make the same mistake twice, but what the hell was she supposed to think with how he was acting towards her and their wedding. Corey's secret calls that he made from the bathroom along with the quick hang ups whenever she entered the room had her thinking the worse. If Corey wasn't cheating, then what the hell was he doing?

They made it to their gate and saw Alexis and Andrea sitting near the charging stations with their phones glued to their hands. They were so into whatever they were doing on their phones that they didn't even see them walk up.

"The seats are for people. Not your bags, bitch." Alyssa tossed Lexi's Gucci bag on the floor.

"Hell naw, hoe. I know you ain't just toss my shit on the fuckin' floor!" Lexi tossed her phone to Drea jumping up ready to fight.

"Calm your ass down, girl. It's just me." They all laughed.

"Bitch, you were about to catch these hands tossin' my shit on the floor." Lexi hugged Lyssa before hugging Stasia.

"Y'all asses were stuck to the phone, how else was I supposed to get y'all attention?" Alyssa hugged Drea before sitting next to her.

"Anyway, I know y'all ready to turn up in Jamaica." Andrea smiled.

"Hell yeah! I can't wait to get there. With everythin' that's been goin' on, I think we all deserve this trip," Stasia answered.

They all murmured in agreement.

"Hey Drea? Did you ever find out who was stalking you?" Lyssa asked.

"Girl, it was Deacon Jones gay ass."

"You lyin!" Lexi gasped.

"Not uh. When D'Mari was in town for my doctor's appointment, I didn't even know what was goin' on until D'Mari spun the car around on some fast and the furious type shit and hopped out with his gun in hand. When I saw who it was, I hopped out the car and stopped D'Mari from killin' his ass." Drea shook her head.

"I know he almost pissed himself when he saw D'Mari." Alyssa tried to hold back her laughter.

"More like shit himself."

They all burst into laughter.

"I'm just glad it's over with. Now, I can stop lookin' over my shoulder," Drea added.

"On another note, how are the babies?" Stasia smiled.

"They're doin' good. We still don't know what we're havin', but they're healthy and so am I," Drea responded as she rubbed her belly.

They talked for a few more minutes until the attendant announced that the flight for Montego Bay, Jamaica was boarding. The Holiday sisters gathered their things and waited for the door to open so they could board the plane. As they made their way onto the plane, they took their seats and waited for the rest of the passengers to get settled. Minutes later, the pilot announced that they were taking off to their destination.

Alyssa placed her ear phones in her ears and listened to her tunes as she stared out the window. Thoughts of Corey filled her head as 'Nobody Else But You' by Trey Songz began to play. It made her think back to the time that they were texting while she was out with Kelly a few months back and he said that he didn't want nobody else but her. The thought made her smile. Alyssa didn't know what was going on with Corey but she decided that she wasn't going to stress herself out about it. She was on her way to Jamaica and she didn't want to bring her problems with her. The situation with Corey would still be waiting for her when she returned home.

After the three-hour flight, they had arrived in Jamaica. Grabbing their things from the overhead compartments, they walked off the plane together and headed to baggage claim. When the sisters had all of their luggage, they walked towards the exit and flagged down a cab. The driver hopped out to help them put their things in the trunk and helped the ladies inside the cab before returning to the wheel. Alexis gave the driver the address to the Villa they were staying in and he pulled off. The sisters chatted the entire way there, only pausing their conversation to look at the clear blue water as they passed the beach.

The driver pulled up to the Villa putting the car in park. He jumped out and opened the door for them before he popped the trunk of the cab. After Alyssa got out of the cab, she stood next to her sisters in awe. The outside of the Villa was beautiful, so she could only imagine what the inside looked like. Andrea paid the cab driver before they grabbed their suitcases and making their way inside. Alyssa's mouth hit the floor as they slowly walked through the luxurious villa. It had six bedrooms, multiple eating and lounging areas, a huge kitchen and large swimming pool as well as a Jacuzzi. The villa had a great view of the sea and the best part about it was that it was a private villa, so they had the whole thing to themselves.

"This villa is dope as fuck!" Lexi beamed as she flopped down on one of the couches in the living room.

"You ain't never lied, sis. We just got in this bitch and I already don't want to leave," Alyssa chimed in.

"Come check out the pool, y'all."

Alyssa and Lexi joined Drea and Stasia out back where the pool was. They stood there for a moment taking in the view as the warm breeze brushed across their skin.

"This shit is beautiful," Stasia stated as she sat in one of the lounge chairs.

"I can get used to livin' like this."

"Don't get too comfy. Let's put our stuff away first then we can figure out what we're gonna do," Andrea stated.

"Aight. I call dibs on the master suite," Lexi said with a raised hand.

"Hold up. How you get the master suite?" Alyssa placed her hand on her hip.

"Because I paid for the trip, bitch. So, I get the biggest room," Lexi stepped closer to her.

"I don't give a fuck what you paid for. I want the master suite."

"Why don't y'all flip a coin or somethin'?" Andrea stepped in between them.

"Cool. I call heads." Lyssa kept her eyes trained on Lexi.

Andrea pulled a coin out of her pocket, flipped it and caught. When she opened her hand, the coin was on tails. Alyssa sucked her teeth as Alexis teased.

"That's why you lost, hoe," Lexi teased her.

Alyssa reached for her sister, but she ran. Alyssa chased Lexi around the pool and when she caught up with her, she pushed her ass in the pool and they all laughed.

"Lyssa, Ima kill you!"

"That's what your ass get." She continued to laugh.

After Lexi climbed out of the pool, the sisters went inside, grabbed their bags and claimed their rooms. Although Alyssa wanted the master suite, she couldn't be mad at the room she chose because it was just as big. The room had a king size bed, its own bathroom along with a dresser and closet. Alyssa placed some of clothes in the closet and put the rest in drawers. She placed her shoes in the closet as well before she opened the doors that exposed the pool. Alyssa felt good about being in Jamaica with her sisters. She wasn't sure of the activities that they were going to partake in while they were there, but she knew her sisters would be down to go jet skiing. Alyssa grabbed her phone from her pocket and checked to see if Corey texted her and smiled when she saw that he did.

Corey: I love you, Alyssa

Alyssa: I love you too

Alyssa wasn't sure why Corey texted her that, but she really didn't care. The anger she had towards him quickly subsided and she couldn't wait until him and the other guys arrived.

Chapter 36

Lexi and her sisters walked arm and arm through Hi-Lo Supermarket in Kingston, Jamaica, grabbing some things they needed as well as some things they did not need. Andrea leading the pack, shopped off pregnancy hormones rather than common sense. They were only on the Caribbean Island for a week, yet they were shopping for a month's worth of food. Granted that they were going to have a house full, but the shit they were stacking inside those three carts were ridiculous.

"Y'all see anything else we might need for the bbq later?" Alyssa asked, grabbing four bottles of jerk sauce.

"Nah, we should be good," Anastasia informed her.

"I just wanna hit up the liquor store cuz everybody knows that... once the Remy's in the system, ain't no telling whether I'll fuck em or diss em," Lexi danced around the aisle as she rapped lyrics to a Jay-Z song.

Drea, Stasia, and Lyssa danced along as the hometown citizens stared at them smiling. Lexi loved Jamaica, in fact her, Bre, and Marcus spent her 21st birthday there. Everyone was so friendly and welcoming, not to mention the unlimited weed she got; she was in heaven. After racking up $376.00 in groceries and charging it to Richard's credit card, may he rest in peace, (NOT), the sisters headed back to the truck they rented, loaded the items in, and headed back to the house.

"I still can't believe what you told us about Bre." Drea said, opening up a bag of chips and a bottle of water.

"Yeah, that is sad," Lyssa added in.

"What's even sadder is the fact that she's so young. I swear to God, I hate cancer," Stasia fumed.

Instead of chiming in, Lexi just looked out the window and agreed with them with a head nod. Bre and her condition had been on her mind heavy since the news was broken to her. She wished that she could take that illness from her ex best friend, but she knew life didn't work like that. Regardless of all the shit Bre put her through, she never wished death on her; their good outweighed their bad at the end of the day. Alexis tuned her sisters out for the rest of the car ride because her mind was everywhere and all she wanted to do was get high, drunk, and swim with some dolphins.

"Ahhhhh my baby herrreeeeee!!" Lexi heard Stasia yell as she squirmed in the driver's seat.

Lexi's eyed popped opened and they had finally arrived back at the house. There were two cars parked in the driveway, which could only mean that the men had arrived. Alexis looked over at Drea who had the biggest smile on her face while Lyssa took off running towards the house, she assumed to greet her fiancé. Although she was alone on what turned out to be a Valentine's getaway, she was happy to see her sisters so in love. Before she could get out of the truck fully, all three sisters had disappeared in the house.

"Don't worry bitches, I got the bags... nah... nah... nah.... It's cool, I don't need help." Lexi yelled out in sarcasm as she went to grab a few bags.

Once she got all she could carry, she walked into the house and found everyone in the living room on the couches hugging and shit.

"Baby Holiday, what's up shorty?" Corey said from the side of Lyssa.

"What up, sis?" D'Mari added in followed by D'Mani.

"What up, lil niggaz?" Lexi said, greeting the three of them before dropping the bags off in the kitchen.

As soon as she sat the bags on the counter, she heard the front door beep, which meant either someone was coming in or leaving out. Moments later, the guys came inside the kitchen with the rest of the bags.

"Y'all must plan on cooking good for us," D'Mani said as he searched through the bags.

"Y'ALL ain't doing shit. Y'all bitches might be though," Lexi replied as she placed the gallon of milk in the refrigerator.

"Damn lil sis, that's how we going?" D'Mari stated.

"Nothing against you, bro, but I'm just saying," Lexi responded.

"Yeah we hear you!" Corey said, laughing and causing the twins to laugh as well.

"What's so funny?" Drea asked as she joined them in the kitchen with Stasia and Lyssa behind her.

"Baby Holiday pressed about some shit," D'Mani responded.

"Shut the fuck up. I ain't pressed about nothing," Lexi said in her defense.

"Y'all excuse our baby sister. She's feeling some type of way because she's here alone," Alyssa said, adding her two cents in.

"First of all, bitch, I can have ten niggaz from each of the 51 states here with me if I wanted to. Not to mention, I can have a couple of the Jamaican mon's walking around this house too so he cool," Lexi snapped

"Woah woah woah! Y'all chill out," Corey stepped in and said.

"Bae, ain't nobody paying Lexi's ass no mind, she'll be ok," Lyssa said, waving off the situation and walking out of the kitchen.

"Right bitch… BYYEEEEE!!" Lexi yelled, just having to have the last word.

"Y'all ass is crazy," D'Mani stated, taking a sit next to Anastasia.

"My sisters, but I love them," Anastasia said, causing Drea to laugh, but Lexi was still in her feelings so she did nothing but roll her eyes.

"Aye lil sis, I got a homie that's flying in later today. I mean I can introduce you to…."

"Nope. Not gon happen. I'm good. Don't waste yo time," Lexi said, cutting D'Mari completely off.

"Damn you ain't even let me finish," he continued.

"Cuz I'm already knowing where you going with this."

"Just hear me out. He's one of my homies from around the way. A real cool nigga. He bout' his business and money. I think you'll like him," D'Mari finally finished his statement.

"I don't like niggaz...." Lexi blurted out.

"Damn you gay again?" Drea yelled, throwing her hands in the air.

"Again?" D'Mani repeated with a confused look on his face.

"Long story baby, I'll fill you in later," Anastasia laughed as she rubbed the top of his waves.

"Fuck all of y'all, ok!" Lexi chuckled a little before walking out of the kitchen and towards the master bedroom.

"I love you, Alexis Holiday," Alyssa yelled from the couch as Lexi walked passed.

"Suck my dick, A," Lexi said, sticking up her middle finger.

Once inside the room, Lexi sat on the bed going through her phone. Her sister was right, she was in her feelings because she was alone and missed the shit out of J.R. He was supposed to be there with her, but he wasn't and it was killing her. Lexi felt a tear escape from her eyes and she quickly wiped it away when there was a knock on the door.

"Come in," she said, shifting her body in the bed.

"You good, sister?" Drea walked in and asked.

"I just don't get it, Andrea," Lexi said, breaking down in tears.

"Oh, my Gooddd, come here," Drea said, pulling Lexi into her arms.

"I finally found someone who I genuinely love. Someone I'll give it all up for, only for him not to give it all up for me. I never asked Jeremy to completely change his lifestyle, I just asked him to not do one thing. This shit is killing me, sister. I love him."

For the first time, Lexi broke down and cried about the situation. She had been holding it in for so long, trying to be the nonchalant Lexi that everyone knew her as; yet, she was dying inside.

"Everything is going to be ok, Alexis. Out of all of us, you are the strongest. You are the fighter. There's nothing you can't get through. I know you are hurting right now, but I promise this pain is temporary. J.R. is missing out on a beautiful soul and if he can't see that, then he is not the one for you," Drea said, dropping jewels as well as tears.

"You right. I don't know why I'm crying over his little dick ass anyway," Lexi said, lifting her head and wiping her tears.

"Wait, J.R. got a little dick?" Drea questioned.

"Hell nah, I was trying to make myself feel better. That nigga working with a monster."

"Girrrrlllllll," Drea said, laughing and playfully punching Lexi in the arm.

Ding….Dong…

The doorbell rang causing the two of them to look at each other.

"Look before you get mad. D'Mani and D'Mari invited Rico ONLY because I told D'Mari that you and J.R. wasn't together," Drea explained, standing up and slowly walking away with her hands surrendered in the air.

"Are you fuckn serious right nowwwwww," Lexi whined.

"What? We thought you liked him?" Drea replied.

"I mean… I wanna fuck the nigga, but I don't wanna be around him for a whole week."

Drea bent over laughing, "Girl, just deal with the man…. DAMN!" she said, pushing her out the door.

Lexi stomped towards the living room where she heard laughter. She turned the corner and her mouth fell to the floor when she saw J.R. standing there with Corey, D'Mani, and D'Mari. The entire room looked at her, but her eyes only locked with his.

"Come give a nigga a hug," J.R. said, biting his bottom lip.

Lexi took off running into his arms. J.R. lifted her up in the air, hugging her tight as she fought back tears.

"Awwwwww…" All three sisters said in unison.

When J.R. finally put Lexi on the ground, she looked around the room at all her sisters who were wiping their faces.

"What are you doing here?" she asked.

"Come in here and I'll fill you in," J.R. replied.

Lexi grabbed his hand and pulled him back in the room, taking a seat on the bed.

"J.R. baby, I can't believe you came," Lexi said, smiling.

"I love you, shorty, I ain't missing out on shit else from here on out," he replied.

"But, I mean… like how…. I thought…. The money…." she stuttered, trying to get her thoughts together.

J.R. laughed before replying.

"I always said that ain't no woman on this Earth going to allow me to stop getting bread…. Well, that was until I met you. I knew killing the twins was going to hurt you down the line and I couldn't live with that shit on my heart. So, the day I took the trip to kill buddie's ass, I got up with the twins. I figured, if they were worth a half a million dead, then them niggaz was worth some real money alive, so why not join them. We linked up and been doing business since then. The half of million I would have made by popping them, I've made more than that in a month by doing business with them. Lexi on some real shit, I love the fuck outta you; if I'll kill for you, then I'll die for you. I ain't never in my life felt this way about a woman. I told you the day we made shit official that if you with me, you won't have to worry about shit and I still mean that. Imma make you my wife one day baby, you believe that."

The words J.R. spoke hit Alexis's heart and she couldn't stop herself from crying, yet again.

"Man, stop all that crying," he said, wiping the tears away.

"I'm sorry, I can't help it," she shyly laughed.

"It's cool, let's go enjoy these Jamaican streets," he replied, standing to his feet.

"These Jamaican streets can wait. Remember for Christmas you said that you wanted a baby?" Lexi asked.

J.R. shook his head up and down smiling.

"Well, Christmas is ten months away. Let's see what we can do," she replied, walking over to the door and locking it.

Chapter 37

Waking up in D'Mari's arms again was definitely a dream come true. The trip to Jamaica had started out awesome and Andrea couldn't wait to see what else was in store for everyone. When J.R. arrived the day before, that put the icing on the cake. Even though Lexi said that she was cool, Drea was ecstatic when J.R. showed up and finally put her feisty ass in check. She liked how he let her think that shit was going her way, but then shut the shit down when he had enough of the foolishness. Drea rolled over, but D'Mari pulled her back.

"Where you goin, baby?" he mumbled.

"I'm gonna get up and cook breakfast for everyone."

"You supposed to be relaxing and shit. You on bedrest. Why you gotta cook?"

"I'm not on bedrest silly... cooking isn't hard work," Drea laughed.

"Besides... I know you're hungry after all that work you put in last night and I wanna feed my man," Drea said.

"Oh, I'm your mans now?" D'Mari pulled her closer.

Drea had never said that to him and it flowed out of her mouth before she could stop herself.

"Don't get quiet now... I like the sound of that," he kissed her on the forehead.

"I wish you weren't all the way in New York," she admitted.

"I can't even lie, ma… I been thinking the same thing. I always heard about these down south women and I done ran into one and she bout to be the mother of my kids. Fuck all that baby mama shit, that ain't how I roll. I'm putting some shit in motion… I don't know how all of it is gonna play out, but I believe that there won't be much distance between us for much longer. Until it's solid, just know that I'll be here at least once a week checking on you."

Drea didn't know if it was her hormones, the love she had for D'Mari, or a combination of both, but as he talked she couldn't help but to cry. He wiped her tears and then he continued to explain exactly how he felt about her. They had talked before, but it felt like that time was different, like it was the beginning to something much deeper.

"I love you, Andrea… and I want my kids to have the same last name as me and their mother," D'Mari said as he rolled over and pulled a black box out of nowhere.

"Oh, my God… are you serious?"

D'Mari opened the box and the sight of the ring damn near blinded Drea. To say it was beautiful or even stunning would have been an understatement. D'Mari removed the five-carat white gold Miadora ring from the box and slid it out of the bed and got down on one knee.

"I know we haven't known each other that long, but nothing else has ever felt so right in my life. Ever since you entered, things have changed for the better. Will you marry me?"

"Yes… yes… I will!" Drea jumped off of the bed and into D'Mari's arms.

After they hugged and kissed, he slipped the ring onto her finger and she felt like the luckiest girl in the world. She never expected for things in her life to take such a drastic turn for the better, but she was filled with joy.

"I love you!" she told him and then headed to the bathroom to take care of her hygiene and relieve her bladder.

Twenty minutes later, Drea was in the kitchen singing and dancing as she cooked. It was after eleven and no one else was up except D'Mari, and he was still in the room. She was sure that everyone would start smelling the aroma from the food soon and start making their way from their rooms. She was glad that they had gone grocery shopping the day before. Drea whipped up some pancakes, waffles, scrambled eggs, sausage, bacon, and she laid out an assortment of fruit. Her phone was connected to the Bluetooth speaker and she had her Apple Music on blasting on Whitney Houston's station because she wanted to hear some good, old school music.

'I Wanna Dance With Somebody' came on and Drea turned up her two step.

"Somebody's in a good mood... the hell you singing and dancing for?" Lexi walked in and grabbed a slice of bacon and asked.

Instead of answering, Drea grabbed her hand and started dancing.

"This ain't the kind of music Lexi is used to dancing to," Stasia popped in and said.

"Fuck yoouuuu!!" Lexi flipped her off.

"This food smells good and I'm starving," Alyssa walked in.

Drea's energy had rubbed off on all of them and they danced to the rest of the song. Lexi grabbed Drea's phone off the counter and the next song that came on was 'Back That Azz Up' by Juvenile.

"Aaayyyeee!" they all sang in unison when the beat dropped.

"Wait a got damn minute... what is thiisss?" Lexi grabbed Drea's left hand.

"That ring is gorgeous," Alyssa snatched Drea's hand from Lexi.

"My big sister done popped that pussy and got a ring," Lexi danced and the sisters' laughter filled the kitchen.

Drea turned around and turned the stove off, and then she began telling her sisters about how her morning had gone. She expressed her true feelings about everything, and it went back to Thanksgiving when they all got together for the first time in years. It had been a very long time since they had a real conversation, and it was long overdue. By the time Drea finished talking, all of the sisters had shed a few tears. Even Lexi's feisty ass. It seemed very therapeutic and she truly hoped that they could continue to enjoy each other without any extra problems or drama.

"What's wrong wit y'all? Somebody hurt... let me get my shit," J.R. walked into the kitchen and said all in one breath.

"Nah… baby, we good. We were just having a sister moment," Lexi told him and then went and wrapped her arms around him.

The other guys appeared one by one, and within the next ten minutes they were all sitting at the table enjoying the delicious meal that Drea had prepared. It was crazy how everything had played out. Just a couple of months ago, J.R. was on a mission to kill D'Mani, but they had linked up and joined forces. Drea looked around the table and smiled. Everything was looking up and she couldn't wait to see the look on Alyssa's face when she found out about her upcoming surprise wedding on Valentine's Day.

Chapter 38

Anastasia leaned against the balcony outside of her room and inhaled the fresh, warm breeze. She closed her eyes and smiled as happiness filled her body. There was a lot of things for her to be happy about. Not only was she free to be with the man she loved, but so were her sisters. Drea was now engaged with babies on the way, Lexi had finally met her match, and was so in love everyone could see it, and Alyssa was getting married. The past few months had been trying on them all, but in the midst of the drama they'd all become closer, and also gotten the men of their dreams.

She'd left everyone inside and had only planned to come out quickly for a moment to reflect, but that moment had turned into a few and before she knew it she'd been out on the balcony for almost twenty minutes. The view and serenity she felt right then wouldn't allow her to leave. She'd been through a lot, and so had her family. To know that all of the bad times were behind them had her damn near emotional, and she didn't really want anybody to see if she did happen to shed a few tears. With a soft moan, she swayed like there was music playing to the sounds of the waves crashing from the beach. She smelled D'Mani's Sauvage cologne, telling of his presence before his arms slipped around her waist and he planted a kiss on the side of her neck.

"What you out here thinkin bout, ma?" his husky voice filled her ears and made her tremble slightly.

"Just how great things are right now," she smiled and placed her arms over his as he rocked them both gently, both gazing out at the bright moon.

"Well, do you mind if I show you how much greater they're going to be?" he asked, causing her to turn to face him with a curious smile.

"It gets better than this?" she cocked her head to the side and teased as she looked into his dark eyes.

"With a nigga like me, of course." He flashed that handsome smile of his and grabbed ahold of her hand leading her out of the house. Everyone seemed to be off doing their own thing, because it was much more, quiet than we she had retreated a little bit ago. They made it out of the house and crossed the street heading straight for the beach. In the distance Anastasia could see some lights on the nearly deserted beach, but she didn't think anything of it. In fact, she wondered if they were going to interrupt whoever had planned the little romantic night on the beach, but as they grew closer her stomach fluttered with butterflies and she couldn't hide the flush of her cheeks.

"D'Mani, where are you taking me?" she quizzed even as the man standing there with a beautiful, white horse came into view. He didn't answer, only stopping just as they reached the sand to remove his shoes, and kneeling to help her slip off her own.

"Stop asking so many questions and come on woman." He sauntered off ahead of her with her hand still in his looking carefree in some khaki cargo shorts, and a black v-neck as his shoes dangled from his left hand. Unable to contain her excitement anymore Anastasia let out a squeal and took off running towards the horse feeling like a little kid.

When she came to a stop in front of it she ran a hand across its white mane and greeted the man standing there. He told her his name was Marcell and that the horses name was Pegasus. Anastasia stood in awe of the majestic horse as she pet it, and then turned her attention back to D'Mani who had finally joined them.

"Damn, just ruin my lil surprise, huh?" he joked.

"I'm sorry baby.... thank you so much! This is so sweet!" she exclaimed jumping into his arms. He let out a low chuckle and held her with one arm, reaching out to greet Marcell with the other.

"Yeah, yeah.... what's up, Marcell?"

"Hello, D'Mani," Marcell said from behind her. He went right into telling them what they needed to do as far as riding and in five minutes Anastasia was mounting the horse with D'Mani standing on the side of her. It felt strange sitting on top of the horse and she gripped the horse's hair tightly scared she would fall off before D'Mani even had a chance to get on. She was surprised when Marcell walked off and D'Mani stayed on the ground holding on to the mane.

"What are you doin? You're not riding with me?" she wanted to know and he shook his head emphatically.

"No, street niggas do not ride horses, girl. You ride, I'll walk."

Anastasia could feel her face begin to frown up until a huge grin appeared on his. "I'm just fuckin with you, scoot up." He hopped right on, behind her, like he'd been riding horses his entire life and clicked his tongue prompting the horse to move forward. They started down the barely lit beach with his arms securely around her waist, going slow at first and then he had them galloping. Anastasia was pleasantly surprised at how skillful he was as he rode through the sand, occasionally taking them to the shore line and letting the cool water hit their feet.

Soon they came to a stop at a scene straight out of a movie and Anastasia couldn't help, but to let out a laugh at D'Mani trying his hand at romance. There was a quilted pad, that almost looked like a bed it was so plush, surrounded by tea candles in glass jars waiting for them. He even had a wicker basket and a throw blanket on top. Climbing down from behind her, he reached out for her with both arms and helped her down as she hid her smile behind her hands.

"Awwww baby," she gushed as her feet hit the sand. He moved her hands away from her face and gazed into her eyes.

"I just want you to know that you can still have the life you dreamed of with a nigga like me," he told her as he caressed her cheek softly. "We had some rocky times, and I'm positive that we'll probably have more, but I promise to make the good always outweigh the bad; you and Kyler are my family now......you ready for this adventure?" he asked with his lips hovering over hers.

"Hell yeah," Anastasia replied barely above a whisper, answering him before his mouth covered hers in one of the most passionate kisses he'd ever laid on her.

"Come on, I ain't got too much longer for this shit before the hood come out of me," he joked, breaking their kiss and enveloping her hand in his as he led her over to their picnic.

Chapter 39

Alyssa woke up the next morning to a breakfast tray full of food and a note from Corey telling her to meet him on the beach when she was finished eating. She couldn't help the smile that appeared on her face after she read the note. The food looked and smelled delicious and Alyssa didn't hesitate to dive in. Alyssa made light work of her cheese eggs, turkey bacon, sausage, and cheese grits before hopping into the shower.

As she began to wash her body, Alyssa couldn't get over how her sisters trip turned into a couples' getaway. The problems that she felt like they were having had pushed so far to the back of her mind that they were really gone. Since he arrived, he had been catering to her every need and giving her all of his attention, which was something that he did often way before they got engaged. Corey was reminding her of all the reasons why she agreed to marry him in the first place and Alyssa was falling in love with him all over again.

When Alyssa was finished in the bathroom, she put on her teal and lavender colored bikini, white cover up and her light purple sandals. Putting her hair in a high ponytail, Alyssa sent a text to Corey letting him know that she was on her way then she sent a text to her sisters letting them know that she was meeting Corey. Alyssa knew that her sisters wouldn't miss her being as though their men had their attention, but she still felt as though they should know. Leaving out her room, she spoke to her brother-in-laws as she passed them on her way out. They were in the kitchen preparing breakfast trays and Alyssa couldn't help but laugh at how much food D'Mari had piled up on the plates knowing the food was for his pregnant fiancée.

Alyssa spotted Corey near the water talking to a man holding two life jackets. They were standing next to two jet skis and Alyssa couldn't contain her excitement as she jogged the rest of the way.

"Good mornin', beautiful." Corey embraced her with opened arms.

"Good morning to you, sexy," She beamed.

"Are these jet skis for us?"

"Yeah. I rented them for a few hours. I always wanted to ride jet skis. So, I figured we'd try it while we're here."

"Aww, bae! You must've read my mind because I wanted to do this since we got here," Alyssa shouted.

"Then what are we waitin' for?" He laughed at her excitement.

The instructor told them how to operate the jet skis as Alyssa removed her cover up and placed on her life jacket the instructor handed her. After Corey secured his life jacket, Alyssa kicked off her flip flops and climbed onto the jet ski. As soon as Corey was on his, Alyssa took off screaming into the ocean and leaving her man behind. The wind whipped across her face as she rode further out into the ocean and it wasn't long before Corey had caught up with her. Alyssa was impressed by the tricks that Corey was doing on his jet ski and even though he seemed like he knew what he was doing, she screamed for him to be careful numerous times.

When Corey informed Alyssa that it was time to go back, she couldn't help but to pout. Corey shook his head at her.

"Corey, I'm having fun. I don't want to go back yet," she whined.

"I know you're havin' fun, bae. But, I wanna chill with you for a minute before we go back to the crib."

"Aight. Can we at least race back then?"

"You don't want no smoke for real, shawty." He grinned.

"Don't try to play me, nigga. Just count off." Alyssa waved him off.

"Aight. 1…2…3… GO!"

They both took off heading back in the direction where they started from. Corey was in the lead, but Alyssa was determined to win. As they came close to the shore, Alyssa zipped passed Corey splashing water on him with her jet ski. When she approached the sand, she jumped off the jet ski and bounced around like Rocky with her hands in the air.

"What you got to say now, Corey?" Alyssa shouted as Corey pulled up.

"Aight, ma. I'll let you have it with ya cheatin' ass," he chuckled as he approached her.

They took off their life jackets and handed them back to the instructor before they took a seat on the sand. Corey wrapped his arms around Alyssa, pulling her closer to him as they stared at the waves while they rolled in.

"What's on ya mind, Lyssa?" he spoke into her ear.

"How everything just seems so perfect." She smiled.

"Me and my sisters' relationship is getting better. We all have good men in our lives, all of us are in love, and we're all here together having a good time. It doesn't get any better than this, bae."

Corey kissed her cheek before she rested her head on his shoulder. They sat quietly for a moment before Corey spoke up

"Lyssa, I just wanna apologize for how I acted before you left," Corey whispered in her ear.

"Don't even trip on that. Let's just focus on moving forward and making the best of this week." She looked back at him and smiled.

Alyssa twisted around in his arms so that she was laying on her back. Corey leaned down and kissed her lips passionately. Alyssa's body tingled as they continued to kiss each other like it was their first time. If Alyssa had any doubt that Corey didn't love her, that kissed did more than confirmed that he did. As much as they wanted to fuck each other's brains out, they decided to wait until later.

After spending a few more moments on the beach, Alyssa slipped on her cover up and grabbed her flip flops before they walked hand and hand back to the villa. As they walked inside, they saw everyone getting things ready for the cookout they were having later on that day. It warmed Alyssa's heart to see everyone smiling, laughing, and dancing as they got things in order. There was nothing but good vibes and love in the atmosphere. Looking back from where they started, Alyssa never thought that her and her sisters would be spending time together like they were, but through all the madness that had taken place between them, it didn't stop them from fighting through it, pulling together, and forming a bond that was on the verge of becoming unbreakable.

Chapter 40

"Alllleexxxxiiiisssssssss"

Lexi heard Drea calling her name for like the nineteen-hundredth time and for the nineteen-hundredth and one time, she was going to ignore her.

"Bae, she gon come banging on the door in a minute," J.R. said through his light manly moans.

Just like she dismissed Drea, she dismissed his ass too. Instead of replying, she arched her back a little more and continued to ride J.R.'s dick. Their sexual moans filled the room as J.R. gripped her waist, causing her to speed up a little. That was all Lexi needed, moments later, she felt herself climaxing, creaming all over his dick. Although she had cum for the second time, she couldn't tap out just yet because he had yet to get his. So, Lexi tightened the muscles in her va-jay-jay, gripped his dick with all she had, and bounced up and down with the last bit of energy she had in her. A smile crept across her face when she saw him close his eyes, only she knew that meant he was coming.

"What the fuccckkk, Lexi. I'm finna cummmm," he grunted, releasing his kids inside of her.

Lexi placed a kiss on his lips before getting off of him and heading to the bathroom.

"Aye shorty," he called out to her, still out of breath.

She whipped her head around in a dramatic fashion and stared at him. J.R. shook his head before speaking, "I think that one was the one."

"What are you talking about?" a confused Alexis asked.

"That nut fo'sho got you popped," he stated.

Lexi hopped in the shower with J.R. not far behind. As soon as he got in, he wrapped his arms around the front of her and started playing with her pussy. Lexi swatted his hand away before turning around and handing him the Dove body wash.

"Damn it's like that?" He chuckled.

"They waiting on us and I'm starving," Lexi replied, rinsing her body off.

After the two of them got out, they both began to get dressed. Lexi slipped on her 2-piece cream and gold Gucci swimsuit while J.R. slid on his gold Gucci trunks. The couple looked themselves over in the mirror before both sliding on their Gucci flip flops and exiting out the bedroom. The entire house was empty as they made their way to the backyard where the pool was located. Just as expected, everyone was chilling around the pool. Alyssa and Anastasia was sitting with their feet in the water while Drea was laid out on one of the many beach chairs. D'Mani, D'Mari, and Corey was over by the grill flipping the steaks, having what seemed like an intense conversation. When Lexi slid the screen doors back, everyone's eyes darted in their direction.

"Well it's about damn time," Drea yelled out first.

"I told yo ass she was gon be the first muthafucker to open her mouth," Lexi whispered to J.R. who smacked her on the ass as she stepped out first.

"Well, look what the wind done blew in," Stasia chimed in as she paddled her feet in the water.

"Chill the fuck out, Damn!" Lexi replied, rolling her eyes as she joined them on the side of the pool.

J.R. walked over to where the guys were while Drea wobbled over to be with her sisters.

"So, none of y'all hoes gon actually get in the water and swim? I thought this was a pool party," Lexi said, as she placed her long weave into a high bun.

"Well, everybody didn't take swim lessons growing up like you, Baby Holiday," Alyssa replied.

"Don't be mad at me cuz mommy and daddy invested in me as a child," Lexi stated with an air kiss to all three of her sisters.

"Invested my ass. You the most fucked up one," Stasia said, laughing.

"Let's not take a trip down the fucked up timeline my sister because I can guarantee you, yo life, especially these last past months, trumps mine."

"Y'all don't start that bullshit," Andrea stated.

"Shut the fuck up, Drea!" All three of them said in unison before sharing a laugh.

The Holiday sisters sat around talking, laughing, joking, and reminiscing about their childhood. About thirty minutes later, the guys announced that the food was ready so the ladies got out of the water and headed inside to get the side dishes that they prepared to go with the meat. Carrying out spaghetti, coleslaw, baked beans and bread, they placed the food on the picnic bench before they began preparing their plates.

"So, what's the plans for tonight?" Corey asked, looking at each sister?

"Well, ummmm we thought about having a little ladies' night," Anastasia replied before taking in a fork full of spaghetti.

"Aw straight up, huh?" D'Mani said, eyeing her.

"Yeah. What y'all got planned?" Alyssa asked.

"Shiddddd. We probably fuck about fo', five, six of these Jamician bitches," J.R. responded.

The whole table erupted in laughter, everyone but Lexi.

"I sholl hope them fo', five, six Jamaican bitches can fight," Lexi said, never once looking up from her phone.

"Aye, J.R., I don't know how the fuck you deal with that one. Lexi ass crazy," D'Mari chimes in.

"The crazier the berry, the sweeter the juice," J.R. replied before getting up from the table and grabbing a soda out of the cooler.

"That boy special. These two belong together," Alyssa laughed pointing at both Lexi and J.R.

"So, what y'all do last night?" Andrea looked at Anastasia and asked while making a second plate.

"Awwww let me tell y'all. My baby had this whole romantic night planned. He had a picnic ready and we rode the prettiest horse ever," Stasia blushed.

"Who rode a horse?" D'Mari looked at his brother and asked.

"D'Mani did," Stasia answered for him.

"This nigga gaaayyyyyy!!!" J.R. yelled, causing everyone to laugh.

"Man, shut the fuck up! I did it for my girl," D'Mani said in his defense.

"Man cuz, I love the fuck out my girl but I ain't riding no horse," Corey replied.

"It's cool. Fuck them, baby," Stasia said, rubbing D'Mani's back.

The crew chilled at the table talking until J.R.'s phone rang. When he got up from the table and walked into the house and answered it, Lexi's mood changed. J.R. was inside for about five minutes before he called D'Mani, D'Mari and Corey inside with him.

"I wonder what's that about?" Drea said, getting up from the table.

"I'm assuming business," Stasia answered her.

J.R. had told Lexi the night before that him and the twins were working close together now. He didn't elaborate on everything, but she knew that it was some real deep street shit that they was into.

Bounce that booty on the floor (Shit)

Shake till you get a lil sore (Shit)

Show em, yo mamma made a hoe (Shit)

Go ahead and get a little low (Shit)

Shake that booty in the car (Shit)

Shake that booty in the store (Shit)

(Shit)

Pop it, Stop it, Drop it, Pop it

The sound of Blac Youngsta's hit song "Booty" that everybody called Toot Toot, broke Lexi out of her trance. She turned around to see Alyssa with the speaker in hand as Drea and Stasia attempted to dance. She laughed to herself and silently thanked God for blessing her with the rhythm that her sisters lacked.

"Fuck you over there laughing at?" Drea asked as she bent over and twerked.

"Y'all non-dancing asses," Lexi replied.

"Well Sexy Lexi, how about you show us how it's done," Anastasia said walking over to where Lexi was sitting, pulling her to her feet. Never being the one to back down from a challenge, Lexi wasted no time showing them how it was done. The four of them danced around the pool until they heard the guys come back in.

"The fuck y'all got going on in here?" J.R. asked?

"Drea, if you don't sit yo ass down, my twins in there probably with a headache and shit," D'Mari added in.

"Alyssa, you need to save all that for our honeymoon," Corey stated.

"And Stasia, I just need you to bounce on my dick jussstttt like that later on tonight," D'Mani finally said.

The girls all laughed, but stopped dancing because they needed to save all their energy for the events later that night. Alexis looked around as everyone made their way to their respective mates. She looked to the left of her where she saw Alyssa and Corey kissing. She couldn't wait until the next day to see the look on her sister's face when she says, "I Do". But right then, she had other plans. Lexi slowly walked over to where Corey and Alyssa were and waited for them to pull away from each other. As soon as their lips parted, Lexi pushed Alyssa in the pool. The look on Lyssa's face as she grasped for air was priceless....

"Paybacks a motherfucker, lil bitch!" Lexi yelled out as everyone around them bent over in laughter.

Chapter 41

It was the night of Alyssa's secret bachelorette party and Anastasia couldn't wait for the fun to begin. They had been having a great time in Jamaica, but it was time to get Alyssa drunk and let her get loose for her last night as a free woman. Anastasia, Lexi, and Drea had a few things up their sleeve for the night, and since the men were out giving Corey a bachelor party of his own, they wouldn't be in their hair... or so Stasia hoped. Knowing the niggas that they messed with, they would definitely come and crash the party to make sure it wasn't no funny business going on. The men had left a couple of hours before so the sisters had free reign of the house to turn up and act ratchet while getting ready without interruption. Anastasia was trying to keep her cool so as not to blow the secret, so that Alyssa would think this was just another night out.

Drea, who was already dressed stood in the bathroom mirror applying a small amount of make-up to her beautiful face, while Lexi twerked next to her in her underwear and curled her hair. Anastasia, who'd mixed everyone a drink stood behind them both beating Alyssa's face while Cardi B's "Bodak Yellow" blasted through the house's sound system. It was obvious that they were lit off of the Patron that Stasia had dumped heavily into their glasses, as they all sang at the top of their lungs and danced around the bathroom putting on their finishing touches.

The sisters were so engrossed in what they were doing that they didn't notice their Aunt standing in the doorway until she shouted, catching all of their attention.

"This my shit! Y'all heffas know y'all ain't right tryna leave me! If anybody know how to turn a party out it's your Aunt Shirley!" She came twerking her way into the bathroom and Anastasia grabbed the remote to cut the radio down.

"Aunt Shirley, what is you doin here and how the hell you get in?" Anastasia wanted to know, hoping that their loud mouth Aunty wouldn't spill the beans about what they were there for.

"How the fuck you think I got in," Aunt Shirley asked, smartly pulling out one of those kits to break into a door. The sisters all looked at her in disbelief, but couldn't help to laugh.

"I didn't know you were comin, Aunty," Alyssa said, looking at everyone confused, at why they didn't look surprised to see her.

"Well, I know y'all ain't think I was gone miss the bachelorette party! I swear y'all so stingy with all the fun," she fussed, rolling her eyes and everyone let out a groan.

"Dang Aunt,y way to ruin a surprise!" Lexi snapped while Drea and Stasia just shook their heads.

"Bachelorette party?" Alyssa asked, obviously even more puzzled about what she was talking about.

"Oh hell! The damn weddin is tomorrow y'all might as well let the cat out the bag, shit! I see the only secrets y'all Holiday sisters is good at keeping is innocent ones. I'ma ask y'all to figure that shit out!" she continued waving the sisters off. "Anyway, Lyssa yes! Bachelorette! Party! Cause yous gettin married tomorrow, and ya mama here, too!"

Alyssa looked around the room at her sisters to see if what their Aunt was saying was true, and by the looks on all of their faces, it was. Anastasia grumbled curse words under her breath at her Aunt and rolled her eyes as Shirley shuffled her way further into the bathroom and grabbed the closest glass to her and took a big drink.

"Well, since Aunt Shirley couldn't stop herself from snitching, I guess I'll tell you, boo," Drea turned to Alyssa with an apologetic look on her face while Aunt Shirley danced around the bathroom.

"Corey has secretly been planning for you guys to have your wedding here in Jamaica. Everything is planned out for tomorrow." She shrugged and Alyssa let out a chuckle as her eyes began to water.

"Is that why he's been acting so strange and secretive lately?" she asked and wiped away her tears. A chorus of "yeahs" went around the room to answer her question and she jumped up from her seat and gave each of her sisters a big hug.

"Awww y'all that's so sweet! I thought I was gonna have to kill him. Thank y'all!!"

"Bitch, they ain't did shit. Your man planned it," Aunt Shirley interjected again.

"Now, where the real drink and the strippers at?" She pulled a thick knot of one dollar bills out of her pocket and waved them around.

"You a mess Aunt Shirley! Ain't no strippers, we're under strict orders..."

"Listen, don't none of them niggas run shit, I know y'all ain't scared of them?" She looked around at each of the sisters, but the only one who was willing to risk it was Lexi.

"All y'all dick whipped except my fave, Lexi." She smacked her lips and looked at them all in pity, while her and Lexi slapped fives and then laughed.

"Ayite Lexi, don't have me get that phone and tell on you, while you tryna act all tough and shit since he ain't around." Drea planted her hands on her hips and hit Lexi with a smirk instantly stopping her from entertaining the shit Aunt Shirley was talking about.

"Bitches always tryna pull my hoe card," she grumbled under her breath but straightened right up. She might have played bad, but the sisters all knew that she was a kitten for J.R.

"Petty asses," Shirley said as the sisters all laughed except for Lexi.

After spending a little time with their mom and Kyler, an hour later they were all finally out of the door ready to see what the night life in Jamaica had to offer, with Aunt Shirley in tow. The first spot they hit was a small reggae hole-in-the-wall bar that had purple and blue strobe lights spilling out into the street. It didn't look like much on the outside, but on the inside, it was packed wall to wall with moving and grinding bodies. The entire club rocked as the live band inside played some reggae rap that none of the sisters had ever heard, but instantly began to move their bodies to. Before hitting the dance floor, Anastasia made sure that she, Lyssa, and Lexi all downed three shots, while Drea had some sparkling water and Aunt Shirley bought a whole bottle of Jack Daniels and waved it around like it was a bottle of Cristal.

"Let's go dance!" Anastasia shouted to her sisters over the music and they all made their way to the center of the dance floor, working their hips the whole way.

Before they even made it to the middle of the room, Lexi started winding her body like a snake and had all of her sisters chanting along with the rest of the small crowd. Anastasia knew her sister was a beast with the moves, but with the added effects of the alcohol she'd downed she stood in amazement. The way she was moving it was no wonder she had been making so much money at the club, she even had Drea out there shaking her money maker. Lexi had all the sisters hyped up.

"Go sister! That's my sister!" Anastasia shouted loudly as she and Alyssa danced with their sisters and hyped them up.

Lexi busted out into a split and moved first one cheek then the other and the whole crowd went wild as she winded her way up off of the floor. The Jamaican girls in there were being put to shame. A commotion on the side of them drew all of their attention away and they saw Aunt Shirley on the top of the bar with her hands on her knees with a crowd of her own around her. Anastasia's hand flew up to her mouth in shock as she first wondered how in the hell Shirley had climbed her ass up on the bar, before she fell out into a fit of laughter.

"Go Aunty! That's my Aunty!" Lexi shouted, egging their Aunt on. They all rushed over to the bar when she went to drop it low and yelled out in pain. Alyssa and Lexi helped their Aunt down off of the bar as she huffed about her hips.

"Aunty, how in the hell did you get up there?" Drea asked, breathlessly, once they'd gotten her onto a barstool safely, bottle still in hand.

"I climbed up there, girl, duh! A bitch ain't got it like I used to tho cause I sure in the hell couldn't get down!" she said, bringing her drink to her mouth.

"Are you okay tho, old lady?" Lexi looked at her with a mixture of concern and humor as Anastasia ordered them more shots.

"Bitch, ain't nothin old over here, but this body! I'm as young as you at heart, tuh!" she spat, picking up a napkin from the bar and wiping away her sweat. They all laughed at her again. Aunt Shirley was a mess and they all knew it. Anastasia handed them all two more shots each and Drea a cranberry juice, and they went back out onto the floor to dance some more.

It wasn't too long before they were hearing people talk about another spot that played hip hop music and the sisters all agreed to take the party there. Thankfully it wasn't too far away since they all had to pile into a cab. The Jamaican driver engaged them in conversation while ignoring Aunt Shirley who was trying to flirt with him. Once he dropped them off, he wasted no time pulling off to get away from Shirley who wasn't trying to take no for an answer.

The music blasted out of the building and they could hear the people inside turning up. Anastasia looped her arms through her sisters and their Aunt and they all walked inside ready to get into more trouble. As soon as they got in they noticed that one of the VIP sections was full of people and it looked like the niggas inside were the life of the party. Deciding to stop at the bar Anastasia bought another round of drinks and they all slammed their shots dancing in place until Yo Gotti's "Rake it Up" came on and Lexi pulled them all out onto the floor. Anastasia stood next to her sisters trying to twerk like she was Nicki

Minaj when she felt a strong pair of arms wrap around her. She froze right up and instantly tried to wiggle free. Anastasia wasn't about to be out in Jamaica disrespecting her man when she'd finally got him. Whoever it was wasn't trying to let her go, but she managed to whip around and looked right into the face of D'Mani. His face split into a wide grin and he pulled her back to him. Anastasia looked around and noticed that JR, D'Mari, and Corey had all of her sisters surrounded. She turned back to D'Mani as he rubbed his hands up and down her body.

"You out here ready to go off on any nigga that touch you besides me, huh, ma?" he asked and she nodded.

"Damn right," she smirked back at him as she felt his hardness against her stomach.

"I ain't gone lie, that shit got me bricked up." He ran his tongue across his bottom lip before sinking his teeth into it and Anastasia's floodgates opened at the thought of him putting that tongue on her.

"We're gonna have to take care of that then." Anastasia was ready to take him in the bathroom and handle it for him, and that's when she knew she was drunk. She laughed at herself for even thinking about doing it, but she was dead ass serious.

"Naw, we got plenty time for that, lets finish hanging out with the fam," he told her and she nodded, only slightly disappointed that she had to wait. Turning so that her back was against his chest, they swayed as the song changed to R. Kelly's "Feelin' on yo booty". A chorus of shouts went through the club and Anastasia grinded against her man. All of her sisters were doing the same thing and a smile graced her face. They were living life and enjoying themselves with their men at their sides. Life was great.

"Ohhhh I see y'all bitches did this on purpose; had us meet these niggas here and now I'm manless while y'all all boo'd up!" Aunt Shirley came out of nowhere and said loud enough for the whole club to hear.

"Our bad Aunty, this shit was a coincidence, but let me buy you a drink," D'Mani said, causing a huge grin to cover her face.

"Come on then, baby! Aunt Shirley ain't turning down no drinks now!" she exclaimed.

Anastasia rolled her eyes as she put her hand in D'Mani's free one and he walked them over to the bar while everybody else finished dancing. They spent the rest of the night getting lit and having fun to celebrate Alyssa's wedding.

Chapter 42

"So, Alexis, you gon' sit yo ass in here and not cook one dish?" Anastasia said from the stove as she flipped the pancakes.

"First of all, y'all woke me up too damn early and this wasn't my idea," Lexi said, grabbing a slice of bacon that Alyssa had placed on the table.

"According to you, this whole trip was your idea," Lyssa chimed in as she stole a piece of Lexi's food and shoved it in her mouth.

"You hoes are so ungrateful. If it wasn't for me, none of this shit would be taking place," she reminded them.

"Bitch pleassseeeeeee..." Stasia screamed.

"Anastasia Holiday, I heard that," Victoria said, walking into the kitchen joining her girls.

Lexi started laughing while Stasia bucked her eyes, she was caught red-handed.

"Mommy, all Alexis do is curse and yet you hear me the one time that I do it," she replied, turning back to the stove, this time flipping the eggs.

"I don't hear, Alexis and I know my baby don't have a foul mouth," Victoria smiled as she stroked Lexi's hair.

Lexi stuck out her tongue and mouthed the word "bitch" to her sister whose mouth flew open.

"Y'all non-cooking ass got this kitchen smelling good," Aunt Shirley said as she walked in wearing a floral pink robe.

"Yeah, it does smell good. Where is Andrea?" Victoria asked, grabbing plates and setting the table.

"I'm right here. I was throwing up this morning. I thought once I hit the second trimester, all that morning sickness crap was going to stop," Drea said, walking in and sitting next to Lexi on the stool.

"Chile, that sickness can last the whole nine months. Them damn doctors don't be knowing what they talking about," Aunt Shirley stated.

The Holiday sisters along with their mother and aunt continued to prep breakfast. The meat was done, but Andrea and her cravings for cheese grits was last minute, so Victoria put on a big pot of grits. The front door beeped causing all the ladies' heads to whip around just in time to see J.R., Corey, D'Mani, and D'Mari leaving out the front door.

"Where they going?" Victoria questioned while she placed a little salt in the boiling water.

"Ohhhh they sooooo dirty. I'll be back," Lexi said, hopping up from the table and heading out the front door.

"Aw nah, y'all trying to start a session without me. Y'all dirty motherfuckers!" Shirley yelled as she jumped up, using her hands to keep her robe closed the best way she could.

Alexis and Shirley reached the front porch just in time to see the guys heading towards the water. From where they were standing, they could see them lighting up three blunts and putting them in rotation.

"Come on, Auntie; they got us fucked up," Lexi said, yanking Shirley's arm forcing her down the wooden steps of the villa.

Lexi jogged while Shirley struggled to keep up. They made it to them just in time.

"Y'all so petty," Lexi said, snatching the blunt from J.R.

"Yeah, y'all know damn well not to leave us out," Shirley replied out of breath.

"My bad, sis and Auntie, we wanted to rap with Corey on some man to man shit before he ended his life tonight," D'Mani stated.

"Nigga, don't play with my sister," Lexi said, giving him the evil eye.

"Man, chill out. Y'all can keep that blunt, but let us have this moment," J.R. said to his girlfriend.

"Aight, we gon leave, but I need to know. Corey are you having second thoughts?" Lexi asked on a serious note.

"Hell nah, I love the fuck out that girl and there is no doubt that I want to spend the rest of my life with her," Corey assured them.

"Aw ok because I'll hate to commit a murder in another country," Aunt Shirley informed him.

"Chill killer, he good," D'Mari added in.

"Aight well it's hot as hell out here. This sand burning my toes. Breakfast should be ready, so y'all need to hurry up," Lexi said as she walked off, handing the blunt to her Aunt.

"It is hot as fuck, which makes me wonder why yo man on the beach in some Timbs." Aunt Shirley said, turning around and looking back at J.R.

"Girl, you can take the man out the hood, but you can't take the hood out the man. Let's go fuck this food up."

Back inside the villa, the Holiday women along with Kyler were setting the table and making the plates. As soon as Alexis and Shirley walked passed, everyone in the kitchens nose turned up.

"What type of shit was y'all out there smoking, it's so loud," Stasia said, fanning the kitchen with her hands.

Alexis eyes darted to her mother who was standing near the stove looking at her with her hands on her hips.

"You know I don't smoke, it must have rubbed off on me since I was out there," she lied.

Andrea, Lyssa, Stasia, and even Kyler laughed.

"What you laughing at punk?" Lexi said, hitting her nephew upside the head.

"Tee Tee Lexi, we gotta work on your lying skills. We'll talk about it later," he replied, pulling up his seat to the table.

Everyone erupted in laughter, including Victoria. Alexis was thankful for Kyler and him taking the heat off of her. After everyone made their plates, the guys walked in and came straight to the kitchen.

"Ah nooooooo, y'all better go wash them nasty hands before y'all touch this food," Victoria said, swatting them away with the towel she had in her hands.

"I just told them that, ma," J.R. replied.

"Really nigga?" D'Mari yelled out as they made their way to the bathrooms.

A few minutes later, they all returned, made their plates, and dug in with the women.

"On a scale from one to ten, how nervous are y'all?" Drea asked the soon to be married couple.

"I'm good," Corey said with a mouth full of biscuits.

"I'm a little nervous, I can't lie," Alyssa admitted truthfully.

"That's normal, baby. I was shitting bricks before I married your father," Victoria stated causing the entire table to grasp for air.

"You were whating bricks, ma?" Lexi blurted out.

"Y'all heard me, but being nervous is normal baby. You are making a life changing decision, but I know in my heart that you and Corey are soul mates and with love, God and prayer, there is no obstacles too big," she replied.

"Amen," Aunt Shirley said causing everyone to grasp for air again.

"This whole villa finna burn down now. Aunt Shirley said "Amen"," Stasia said.

"Well, I'm just happy that my sister found someone she loves," Drea added in.

"Thanks Drea, but I'm happy for you, too. As soon as tonight is over, we will be planning your wedding next," Lyssa said, looking between Andrea and D'Mari.

"I can't wait to see all my daughters happily married," Victoria grinned.

"Well, I know you gon be waiting a lonnnggg time for one of them," Shirley said taking a sip of her tea.

"Which one?" Anastasia and Alexis asked in unison.

"Not my fav," Shirley said, eyeing Stasia side-ways.

"You gotta be talking about your fav cause she's the one that need taming," Anastasia shot back.

"Taming? Bitc--- Girl, I ain't no animal," Lexi replied, rolling her eyes at her older sister.

"Ok y'all, it's over with," Victoria announced.

"And besides, I think Lexi has met her match," Mrs. Holiday continued, winking her eye at J.R.

"Yeah me, too, mommy. J.R. came in and put his foot down," Andrea added in.

"J.R. ain't came in and did shi…" Lexi stopped when she noticed the look he was giving her.

"Yeah, he did though, sis; you stopped dancing and all that," Lyssa said.

"Dancing? Lexi was a stripper?" D'Mani blurted out.

The entire table looked at him like he was crazy.

"What? My bad, I wasn't around then."

"Yeah baby, but J.R. ended all that., Stasia explained to him.

"Okay, could we discuss something other than Alexis right now?" she said, clearly annoyed.

"It's cool, bae. You went from a worker to being a boss," J.R. said, going inside his pocket and pulling out a sheet of paper.

"Here! Happy Valentine's Day," he stated, tossing the paper across the table at her.

Lexi grabbed the sheet of paper and opened it. She scanned over it for a while before letting out a loud scream.

"WHAT?" everyone asked around the table.

Lexi jumped up and ran over to J.R. hugging him tight while he was still in his seat.

"WHATTTTTT?!?!" they all asked again.

Lexi held up the sheet of paper in the air and danced around.

"I'm a boss, you a worker bitch, I make bloody moves!" she rapped and danced around the kitchen.

Drea snatched the paper out of her hands and she too screamed.

"If one of you heffas don't tell me what's going on, Imma start beating some ass," Aunt Shirley stood to her feet and said.

"Sorry y'all, but it's a contract. J.R. brought Lexi her own strip club."

All the girls including their mother stood to their feet and screamed while the guys congratulated J.R. on the boss move he made.

This was the best Valentine's Day gift Lexi has ever received. While she celebrated and danced around with her sisters, mother, and aunt, she thought of ways to make Club A4 the dopest club in the "A".

Chapter 43

Jamaica had been nothing short of amazing, but it would be a lie if Drea said she wasn't tired as hell. All of that partying had taken a toll on her pregnant ass, but she would do it all over again because the smiles on everyone's faces made it all worthwhile. It was finally 'Love Day', which was the day of the wedding. Breakfast was over and the ladies had a spa appointment at one o'clock that they were headed to. Drea had taken it upon herself to get some shirts made for the ladies and they turned out cute. They were white tee shirts with purple writing since their dresses were lavender. She wanted the words to show up on each shirt, and it worked out perfect.

"Drea, I take back everything I ever said about you since you bought me a shirt, too. You ain't all that bad after all," Aunt Shirley said as she walked into the living room wearing her shirt that said 'Drunk Auntie of the Bride'.

"You're welcome, Aunt Shirley," Drea laughed.

Everyone had made their way out of their rooms and it was time to head out.

"Wait… let's take some pictures before we go. Where the guys go?" Anastasia inquired.

Lexi yelled out to J.R., and he appeared about a minute later.

"Snap these pictures for us pleeaasseee," Lexi's extra ass whined.

Ten minutes and about a hundred pictures later, they were all outside and piling into the Yukon that D'Mani rented with Stasia behind the wheel. They navigated their way to Escape to Exhale Spa while laughing and talking shit the entire way. Even Victoria let her hair down and laughed at her sister's jokes instead of telling her to shut up like she normally did.

"Stasia, did you see Richard the day before and the day of your wedding?" Aunt Shirley asked after a few minutes of quietness.

"Ummm… no. I was told I wasn't supposed to."

"Oh… well Lyssa you might be good since you saw Corey. You better do everything the opposite of what your sister did," Aunt Shirley called herself whispering, but everyone heard her and agreed with laughter.

"I'm very proud of all of y'all… I know we made things hard on y'all growing up, but we only did what we thought was best. Some of it was wrong, but to see how much each of y'all are growing and doing so good makes me happy. I just wish… I wish that Abraham was here to see," Victoria sniffled.

"It's okay mommy… we all still love you very much, and daddy is watching over all of us. He's still proud," Drea reached to the front seat and tried to comfort their mom.

"You wasn't really that hard on us mommy… they just some lil bi… I mean babies," Lexi chimed in.

"Oh, hush you lil mama's girl," Stasia cut her eyes at Lexi through the rearview mirror and Lexi flipped her off without Victoria seeing her.

"Y'all girls know I talk a lot of shit… and Ima do it til the day I die, but y'all do have some of the best parents in the world… they did some foolish shit, but parenting is trial and error. Look how all y'all done turned out. It's more than I can say for mine. Shit, where my drink? That's why I drink so much. My two been tryna kill me they whole lives," Aunt Shirley said and then grabbed her flask and took a few swigs.

"Awww Aunt Shirley… you got me," Lexi leaned over and hugged her.

"You know you my fav," she called herself whispering, but just like always, everyone heard Shirley's big ass mouth.

They arrived at that spa and were greeted immediately. As soon as they walked in, Drea knew that they had picked the right place. The atmosphere was so serene. The ladies were led to a private room and given some plush white robes and slippers to put on. Everyone got manicures and pedicures first, followed by facials. They drank mimosa's while waiting to receive their full body massages.

"Are you ladies ready?"

"Wait… it's gon be men giving the massage, right? I don't want no woman seeing all my goodies. One of these in here might, but I ain't gon call her name because she my favorite," Shirley said and winked at Lexi.

Everyone erupted into laughter yet again while shaking their heads at the same time.

"We have both men and women masseuse, but you all have men. Follow me," the friendly Jamaican girl smiled.

They followed her and were instructed to lie down on the tables and get comfortable.

"Are you nervous, Lyssa?" Stasia quizzed.

"We've really been to turnt up for me to be nervous, but now that you mentioned it… my stomach did just do a flip."

"That's just all them drinks from last night," Lexi chimed in.

"I'm not gonna even ask how much you girls drank… I'm just glad y'all were responsible," Victoria said.

"Everyone was responsible except one of us, but I ain't gon tell on…"

"Girl, you better hush if you wanna make it to yo wedding tonight," Shirley cut Lyssa off.

Before anyone could say anything else, six fine ass Jamaican men walked in wearing nothing, but shorts. It looked as if they had bathed their ripped abs in baby oil and each of them had dreads that were neatly done and hanging down their backs.

"Alllll y'all here for me… fuck the rest of these hoes. They got men. I need all of y'all!" Aunt Shirley beamed.

To make Aunt Shirley feel good, each of the guys showed her some attention, and then they broke away and gave everyone their massages. Everyone left feeling refreshed and rejuvenated.

"The MUA should be at the house by five. Since we have a few hours, do y'all wanna grab something to eat?" Drea asked.

"Yeah, let's get some authentic food," Lexi replied.

"Works for me? Who is the MUA?" Lyssa quizzed.

"Her name is Haley Love and she is a beast. She's actually from Louisville, Mississippi, too. She recently went to Atlanta and her career has taken off. Y'all should look her up on Facebook. I'm glad I was able to book her."

They found a local restaurant that didn't have a long wait time and ordered some samples of a lot of shit that they couldn't even pronounce so that they could share. They went over the details of the wedding and everything and talked about how beautiful it was going to be. A night wedding on the beach was something you only read about in books, but the Holiday sisters were about to live it. An hour and a half later, the family headed back to house so that they could beautify themselves and get Alyssa married.

Chapter 44

As the hours passed, Alyssa couldn't help but to be anxious. After learning that she was getting married the night before; it was natural that she shed a few tears. She was at a loss for words that Corey had her sisters plan a surprise wedding for them and she felt bad for thinking that he was cheating. Alyssa was the perfect definition of calm on the outside, but the knot that started out small that morning seemed to grow throughout the day.

Haley, the MUA, arrived at five on the nose with her team and they got started on the girls immediately. They did the girls hair and make-up two at time and when six o'clock rolled around, their faces were beat to perfection and their hair was slayed. Aunt Shirley and Victoria were the first ones dressed and they helped the Holiday sisters get ready. Alyssa remained in her robe as she smiled at how beautiful her sisters looked in their lavender halter bridesmaids' dresses. When Anastasia was finished getting dressed, she left out the room. Alyssa was a little upset that she didn't have her wedding dress and wondered what she was going to wear.

"Alyssa, you're supposed to be happy, baby. Why are you frownin'?" Victoria sat next to her daughter, grabbing her hand.

"My sisters helped me pick out the perfect wedding dress and since I didn't know about the wedding, it got left behind," she sighed.

"Do you really think that we were gonna let Corey bring his ass here without that dress?" Lexi stared at her sister through the floor length mirror.

On que, Anastasia entered the room with Alyssa's wedding dress and jewelry in hand. Alyssa's frown was instantly turned upside down. Jumping to her feet, she snatched the dress out of her sister's hand and proceeded to get dress. Once her dressed was zipped, Alyssa traded places with Lexi at the mirror to admire herself and she almost cried.

"You look so beautiful, sis," Drea complimented and fluffed out the bottom of Alyssa's gown.

"All of my girls look beautiful," Victoria sniffled.

"Oh, how I was wish y'all father was here to witness this. I know he's smilin' down on us right now," Victoria dabbed her eyes with a tissue.

"Come on, y'all. We can't be fuckin' up our make-up and shit. We still got pictures to take. So, let's go already," Aunt Shirley rushed them.

Alyssa chuckled as she dried her eyes with a tissue as well. The sisters grabbed their flower bouquets and made their way out of the room. Alyssa trailed behind as she watched her sisters get everyone ready to walk on to the beach. The ladies locked arms with their spouses and seconds later, 'A Couple of Forever's' by Chrisette Michelle began to play from the beach and Kyler, looking handsome in his suit, was the first one to walk out. Next up was Anastasia and D'Mani, then Drea and D'Mari, followed by Lexi and J.R. Alyssa and Victoria stood behind Aunt Shirley and when she missed her que to go, Victoria pushed her forward and Alyssa couldn't help but laugh as her aunt strolled down the path.

Alyssa and Victoria walked barefooted onto the beach and her mouth hit the floor at the sight of the beautiful decorations. Tiki torches were lined up on each side of them creating a straight lane to where everyone was standing near the water. Rose petals decorated the path and at the end, there was a rectangular arch that was decorated with white and lavender roses. There was a table off to the left that was decorated with plates, cutlery, candles, and flowers and the DJ was to the right. As they got closer to the end, Alyssa scanned her family's smiling faces before she locked eyes with Corey who was smiling as well. Although Alyssa had seen him in a suit plenty of times before, Corey looked like a whole snack in his black tuxedo, that she couldn't wait to rip off him later.

When they reach the end of the path, the music faded out as they stood under the arch. Corey stood on the right side of Alyssa while Victoria remained on her left.

"Who gives this woman away to be married to this man?" the handsome, middle-age minister spoke.

"I do," Victoria stated proudly.

Victoria placed Alyssa's hand in Corey's and kissed them both on the cheek before standing next to Aunt Shirley. Standing hand and hand, the minister began the traditional wedding speech and as he spoke, Corey and Alyssa couldn't take their eyes off each other.

"I believe the couple have prepared their own wedding vows." The minister nodded towards Alyssa to go first.

"Corey, I didn't fall in love with you. I walked into love with you, with my eyes wide open, choosing to take every step along the way. I do believe in fate and destiny, but I also believe we are only fated to do the things that we'd choose anyway. And I'd choose you; in a hundred lifetimes, in a hundred worlds, in any version of reality, I'd find you and I'd choose." Alyssa choked back tears.

"Alyssa, I choose you to be no other than yourself. Loving what I know of you and trustin' who you will become. I will respect and honor you always and in all ways. I take you to be my wife, to have and to hold... In tears and in laughter... In sickness and in health... To love and to cherish, from this day forward. In this life and the next..."

Alyssa could hear the women sniffling and she couldn't stop the tears that fell from her eyes. The minister asked for the rings and Kyler stepped up and they removed their wedding bands from the pillow he was holding and placed them on each other's fingers.

"By the power vested in me, I now pronounce you husband and wife. You may kiss your beautiful bride, son." The minister smiled.

Corey gently grabbed her face and kissed his new wife passionately. Their family cheered for the couple as they walked back down the lit path, followed by their family. It was completely dark outside, but the bright, shining stars and moon provided light for them as well as the torches and candles that were lit. As they took a seat at the table, the caterers brought out their appetizers of stuff mushrooms and shrimp cocktails along with a few bottles of champagne. The family congratulated Alyssa and Corey on their new marriage before they laughed, talked, and drank the night away.

While they waited for their main course, the DJ played 'You and I' by Avant featuring KeKe Wyatt, which was the couple's first song they wanted to dance to as husband and wife. As they slow danced under the starry sky, Corey kept his eyes trained on Alyssa as he recited the lyrics of Avant and Alyssa did the same, she sang Keke Wyatt's part. They danced until the song went off and returned to the table to eat. The lobster and steak meals they ate were beyond delicious and they were all to stuffed to eat dessert.

As the evening continued, they all danced the night away on the beach and the love and feel good vibes of the wedding only added to the environment that they had created since they arrived in Jamaica. Throughout the past few months, the Holiday sisters had endured more than any one family could handle. The feud between the sisters, their individual secrets and problems, the passing of their father, the family secret of Andrea not being Abraham's biological daughter, and the drama that popped off at the funeral was enough to break up any family. But, instead of letting their problems defeat them, they defeated their problems, which in the end, brought them closer together. Alyssa loved each of the sisters the same and she knew that there was nothing but great things in store for their future.

"Aye… now that y'all got all that love shit outta the way, DJ, play that 'Thug Holiday' by Trick Daddy!" J.R. said

"That definitely describes our family don't it, baby?" Lexi chimed in.

When the beat dropped and the lyrics began to play, everyone bobbed their heads to the beat and sang along. They hadn't heard the song in forever, but it was one of those songs that you just remembered. When LaTocha Scott's part near the end came on, Aunt Shirley stood up and sang and shocked the shit out of everybody.

"So many tears, throughout the years

Somebody tell me what's going on

And so many liiives, but only God knows

About the pain deep inside

It gets so hard, you got to keep your head up

I know your're fed up, but stay strong

Here's a message from coast to coast

Cause when then thugs really need it the most, THUG HOLIDAY!"

"Y'all thought Aunt Shirley didn't know bout that didn't ya? I coulda married Trick Daddy if I wanted to," she said and took a sip from her flask.

Of course, everyone laughed at her ass like always and enjoyed the rest of the night while silently wondering if the next holiday would be as peaceful for the Holiday sisters.

Don't forget to leave us a review please!!

Made in United States
North Haven, CT
15 February 2022

16141970R00170